KINGDOM OF RUIN

Dragon of Eriden Book 4

SAMANTHA JACOBEY

Lavish
Publishing LLC

First Edition

Dragon of Eriden Book 4

2018 Lavish Publishing, LLC

All Rights Reserved

Published in the United States by Lavish Publishing, LLC, Midland, TX

Cover Design by: Victor R. Sosa

Cover Images: Canstock

Paperback Edition

ISBN: 9781944985615

www.LavishPublishing.com

Contents

Prologue

SLITHERING BACK AND FORTH, Gwirwen glared at Ziradon through the massive stone bars that formed the deposed king's prison. His supporters had helped him construct it nearly two decades ago, and he had held the title of Supreme Dragon ever since. "A moment in time for a dragon," he grumbled to himself. He wanted more, but the chaos around him whispered his end was near.

Charging one of the gaps, Gwirwen shouted, "Answer me!" The scent of a mortal of the rim burned his nostrils. "Who has been here?"

Within the fortress, Ziradon gazed at him with cold emerald orbs. "You know who it is," he growled, not bothering to deny it.

Kaliwyn, still trapped in the mortal body of Amicia, had presented herself before him only hours before. Leaving as quickly as she had come, he had lain deep in thought since her departure. Contemplating his life, and hers, the realization of their existence had become clear.

He had not known of her importance until she had stood before him, powerful enough to hide in plain sight. Cunning enough to fool even the most prepared. He feared what lay ahead, and he had feared little in his seven-hundred years.

"Why did you not kill her when you learned she had returned to Eriden?" Ziradon asked in his gravelly voice. "Did you think you could end her at any time, and enjoy toying with her from the shadows?"

Gwirwen's heart beat hard against his chest, but he resisted the urge to blast the former king with a wave of fire. "I have no fear of your puny dragoness."

"And that shall be your downfall," Ziradon nodded.

1

"Tell me of her treachery," Gwirwen growled. "Does she think she can free you? I assure you, she will not!"

"You are a fool," Ziradon replied, almost calmly. "I begged you to spill her blood upon the soil, but you refused. Your arrogant self-importance has brought us to this place."

"Hmph," Gwirwen sneered. "As the Supreme Dragon, I know my worth."

"You know nothing!" his prisoner snapped, charging the divide and meeting him nose to nose.

Ziradon had once been a hefty beast; a force to be reckoned with. Now, after years of imprisonment and malnutrition, his body had grown thin; frail and weak. A dragon's heart still thundered within him, but his aged bones and emaciated frame were no match for his adversary, even if he could get to him.

"You dare challenge me, even now behind the walls where I have held you," Gwirwen sneered. "Tell me again how all of this is my fault," he taunted, unable to refuse the temptation to gloat.

"You squandered chance after chance to remove her," Ziradon obliged. "You could have put an end to me and my line forever, but you thought you could handle us. Your choices were wrong, and it is you who has brought all of our land to this dark place."

"What dark place?" his nemesis laughed, sitting back on his haunches and staring at him. "Surely you do not believe such tales? The creator and the destroyer – bah! And here I had once thought you wise."

"I was wise in my council," Ziradon clipped, "on the night you laid our fate. She was a sweet and kind dragoness, and you have transformed her into a monster."

"A monster," Gwirwen continued to prod, basking in his ability to torment his predecessor. "I should kill you now and be done with it. I grow weary of your presence."

"Kill me; don't kill me. It matters not. Every choice you have made has brought us closer to the edge of destiny."

"If my choices are poor and I such a fool, what does that make you? I was your adviser, after all," he laughed airily, enjoying their téte-à-téte.

"No, you were my friend, and you betrayed me. I did not keep you close because of your ability or cleverness, but the truth is always hidden from those who refuse to see. Kaliwyn has returned, and in your stupidity, you have allowed her to grow strong. She has surrounded herself with friends, followers loyal to her command and her cause. The destroyer has come, and Eriden will fall."

ONE

A Meeting of Means

"I NEED A MOMENT," Piers informed his young crewman, watching him as he gathered necessities for his assignment.

"With me?" Reynard asked anxiously, glancing around to see who else was close enough to overhear.

"With the siren," the Mate replied, giving the tiny creature a smile.

Her hands folded in front of her chest, Oldrilin stared up at him with wide blue eyes, her small frame slouched timidly. He would never harm her unless provoked, as Piers Massheby was not that kind of man. But there had never been real friendship between them; she knew he had tolerated her at best. "Yes?" she replied, her lip trembling.

Kneeling before her, Piers ran his hand roughly over his beard, smoothing it as he took a few deep breaths. "I have much I need to say, but only a small part of it will matter. First, I wish to apologize, both to you and your kind. When you stand before Olirassa, please tell her my distrust was misplaced. After our travels through Eriden, my eyes have been opened to the truth."

"Yes, this will be said," the siren agreed. Offering her hand, her surprise at his words quickened her pulse.

Clasping her tiny fingers, he stared down at her round face with a small nod. "Next, you must let her know that the fight is finally coming. We will need all who will stand on our side, and I believe that includes the sirens. As I said, I think I understand her reasons for helping us when we came here, and that makes her a part of our cause."

Lin nodded slowly, "I shall say this as well."

3

"And lastly, tell her not to give up hope. Amicia... Kaliwyn... grows strong and understands the importance of her place. She will do all that she can to preserve the realms of her homeland," he finished with a strained smile.

"Of course," the mermaid agreed, matching his grin.

Using the appendage, he drew the creature close, wrapping her in a warm embrace. "Be safe, Oldrilin. Be quick in your journey and return to us with what news you can of your friends."

"Are we ready?" Meena interrupted as the group gathered on the other side of the northern part of their shelter.

"Yes, I believe we are," the Mate agreed.

Lifting Oldrilin into her pouch with her back against his chest, Rey prepared to leave by slinging his pack over his shoulder. Inside, it held his blanket, a water-skin, and a few days rations; enough to tide him over while he awaited their minia-ture spy's return. Following, as the group began their trek through the marshes to stand before the elders of the gnomes, he watched for his opportunity to duck away and take his own path.

Tromping through the swamp in single file, Amicia guided them through the trees. "How do you know the way?" Zaendra asked as the sun disappeared, and darkness brought a chill to the air.

"I feel them. These are very powerful creatures," Ami explained. "I believe more so than any we have encountered yet."

"Or perhaps you are simply more sensitive to their presence with the discovery of your own power," Meena theorized.

"That could also be true," the blonde agreed with a sigh. Pausing, she indicated the dancing firelight ahead. "This is the village, either way." Glancing around at those who gathered around her, she noted that Rey was not among them. He had split off to make his way to the coast and would not return until Lin's mission was complete.

"What exactly are we going to ask for?" Animir inquired.

"The world," Amicia giggled. "Don't worry. I have a speech prepared."

Grinning at her, Piers nodded, "You have become a fine leader and diplomat."

Hayt snorted at the word, "I thought it would be me who parlayed for our truce."

"And indeed, it shall," Ami stated confidently, offering him her arm. "Walk with me and let us show a united front. If they remember your alliance of old, it will help us gain their confidence today."

Sliding his appendage through hers, the dwarf walked beside her through the last of the thicker forest. Before them, the area opened into a clearing, where small stones and logs sat scattered in a set of rings around the fire. Seated upon them, dozens, maybe hundreds, of small bodies sat awaiting their arrival. The woods around them thick and old, large trees had been hollowed or the ground beneath sculpted to create small dwellings like the one Sevoassi had held in the northern woods.

"My queen," Thirac greeted with a slight bow of his head.

"Good evening," she replied crisply, her green eyes flittering over his people. "I did not expect so many."

"Word of your arrival has spread," the gnome sneered, sending her heart into a flutter. "All wished to lay their eyes upon you."

Coming in behind, the rest of their group huddled together. The air heavy inside their village, they had come to expect a warm welcome, as almost all in Eriden had proven to be less venomous than rumor held.

Not this time, Amicia observed silently. *These creatures are just as dark and ominous as promised.* Squeezing Hayt's arm, she gathered her nerve, then pushed forward, "You remember Hayt?"

"Yes, of course. But it is your words we shall hear, princess," the short leader replied, wafting his hand around at his company. "We have waited many moons for you to stand within our presence."

Her eyes searching again, his words gave her gut a twist she could not place. "As you wish," she whispered, reluctantly releasing her grip. Licking her lips, her mouth felt dry as she stepped forward, leaving her companions. Glancing back at them, she could see their fear evident in their huddled mass. Grinning at the Mate and Animir encouraging them to relax, she felt calmed by their regard for one another and for her.

"Good gnomes of Falconmarsh," she began, holding her arms wide and presenting herself before them. "I am Amicia Spicer, mortal of the rim," she introduced herself confidently. Hearing the ripple of small voices, she added, "also known as the dragoness Kaliwyn, heir to the throne of Eriden."

The crowd erupted into louder unrest as her words were measured. Not to be dissuaded, she continued, "As you know, we have been in Eriden for some time, traveling on a great quest. As I have learned of my identity and my ability, I have also become aware of my place, a position of great importance throughout the land."

She paused, casting her eyes across the sea of bodies. Their presence strong about her, it was hard to discern their intentions as their powerful emotions rose and fell, but she carried on. "To fulfill our task and make things right within the kingdom, we require the support of its inhabitants. Great evil looms over us all, and only by working together may it be defeated. Therefore, we have a few requests of your people. First, we seek refuge here in the marsh until we have prepared for the battle ahead. Second, I am in search of a cure for the curse that has bound me in this mortal form."

The whispers louder, the air crackled as anger and distrust filled the clearing. "She is weak."

"She can't regain her form?"

"This is a lie!"

"How will she fight?"

"We cannot interfere."

"Gwirwen will never allow it."

Their voices overlapping, their doubts remained obvious. Listening to them bicker among themselves, Ami drew a deep breath, unsure what should could say that would allay their fears and win them to her cause.

Amid their unrest, a large form swooped in and sent them scattering. Diving low over the rows of gnomes, Lamwen released a deafening roar before pulling up and landing beside the self-proclaimed queen of the land.

"You will hear and obey!" he shouted, snarling at the creatures who had scattered at his displeased entrance. Hiding among the trees, the whispers rippled once more before small pockets of gnomes trickled back into the central location.

"You declare her words are true?" a small voice shouted.

"Of course they are true! Can you not see the dragon's light within her?" he snapped. His large head panning, his eyes roamed, peering into the darkness. "I once held rank as captain of the king's guard! I am Lamwen, and you know my words are just. I stepped away from that place in favor of our queen and devoted my days and nights to her protection since her discovery. If you do not trust her words, trust mine, for I have stood before you many times. Gwirwen is not invincible. Kaliwyn will be his downfall, and we only need have faith that our future will be secured."

The conversation rising once more, the gnomes poured into the courtyard in even greater numbers, as those who had hidden among the trees before joined their brothers. "Speak then. What would you have of us?" a loud cry beseeched.

Her voice shaky, Ami tried again, "As I said, we need shelter, and any who have knowledge that could be useful in my restoration are called forth. If you are willing, we will ask you to fight as well, when the time comes to make our stand."

"Fight," Thirac laughed. "Do we appear as warriors to you?"

"You appear as the inhabitants of Eriden," Ami countered more confidently. "This is our home, and Gwirwen threatens to destroy it. He has turned against our realms one by one. Eventually there will be none left to stand against him, while the rest cower in fear. If you intend to remain here, then you should have no hesitation in the fight to restore our beloved Eriden. Let no realm hold more worth than another, for all are equal in my eyes."

Her words sharp, silence fell across the sea of small bodies. Thinking of the night they had stood at the center of the sacred rings of the glen, Amicia smiled.

Spreading her arms, she drank in the power of the small creatures surrounding her, lifting her chin and closing her eyes as the moonglow splashed across her delicate features.

"You are a powerful queen," Thirac observed, disrupting her trance.

"Then you will do as I have asked?" she replied without altering her position, still sapping their strength in the cold white light.

"We will consider you our guests in the marsh," he acquiesced. "As to the rest, we will discuss joining your fight."

"And what of my imprisonment?" she snapped, pulling her head up to glare at him.

"We have no power over such things," the king confessed. "However, we have tools at our command which may aid in your recovery and your cause. Soon, you will be given service in these things. You have my word on it."

Next to her, Lamwen had been studying the gathering, and at that moment realized their group to be incomplete. "Where is the siren?" he growled. Turning in a slow circle, her presence could not be confirmed.

Looking past them, Thirac also studied their group of newcomers. "You did have a siren. Where has she gone?"

Glaring at the dragon, Piers waited until their eyes met, then leveled, "She has made a journey but will return as quickly as possible."

"And where has she gone?" Lamwen pushed, his glowing orbs narrowed to slits.

"To Riran," the Mate informed him calmly.

"You do not trust me," the dragon hissed in disbelief.

"Well," Piers shrugged, "prudence demands caution. If you have spoken the truth, our friends will return with confirmation of the mermaids' situation."

"What situation?" Thirac shouted, disturbed by their seeming to be divided.

"Lamwen has seen that the elves are moving to claim Eriden for their own," Amicia informed him flatly. "We have dispatched our siren to verify this and to deliver a message to our allies. We will need to gather our forces as much as we are able, but I am afraid time and distance are against us in this cause."

"And you did not feel the need to speak of such treachery?" the king spat, glaring at Animir.

"I –" the elf began, but Amicia cut him off with a wave of her hand.

"We would have shared the intelligence once the invasion has been confirmed. For now, I have spoken of what must be completed at this time, for if I am unable to regain my dragon form, then all our plans for the future will be affected."

"I see," the gnome glared at her, impressed with her strength. "Very well then. Return to your camp and bring us news when it has been won. We will likewise search our history in case a transformation has ever been achieved in days gone by. If we can help with that regard, we will inform you at our next meeting."

Bowing to him slightly in agreement, Amicia could tell the king was upset. His small frame hunched, he gathered his cloak around him as he disappeared into the trees on the far side of the crowded clearing, the rest of the gnomes reluctant to vacate the area.

"Wait," Animir called, taking a step forward as if to chase him down.

"Let him go," Ami commanded, catching his arm and preventing his pursuit. "We have what we came for; permission to reside in the marsh. The rest, we will formulate without the help of these creatures if we must," she declared, shifting her eyes to take in the small forms that again spoke to one another in whispers.

"Let's get out of here," Piers agreed, his arm around his wife as he guided her the way they had come.

Tromping through the thick marsh, Rey made small talk with the siren strapped to his chest. "Are you excited about returning home?" Catching a limb, he held it away so she would not be struck as they passed.

Facing away from him so she could see where they were going, Oldrilin grinned, "Home to Riran."

"Yes, Riran," he agreed, testing his footing on a slick-looking expanse of moss-covered stones. Taking it slow, he observed, "Man, this place sure is treacherous."

"Gnomes are small," she replied.

"I guess," he chuckled. "Does that mean they don't have far to fall when the earth gives way beneath them?" Reaching the other side of the hazard, he again picked up the pace.

"Rey Daye funny," she giggled. "Lin has an important message for queen Olirassa. We must hurry."

"Yeah, I know," he grimaced. "I'm doing the best I can. But don't hang out there too long. We'll be waiting for you to get back, and I'm not looking forward to laying around alone while I do."

"Rey safe," she sighed. "Oldrilin will hurry most certain."

Ahead of them, the trees parted, and a wide rocky shore spread before them. "Well, it's about time," Rey grinned. "Ok, this is it. Let me get us to the water, and you can be on your way. And we need to find a landmark, so you will know where to come ashore when you get back." An idea springing to mind, he gasped, "Man, I wish we had perfected that telepathy thing. Then you could just let me know you're back."

The siren had spoken to him once, but only once, and the message had been short at that. "I will try," she agreed, doubtful they would be able to connect, as neither of them were practiced at using it.

Moving down the shore, the pair searched for the right location for her to enter. It needed to be one she would be able to recognize when she returned. Seeing a peninsula that stuck out a fair distance, he pointed, "Looks good, huh?"

"Yes. Looks like land," she agreed.

"Looks like land," he mocked. "I know it's land, but will you see it from out there?" he asked, swiping a hand to indicate the dark water before them.

"I see it good, Rey Daye," she agreed.

"Then this is our spot," he discerned with a shrug.

Dropping his pack at the edge of the trees, Rey pushed forward. Reaching the water, it crashed in huge waves against the shore. The moonlight splashing across it, the air felt cold, and the boy was glad he wouldn't be the one going in. "Are you ready?"

"Ready, Rey Daye," she sang, feeling joy at the prospect of returning home after so many moons away.

Pulling the bindings to her pouch from his shoulder, he lowered her to the ground and helped her step out of her carrier. "This is it," he beamed, hoping she would be reassured at her first attempt to transform.

Swinging her hands in a wide arc, she clapped a few times before her, then stepped into the water and dove into the rough surf. Gone in an instant, the speed of her disappearance sent his heart racing.

"Lin!" he shouted, having at least expected a goodbye.

A moment later, a large black fish turned straight out in front of him, a few yards from the rocks of the shore. "Oh, thank God," he breathed.

Turning a few times, the ebony fins slapped the water, and he laughed. "I see you. You're good. Go on, and I'll meet you here at this point when you get back."

The point he referred to was the small peninsula of land that jutted out a bit farther into the sea. Standing upon it, water flanked him, and a cold wind beat against his thin frame, adding doubt to the back of his mind. Turning to face the beach, he hoped that she would see it, as the line of trees on the shore held no discernible features as far as the eye could see.

Staring at the abyss for a few minutes, she did not appear again, and he knew that she had gone. How many days it would take her uncertain, all that remained was to return to his gear and make camp. Normally a patient man, he knew this wait would be particularly difficult, with so much of importance hanging in the balance, not to mention his special little friend who might never return.

TWO

A Sprinkle of Magic

THE OCEAN COLD, Oldrilin's sleek, black body sliced through the waves. It had been many moons since she had last transformed, but she used a sprinkle of magic and made the shift as if it were nothing. Taking one look back, she rolled to see Reynard standing on the shore, and panic coursed through her veins.

Goodbye, Rey Daye.

Turning south, she dove, her scales shimmering as she wriggled back and forth in practiced motion. The sirens seldom took to the water at night, but this was no ordinary occasion. Oldrilin knew the fate of her people could be at stake, and she would face her fears of the cold, dark water to help them.

Must make Riran.

The daunting distance would be a great challenge to achieve, especial after spending so many days upon the land, followed by such a long swim. With the gnomes of Falconmarsh situated high on the eastern coast of Eriden, she would not arrive in the mermaid lagoon until close to sunset the following night. How far did not matter; she had to get there.

Go far to save my friends.

Using the thought as her mantra, she focused on pushing herself. Which friends was she swimming to save? She had so many these days. The new ones she had roamed with and those she had left behind. Would Olirassa still be queen? If the elves had invaded them, anything could have happened. Worry tormented her thoughts, and her heart sang with pain.

Must deliver Piers's message.

It warmed her when she thought of her friend and leader; the human male who had guided their group through one catastrophe after another. But they had always come through in the end. He had never spoken to her so kindly as he did in their parting. Rey had always been her best and Bally close behind.

Oh, Bally, why did you go?

Her mind on their lost comrade, her pace slowed. Picturing his small circle of trees and giant stone marker, her heart ached. She had cried her pitiful song at his memorial, but she doubted if the others knew how much she missed him. The salt water caught her tears, and she mourned him once again before tearing her mind from the woeful thoughts.

Focus. Swim. Don't think. Don't weep.

Determined, she pushed the memories aside. Holding on to Reynard Daye and all the time he had carried her, she imagined he was doing so at that moment. Her mind safe in her pouch, she undulated through the salty water, pushing ever harder and faster towards the southern shores.

"Oldrilin? Is this her?"

"I think it is!"

"Shh – do not let the elf hear."

"Quick, get her onto the shore."

"Hide her in the trees."

"She's freezing."

"She must be exhausted."

"Where did she come from?"

"Where has she been?"

"Quiet, all of you," Olirassa commanded, taking charge and shooing the swarm of tiny bodies away. "Bring her to lie on the moss. Who will fetch the nectar?"

"I will," a volunteer spoke up, her tiny feet pattering on the path to the great waterfall.

"The elves have plundered our meadow," another sobbed.

"There will be enough," the queen soothed, lifting their lost sister's hand. "We will sacrifice what we can find and nurse her to health with our last drop if we must."

Her eyes fluttering, Oldrilin laid her arm across her face to shield herself from the sun. Blinking against it, she turned her head and looked side to side. Spying a small mermaid to her left, she giggled, "Oldrilin found Riran?"

"Oh, Lin!" a small voice sang. "She's awake, my queen!"

"Shh," Olirassa hissed, looking around anxiously. Seeing the elf had not noticed, she grinned, moving to sit so the sun lay behind her and fell as shadow across her old friend.

"I am home?" Oldrilin pushed, her sounds weak.

"Yes, you have returned to the alcove. Here, sip." The sovereign offered a shell of the precious, healing liquid.

Taking a long drink, the cool water felt good against her swollen lips. When she had finished a second, she lay back against the cool, moss covered sand. "I was frightened, to not transform," she whispered, holding up her hand to test her fingers.

"You are safe," Olirassa smiled. "You were found yesterday, here on the beach when we came in for the evening."

"Yesterday!" Lin gasped, trying to sit up. "Oh, no, I've been too long! My poor Rey Daye…" she lamented as she gave up her struggle and rested once more.

Her eyes roving up and down her prone position, the queen sighed, "You speak of the mortal, Amicia's friend. They are the ones who took you from us?"

"Yes," Oldrilin agreed with a small nod, "but no. I was hurting the night of the dragon's fire; I couldn't swim. Rey Daye saved me, wrapped and carried away," she explained. Pulling hard, she made it to a sitting position. The sun no longer behind her friend's back, she was able to see her clearly for the first time. "Oh, what happened?" she gasped. "So sad."

Her hand absently adjusting her mane, the queen sighed, "Oh, Oldrilin."

Olirassa's appearance had changed greatly since the night of the birthday celebration ball. Her hair still a golden brown, it only grew from portions of her scalp, with large places of rough skin covering much of her small head.

"I was burned badly the night of the dragon attack," the queen explained, wafting a hand to indicate her followers. "Many of us were. Hurt beyond the power of the nectar. We were healed, but we were changed."

"Oh, sweet Eriden," Lin wailed softly, tears forming in her clear blue orbs. "So sorry to see."

"Yes, we lost many friends on that fateful night," her matron sighed, then her features brightened, "but one who was lost has been returned."

"Returned, yes," Oldrilin giggled, then suddenly recalled why she had been gone. Her smile removed, she cut her eyes over to see the pair of elves standing watch at the remains of a tree that once marked the entrance to their lagoon.

Inspecting them, she noted they were not as tall as Cilithrand or those of the ruling class like Animir. Shorter, they were closer in height to their servants; but still giants to creatures such as the sirens. "So, Lamwen speaks true."

"Lamwen?"

"The watcher dragon. He is a friend of Amicia. I have come to see if his words were right. It seems so," she moaned, shaking her head side to side.

"Yes, they have been here only a short time, but our lives they have disrupted much," Olirassa agreed.

"I have a message, my queen," Oldrilin pushed, wishing to stand.

"Don't move!" Olirassa warned. "It would be better we remain here, quiet, while you share," she explained as she cut her bright green eyes over at their invaders as well. "We have feigned obedience, but they refuse to leave us. They make camps to remain, to build an elf city by the sea."

"Very well," Oldrilin nodded, glad of the news she would report at her return to the others. For now, she had a message to deliver. "Piers sends his regrets; wrong he was to stand against us in distrust."

"The Mate," Olirassa growled, shaking what remained of her long brown locks. "He, we should have devoured."

"He has said his sorry," Lin persisted, shaking her head dolefully. "He has seen the truth in our days of journey. He wishes to know if you will be allies to stand against Gwirwen."

"We have always stood against him," the queen hissed, "in our own way. Is there a plan?"

"Only be strong," Oldrilin sighed, shaking her head. "You must be ready for the time we fight; Ami will call for you when the need is arisen."

"Yes," the queen agreed, offering her hand.

Taking it, Oldrilin smiled, "Then the deal is struck, and I must depart."

"Depart," the siren who had been tending her spat. "You must rest, Lin. You have been weakened greatly, away from the water so long."

"But I must return to my friends," the mermaid cried, her lip forming a small pout. "I shall reply to the message and give our word. And tell them of the elfs who should not be."

"We must let you go," Olirassa agreed, "but not today. You will take the nectar through the night and go out with us at first light. Slip away quietly, that the Cilithrand will not know you have come or gone."

"Lady Cilithrand asked for me?" Oldrilin inquired in a shaky voice.

"When the elves first appeared," the queen explained. "They hunted for you by name, but we told them you were not here, and we had not seen you since the dragon's fire rained upon us."

"Then I will hide and not let them see," Lin agreed with a generous nod, her voice low. "Thank you, my friends. I will do as you say and leave quietly on the morrow." Lying back against her cushion of moss, she closed her eyes to rest. She would need her strength for the return trip as she carried the truth and words of hope back to her friends and her Rey Daye, who waited for her on the shores of Falconmarsh.

THREE

Heart of Darkness

"I THINK THAT WOULD BE UNWISE," Meena advised, her hand occupied with stirring a pot of breakfast mash. The group had spent the night in fitful sleep with Rey and the siren gone, and the path Amicia would lead them down the morning after troubled her.

"Oh," Ami clipped, taking her seat on the rock before her bed. The blackened hamar gem in her hand, she stared at it, amazed at the transformation. "Well, you must understand that this is my choice to make," she informed them, a hint of lording in her voice, as if they were now beneath her.

"Is it, love?" the Mate cut in, standing to tower over her. "Seems I've been deposed," he growled, glancing at his wife. "But perhaps my years of wisdom will carry a little weight."

Ami glared at his surliness, a little deflated by his tone. "You always have my ear even if I do not heed your urging."

"Is that so," he growled, taking the empty spot next to her. He pointed at the stone as he spat through gritted teeth, "That thing killed Bally. She's an evil witch that serves no purpose to the rest of us."

The air tight in her lungs, the girl turned his words. "I know this. But I also know that we are all capable of dark, even depraved acts, at least in the eyes of others if not ourselves. I'm not saying we should make her a part of the group." She cut her eyes over at him, lifting her chin enough to meet his cool, dark gaze. "I just think it would be wise to win her over or remove her from the stone."

"There would be no winning," Meena corrected, taking the corner of the adjacent giant rock so she could sit close as well. "She could never be trusted."

"Kedoria is a dark elf," Animir joined in from the other side of their fire. "They serve no master among the living."

"And so, you think this idea folly as well?" she accused, sitting up straight to glare at him, then at Hayt and Zae.

The dwarf and nymph couple remained silent during the discussion as they sat on the fourth stone in front of their bed. Holding hands and their tongues, they felt no need to join the debate, as nothing they could say would soothe the heated argument, and neither cared to add fuel to the flame.

"I do," the elf replied, less afraid of taking a stand. His lips forming a puffy pucker, he held the odd countenance to emphasize his point of view.

Standing, Amicia's heart ached. Leaving them, she ambled down the line of the trees until she arrived at the designated trail. Rey had marked it the day the memorial had been erected. The ceremony had taken place as if they wanted to say their goodbyes and forget about the young man who had once walked beside them.

On the contrary, the sacred place was visited every day, several times a day, and the trail had become familiar to them all. Wiping at a tear as she cleared the ring and stood within the circle, she whispered, "Hi, Bally."

Holding up the gem, she spoke to him as if he would reply. "I've got a bit of a problem, and I was hoping you could help me riddle it out. The dark elf that Animir captured, Kedoria, occupies my hamar gem. She is a powerful witch, and I wish to turn her and use her against our enemies."

A gust of wind pushed against her, lifting the few hairs that framed her face and causing them to float. The feel of them brushing her skin gave the girl a tingle, and she panted, her lungs gasping in spasms of excitement that he might have heard and even responded.

"If she refuses to take up our cause, I may not be strong enough to destroy her. The best I could do is free her and allow her to return to the darkness of the caverns. We would be safe, mind you. She cannot or will not come out this end, and the dwarves have blocked the other with their magical enchantments. She would be a prisoner there for all time, or inside the stone even, if we do nothing," she argued, her eyes misty by the end.

"They've imprisoned my father, you know. Or perhaps you don't know," she added, catching the hairs and pulling them out of her face with a twisted smile. "I got to see him, Baldwin. He was a magnificent dragon, but he has wasted in his cell until he is scarcely scales and bones. It was pitiful to stand before him, and I would not wish that upon anyone, to sit and decay while one still draws breath," she huffed, "not even my worst enemy."

Staring down at the gem, it felt heavy in her hand, and her choice was clear, as if her young friend had whispered it in her ear. "I must do this," she agreed, sucking her lips in and chewing them for a moment. "Either she will join us, or she will be banished, but I cannot hold her imprisoned here within my grasp. Thank you," she smiled, turning to rejoin to the others.

Arriving at their fire, the group less Lin and Rey ate their breakfast in silence.

"Are you ready for your bowl?" Meena asked tenderly.

"No. I must deal with the dark elf first," Amicia spat. "Animir, would you join me?"

"My lady?" he replied, glancing anxiously at the others. Seeing she intended for him to follow without further debate, he slid his hand over and placed his bowl in Oldrilin's empty seat on the rock.

"They can't help you," Amicia clipped. "This is my call. Come with me and let's settle this once and for all," she commanded, turning her back as she walked away.

Strutting towards the cave, which would eventually lead to the fallen kingdom of Asomanee, Amicia gripped the darkened stone. Squeezing it firmly, she wriggled her fingers as she left the bright light of day behind her, Animir at her heel with his long bow and a few arrows in hand.

"My lady, I must insist upon my position, as I have stated quite clearly. This is not a sound course of action," the elf beseeched as he followed her into the darkness.

"Sound or not, this is the course I have chosen. Either she will join us or return to the depths below, but either way, I must have use of the gem returned to me," the girl explained with a tight jaw.

"Meena says –"

"I know what Meena says," Ami sighed. "Yes, the power is mine, and I am stronger each day; but the hamar holds some magic of its own. It augments mine, and they resonate and increase my strength as well as my focus. Besides, Kedoria has her own magic. If she were to agree to help us, it would add to our number, and we will need all the allies we can get." Lifting the darkened vessel, she stared into its immutable black. "You will be able to return her if the need should arise?"

"I believe that I will," he agreed with a firm nod. Using the end of his weapon, he drew a large circle on the ground. Kneeling, he used a stiff finger to add the runes for the four corners, followed by others for protection around the edges, mimicking the original he had drawn at the other end of the tunnel that exited the cave and led to the abyss beneath them. "I used a similar device as this when I captured her before. I am confident she is bound by magical law and we will be protected when we stand within it."

"Magical law," Ami whispered, her lips twisting into a crooked grin. "I feel I have much to learn in the magical arts."

"Indeed," Animir agreed, dusting his hands against one another as he stood. Holding out a flattened palm, he waited for her to turn the stone over to him.

Studying her profile, he grimaced, "I am sorry I did not warn you before you took your vow with Reynard."

Distracted from gazing into the gem, she stammered, "What? Why would you say that?" she demanded, lifting her chin to glare at him.

"I feel as if I should have, in hindsight. Now that your true nature has been revealed, I sense you are in pain." He could have said her unhappiness had affected her judgment but swallowed that detail for the moment.

She shook her head slowly, as if to dismiss his words. "Only for my people," she soothed, forcing a brief smile. "I will one day rule this land, and I must make my choices align with the good of the kingdom." Offering him the hamar, she indicated it with a nod, "My father has been imprisoned for two decades; a fact that tears at my heart beyond words. It would be easy to do the same with my enemies, but it would not be right. I will not see the queen of the daemons treated so unjustly. Either she will join us or she will return to her realm, but we will hold her no longer if we can help it."

"Yes, my queen," he agreed, accepting the gem. "Stand within the circle. If she attacks us, try to stay inside it. Only flee for the sunlight outside as a last resort."

"I understand," Ami replied, taking her place beside him within the ring.

Raising his arm, Animir chanted softly, his drawn lips moving as he whispered the spell that would release their nemesis. A bright flash of light halting his words, he held up an arm to shield his eyes, then blinked at the dark figure standing before them.

Her hair bright red, Kedoria's short mane burned. Her clothing dark against her pale flesh, she turned slowly to face the couple who had restored her physical form. "How dare you," she growled, her cold grey eyes fixed on the girl.

"I have decided to grant your freedom," Ami replied, getting directly to the point. "That is all that I dare. Your choice is simple. You may join us in the fight against those who would destroy our kingdom, or you may return to the darkness below."

Holding up an empty, bony hand, the daemon hissed, "What trickery is this? Why would you allow me to go?" Studying her adversary, the witch pondered what could have transpired while she had been trapped. Reaching out with her power, she probed the girl before her, poking at her through the protection of the charmed circle in which she stood. "You have discovered yourself," she surmised more quietly, lowering her appendage.

"Yes, I am aware of my station within the realm," Amicia agreed. "That is why I have come to make you this offer."

"I cannot help you," Kedoria bit sharply. "I am forever a prisoner of the darkness even if you do not hold me within the enchanted gem. Not even by the light of the moon am I permitted to exist."

"What of your minions? Are they also bound by such constraints?" Ami asked doubtfully.

Shifting her gaze to the elf, the dark queen studied the pair in turn. "You hope to deceive me," she proposed.

"No. If we wished to destroy you, we would have called you forth within the marsh and been done with you," the elf explained. "We understand your limitations, and my lady is willing to work within your needs if you would be willing to serve her."

"Serve her," the dark elf scowled. "Galiodien would never allow such a thing."

"Galiodien is dead," Amicia spat. "Centuries you have remained in the darkness of the dwarf caves, cut off from all that has happened. His daughter, Cilithrand, sits upon the elven throne. It is she that we must face if we are to hold our lands and protect our people."

"I see," Kedoria hissed. "And you believe my oath to him died with him. Foolish girl!" She threw up her hand, sending a wave of energy towards them as if to test the barrier between them.

With a quick flick of her wrist, Amicia blocked the unfriendly charm, dispelling the curse around them. Smiling, she felt a hint of pride at her quick reflexes and obvious abilities. "I do not wish to hold you prisoner any longer, and therefore a choice must be made. I understand you may not venture into the light, but there may yet be times you might prove yourself useful to us."

"And you will carry me in your pocket, letting me out when you see fit," the witch scoffed.

"Yes. Obviously, you do not require food, water, or sustenance. Can you sit by a warm fire, or is all light forbidden?" Amicia asked in a soothing voice.

"The light of the sun," Kedoria replied stiffly, "even as it is reflected by the moon, eats away my flesh. I must remain within the shadow if I am to survive."

"Then I dare say a warm fire might do your decayed heart some good," the girl smiled at her, genuinely pleased at the idea of including the powerful creature in their number. "Return to the stone, and we will call you forth in the evening that you might meet the others." Taking the gem from her companion, she held it up in front of her.

Her beady eyes wide, the dark elf glared at Animir as Amicia raised the stone, offering it to her. Blinking rapidly, she considered her options, then lowered her chin. "I will come with you and take up your cause in exchange for whatever freedom you can afford me, but do not be foolish enough to think that we are friends. I will bring forth my favored minions that they might join me." Turning to the sloped tunnel that connected the cave to the chambers below, she stood in the mouth of it and shrieked loudly.

Covering her ears at the shrill scream, Amicia squinted at the spectacle, curious if any of the daemons would indeed present themselves. To her surprise, they in fact did, and four small blobs of fire and ash came out of the darkness. The tallest of them scarcely two feet in height held up a tiny hand, which burned with small orange flames. "Do they have names?" she asked.

Curious once again at the girl's behavior, Kedoria indicated each in turn, "Falissi, Alelia, Liranni, and Cadeilia."

Catching a giggle, Animir snorted a short laugh before he squelched it. "Surely you do not think we will need names for them, my lady."

"Of course we will," Amicia corrected, indicating the gem once more.

In a flash, the four small shadows vanished in a puff of smoke as they were absorbed by their queen. Safely hidden within her body, they were a part of her, and she carried them with her when she returned to the gem in a final brilliant flash of light.

Leaving the cave with their new helper safely back inside the hamar gem, Amicia smiled at the bright sunlight. At the circle, she took up her bowl and filled it with mash. "We have our first real ally," she announced. "When darkness comes, we will be able to share with her our plans." Sitting, she ate hungrily, the weight of the issue resolved and lifted from her mind.

"Only tell her what you must," Piers warned, his eyes fixed on his bride. "I fear trusting her may cost us dearly."

Blinking at the Mate, Meena said quietly, "You have insisted upon bringing her into our group, but I pray you will not call her forth until she is needed."

"You fear her, even as she is locked away," Ami noted. "How can she harm us?"

Shaking her head, the other woman did not reply.

Sighing loudly, Amicia stood, pulling the gem from her pocket. "Very well. I will not force her upon you so quickly. I will place the hamar in my bag, and we will give you a few days to adjust to the idea of her joining us."

"As if a few days could allay my concerns," Meena sighed.

Rolling her eyes, the girl shoved the darkened stone to the bottom of her pack, next to the red orb. Feeling the sphere, she grinned at the thought of the two objects resting side by side, hidden from view. "You'll get over it," she laughed, taking up her bowl and resuming her meal with a satisfied twist on her lips.

FOUR

Lay in Wait

THE COOL AIR of the swamp around her, Amicia lay in her new bed and listened to the noises of the forest. She had slept in it alone the night before easily enough; her day had been long after discovering her inner self, seeing Rey and Lin off on their mission, and not to mention standing before the gnomes.

Tonight, she felt alone. She really hadn't expected her new husband to return so soon, as Riran was miles away to the south, a distance that the small mermaid would have to swim twice. *And I'm certain she will want to spend some time with her people.*

Thinking of the sirens, Ami toyed with the merdoe through her shirt. Their gift had been special, and now that her hamar gem was occupied by the dark elf, she relied upon it heavily to help her focus her magic.

After a few minutes of random thought, she rolled onto her side and stared at the empty half of her bed. She had missed Rey during the day, and the night even more so. She had taken her vow with him, and as the idea of it might have been short-sighted, it only felt right that she should hold to her word.

"Rey, I wish you could hear me," she reached. It would have brought her great comfort if he had replied. When he did not, she threw back her blanket and crawled out of the small structure.

Glancing around their camp, she sat still and listened. Only the birds, bugs, and sounds of the marsh stirred. In the other beds, her friends slept soundly, their breathing and snores a testament to their peaceful slumber. Sitting back on her mattress, she slipped on her boots and quietly crept out of the square formed by their leaning shelters.

Taking the familiar path, a sliver of moon lighted her way. Drawing her sweater around her, she thought about their day. They had kept busy, she and Animir both practicing their magic under Meena's guidance. The gnomes had promised their aid, but they were nowhere to be seen. Resistant to wasting time waiting on them, the wan had insisted there was progress to be made, and indeed Ami had felt the older woman's knowledge an asset even if she did not always heed her advice.

Amicia had come to suspect the tiny creatures watched from the woods, as even now she did not feel completely alone. The idea of it might have unnerved her if she had not felt inexplicable and unwavering trust in their new diminutive friends. *I hope they will honor their word soon enough, but for now, we wait,* she sighed, arriving at Baldwin's memorial. Staring at it, the words the Mate had carved in the stone brought tears to her eyes.

"You do not sleep, princess?" Lamwen joined her thoughts.

"Good evening," she smiled, comforted by his presence. *"Not tonight I'm afraid. Too many things to distract me from my slumber."*

"Come. Lie with me then and let us pass the darkness together," he beckoned.

Shaking her long blond locks, Ami's gaze swung around the circle of trees. *"Which way?"* She had yet to see the place her large friend had taken up residence within the marsh.

"To the north, probably in a straight line, in fact," he directed.

Still toying with her magical shell as she clomped through the moss-covered rock and mush, she recalled the trek she had made to see him in the dead of winter. *How odd to be such friends with a dragon,* she mused, a faint grin on her lips. Then recalling what she had learned only the day before, her countenance darkened. *I am also a dragon.*

Her emotions had run wild over the last day or so, as if caught out on the sea in a violent storm. One minute, she crested the waves at the highest point with pure joy coursing through her veins. The next, she crashed into a crest, and sorrow deeper than any she had ever known pressed in around her.

"Lamwen," she said gently when she entered his small clearing. His massive body spread on the ground, his pale green scales shimmered beneath the glow of the moon, stealing her breath for an instant.

"Princess," he replied, raising his wing and offering her the warm comfort of his underside.

Walking towards him with purposeful steps, she rested her hand against his neck, imagining the smile within him as her fleshy palm caressed his rough scales. "What a pair we have become," she sighed, dropping the appendage and turning to sit on the moist ground. Her back leaned against him, she sighed.

"You are troubled," he observed. "You miss your mate," he guessed, unable to hide the pain the idea of it brought him.

"Indeed," she huffed again. "I made my vow with him, and I cannot deny I love him deeply."

Wrapping her gently with his wing, he agreed, "And rightly so. Do not feel you are judged for your choice, sweet Kaliwyn. For it is the tenderness of your heart that makes you strong."

"I don't see how," she coughed. "All my soft heart has brought me is pain," she lamented, thinking again of all she had learned as of late. Arriving at her visit with her father, she asked, "Do you think Ziradon would be displeased to hear I had pledged myself to a mortal?"

"I should think your father will love you either way," Lamwen replied.

"I hope that it is so," she agreed. "We have much to do, and yet we lie here in wait, making little progress."

"Your power grows as you train," he pointed out, having observed them most of the day. "Your Piers works with the dwarf and nymph, sparring and giving them pointers, as his wife does with you and the elf. I think your fight shall be valiant, whatever the outcome."

"Still, I grow restless for the battle to come," she yawned. "And I have secured a strong ally, so there is more to us than our small group and a hand full of dragons."

"The dark elf."

"Yes, Kedoria. She kept four of her minions as well. I know my choice was not popular among the others, but I believe it was the right one." Stiffening, she realized she had not asked his opinion on the matter. "What say you of it, Lamwen?"

"I say she is a dark creature and agree her power is great. Whether she will betray your trust is hard to judge. As you are well aware, even the closest friend can turn against you," he advised, enjoying the warmth of her back against his belly. "Are you comfortable, my queen?"

"I am," she giggled, rubbing the stretched part of his wing and tracing the scar from his brush with the satyrs. "You speak of Gwirwen and my father. He is the friend who betrayed him."

"Yes, they were close for many centuries."

"He will pay for doing so," she promised through clenched teeth. "You were not near enough to see how Ziradon has suffered."

"I have been to his cage before. His body has lost much of its previous glory, but his spirit remains strong. You will try to free him, yes?"

"No," she cackled. "There will be no try. That task is high on my list of priorities. Once I am out of this skin and back into my scales, we will make for the prison and bring down his walls, be assured."

Lamwen smiled inwardly at her bravado. He loved her dearly at that moment, and a single tear escaped his eye, running over his scarred face and making its way down to his leathery neck. A lump in his throat, he asked, "Will you be able to control this dark creature you have aligned yourself with?"

Hearing the change in his voice, she gasped, "Surely you do not speak of Rey?"

"No, my princess," he laughed, in spite of his emotional state. "Your mortal is quite harmless, I am certain. I speak of Kedoria. Will she follow your command?"

"I'm uncertain. I will not control her at any rate, as I have no desire to bend any to my will. It will be her choice, as much as it is yours or any others to follow my command," she informed him tartly. Her heart beat wildly inside her chest at the anger he had stirred. "This isn't helping me sleep by the way," she rebuked.

"Oh, is that why you have come?" his laughter rumbled. "To sleep against me as if I were made of feathers?"

"Feathers," she grinned, thinking of the beds in their spire at Jerranyth. "Only once have I had a bed so fine, but the price of it was steep. You make a sweet place to rest, love; feathers or not." Her eyelids heavy, she closed them gently and rode the waves of his deep breaths.

Aware of her drift towards slumber, despite her protests, Lamwen held further comment. His own thoughts turning, there was much left for them to do, indeed. But for now, they would wait, while they trained and grew their numbers. *We must do it quietly, after all,* he silently observed. Thinking of the prophecy, he tightened his grip on her. *Sleep well my destroyer, lover of dragons and men.*

FIVE

Wanderers Return

COLD ROCKS BENEATH HIM, Rey sat on his small peninsula on the east side of the gnome marshes. The community of Falconmarsh behind him, he had yet to see the actual village for himself. He and Oldrilin had left their group the night Amicia was to stand before their gathering in search of their own quest.

Arriving at the water's edge, he had watched his tiny friend transform into her magnificent fish form before she swam away, five days ago now. *Five long days,* he lamented to himself, during which time he could have explored much of the area if fear had not prevented him from doing so.

They were close enough to Adiarwen that he dared not be seen by a passing dragon. His mission was too important to risk it, as being caught off guard by one of the beasts would have been disastrous to their cause. Only sitting out on his little swath of rocks in short intervals, he kept a watch out on the horizon, in case any of them should approach that he might hide before they drew near.

Catching a handful of the smaller rocks that wedged themselves between the larger, he bounced the gravel in his palm, then tossed the small stones into the water one at a time to watch their minuscule splash when they hit. He had eaten his rations sparingly and had managed to hunt a few meals while he was there, but that was the extent of his wandering, as he wanted to be close at hand for her return.

What if she doesn't come back? he thought again for the umpteenth time since his camp had been made.

They had not discussed exactly what he would do in that instance, but it was approaching the edge of what could be deemed a reasonable amount of time to swim down and back, even allowing for a bit to be spent in Riran while she was there. *This could be serious,* he surmised.

Picturing her black, scaled form, he could imagine a larger creature attacking her in the dark waters of night. Frozen in fear, his trancelike state stared into oblivion as he watched a shark with pointed teeth tearing her to shreds, or worse swallowing her practically whole with a few quick bites.

"Sharks," he muttered, thinking of the fins they saw regularly from their ships. Would there be any close to Eriden, or would the great barrier keep them centered around the rim of mortals?

A good question, he didn't have an answer for that. Deciding he could call it a dubious event, he dismissed the thought and imagined that she had in fact arrived in Riran. What then?

Elves.

If Lamwen had been correct, the beach he had last seen by moonlight the night of the birthday ball could be swarming with them. Would they recognize his small friend?

She had been in the infirmary when we were there, that and the suite. Even when they visited the enchanted gardens, few had laid eyes on her. *Unlikely any of them would know her,* he concluded.

Arriving at another sad notion, he pondered, *what if she chose to stay?* He knew she had missed her home and siren kin. If she had arrived but been overwhelmed at being home, she might have decided not to risk the return swim.

Scowling at the waves as he considered this, a large flat fish flipped in the water before him, disappearing into the depths before it rocketed out into the air. Spinning a few times, it slung water around it before it dove, nose first back into the abyss.

"Lin," Rey shouted, getting to his feet as quickly as he could on the slippery rocks. "Oh my God. You're back!" Looking around, his eyes dancing over the tops of the waves, he waited, but she did not appear again. "Where are you?" he panted, eager for her to leave the water and join him.

"Happy Rey Daye," her sweet voice called, catching his eye from the other side of the narrow strip of land.

Kneeling, he waited as she picked her way to him, each of them wearing large grins. When she reached him, he scooped her up, hugging her tightly as he carried her to the safety of the more solid, marshy ground.

Tears on their faces when he put her down, their joy at being reunited was evident. Helping to pack his things, they quickly prepared to head home while she shared a few tidbits from her adventure, while saving most of what happened for the group.

When they were ready, Rey placed her pouch onto his chest and helped her to climb in. Facing out so she could see where they were going, the pair set off on their march across the swamp.

"Well, it's been five days," the Mate announced, taking a seat to claim his spot at their new table. A long flat surface about three feet wide and ten feet in length, it held a bench for each side that would accommodate their party perfectly. He had completed the construction earlier that day, placing it to the north of their structures and running parallel to the forest and the mountains across the way. Smiling at his craftsmanship, the stew his wife had prepared would be their first meal upon it.

"Aye," Amicia agreed, seated on the large rock before her quarters and braiding her hair. Doing so reminded her of Reynard; well, everything she did reminded her of Rey, and she fought the urge to cry all the more.

"I smell dinner," a voice called from the woods a moment before a scruffy man cleared the trees, a small dark-haired siren strapped to his chest.

"Rey!" Zaendra screamed, leaping up from her seat next to the Mate to greet him.

Giving the girl a hug, the young man squeezed her tightly from the side so as not to squish the mermaid in between. Then releasing her, he knelt to place Lin's feet on the ground. A circle of friends had formed around them, and he rubbed his hands anxiously on his pants as he stood to face them.

He had had five days to consider his actions and those of the girl who had taken his name. It didn't take much to realize she might harbor some regrets, and he wasn't all that anxious to find out if Animir would share his bunk that night.

As the group parted, Amicia awaited outside the crowded space. A gap opening between them, everyone watched and waited to see what the verdict would be. Their eyes meeting, Rey grinned, not moving as he took her in; "You look beautiful, love."

"And you," she beamed, not afraid to take the first step, or three as the case may be. In his arms in an instant, she wept openly; "Dear God, you're really here!"

Uncomfortable at the display, their friends quickly disbursed, giving them some room and a few minutes to say their hellos in private. Hugging her against him, Rey lowered his mouth to hers, searching for relief of his fears and doubts.

Her heart pounding inside her chest, Amicia opened herself to him. If she had ever held misgivings in the connection between them, they were swept away by the raw emotion that flourished within her. "I was so afraid I would never see you again," she whispered when he finally broke off to breathe.

"Oldrilin did the swimming," he laughed. "I just sat at camp for a few days and waited." His forehead pressed against hers, he whispered, "It was a very long few days, to be certain."

Feeling a tug at her pant leg, Ami looked down to find Lin staring up at her. "Ami miss Lin as well?" she asked in her tiny mermaid voice.

"You know that I did!" Amicia grinned, kneeling to take her small friend into her arms. "I see you made it back all safe and sound. So, tell us; what did you discover?"

"Allow me to serve the bowls," Meena suggested, indicating the table. "You pour the water and sit, and we will be ready to hear in a few minutes; I'm sure the story will keep for that long."

"Where's Lamwen?" Hayt asked. "He will probably want to hear the tale as well."

"I'll call to him," Amicia agreed, reaching out to her large friend. *"Lamwen, we have need of you. Rey and Oldrilin have returned."*

"About time," he growled. *"What's the word?"*

"We don't know yet. We await your arrival that we all may hear at once," she explained, grinning brightly at her husband as she did so.

Zae serving the cups and Meena the bowls, the group quickly gathered around their table and sat on the two long benches, Rey claiming the tent end facing the mountain with his bride across from him, facing the trees. Taking small bites, the air around them crackled with excitement as the dragon arrived and came forward to sit at the clearing end of the row among the moss and grass.

"So kind of you to wait for me," he bowed.

"Nonsense," Piers clipped, his eyes darting over to their large friend. "You are one of us now, Lamwen."

His pulse slowed, the dragon narrowed his gaze as he stared at them, considering that sentiment. "Never has a dragon resided among other than his own kind," he confessed in a deep voice. "We would rather live alone as outcasts than in the midst of those beneath us."

Bothered by his statement, Amicia placed her hands in her lap and looked up at him. His eyes large and round, they appeared distant, almost sad. "Tis true, love. You have a place at our table even if you do not fit within a chair."

"I thank you, princess," he agreed, lowering his head and eyeing the returned pair as the siren sat beside him on the bench. "Shall we hear of your adventures, siren?" he growled, confident he would be deemed honest at any moment.

"Alas, what you have said is true," she whined. "I saw the elves with my own eyes."

"That's unfortunate," Hayt growled, chewing at his meat.

"Indeed," Animir seconded, also scooping at his meal.

"What of Olirassa?" the Mate prodded. "Has she accepted my apology?"

"Oh, yes, Mate," Lin sighed. "She was most gracious and agrees to help when they are called."

"Are they well?" Amicia asked, concern growing in the back of her mind at how little had actually been said. *But then again, Lin has never been much of a talker,* she mused.

"The sirens have suffered greatly," Oldrilin explained, shaking her head as tears spilled onto her cheeks. "They were burned by the dragons, with scars that even nectar cannot heal."

Uncomfortable, Lamwen stiffened and growled, "Is this what I was called to hear?"

"We know you can't take it back," Amicia soothed, "even if you wanted to. Do not feel judged by your past actions under the direction of Gwirwen. We all know who is responsible for the plight of the sirens."

"Hear, hear," Rey cheered, lifting his cup of water as a toast to the truth in her words.

Watching as Ami and Rey shared their meal, facing one another at the far end of the new table, a fire burned within Lamwen's chest. He could see the connection between them had only grown stronger in the man's absence, and he knew he would need to take great care if he wished to hide the jealousy within his heart.

"I will feel responsible until I can make amends," the dragon countered.

"And soon you will get your chance," Ami challenged, smiling up at him.

Meena and Piers exchanged a glance with one another; if they had thoughts on the topic, they remained hidden, as they had larger issues to discuss. They had convinced the girl to keep the dark elf caged until Rey's return, in hopes that he could convince her that bringing Kedoria out would be a mistake.

Daring to broach the subject, the Mate made his comment smoothly, "I guess you feel Kedoria will as well."

"Kedoria," Rey parroted between bites. "That name sounds familiar."

"That's the dark elf," Meena dropped evenly, no longer actually eating her stew. Lifting a spoonful, she spilled it over the side and back into the bowl anxiously.

"The dark elf," he paused, his next bite frozen in midair. "The one from Asomanee?" he gasped. When no one replied, he glanced from face to face until his gaze landed on his bride. She was the only one still eating, and she did not meet his stare.

"Ami, what are they talking about?" he pushed.

Licking her lips, she placed her utensil on the table next to her bowl. Her voice calm, she replied, "While you were away, I invited the dark elf to join us."

She could have gushed on with her reasons why, but she had two things on her side she hoped would be enough; one, the creature held great power and they would need all the help they could get. The second and more important, Amicia was in charge, and in the end, the decision was hers to make.

"You mean you want me to share ranks with that thing that killed Bally?" he gasped, then wafted his spoon at the dragon and spilled the portion. "As well as the dragon who attacked the sirens, and us for that matter?" Clenching his jaw tightly, he waited for her reply. He had missed her so much, and in an instant, his rage threatened to spoil their reunion with a few choice words. When the pause grew long, he pushed the bowl back and stood. "I'm done."

Walking away from them, he skirted the dragon with a cold glare and entered the forest on the worn path, arriving at the place that had become all too familiar. Wiping at his eyes, his feelings churned. *I thought I knew her,* he sobbed. *How could she do this, like she has turned against all that we stood for.*

A short time later, a branch cracked behind him, and he stiffened. "I do not wish to speak. Please go."

"Even to your wife?" a small voice replied.

"Especially to her," he growled. "It would be unwise to share words in my state."

"You are angry," she observed, sidling up to him. "That is fine. Then you will listen."

"Bah," he grunted, still not looking at her. Wrapping himself tightly across the chest, he waited, knowing she would not give up so easily.

Gathering her courage, Ami licked her lips. Having arrived next to him, she could see his profile, with his firm jaw and the dents in his forehead where he scowled.

"We have all done things we regret, husband. Things that may even have hurt other people. Those things do not make us good or bad. They are simply things that we have done and actions we have taken. They do not define who we are. As you would follow any order given by the Mate, Kedoria believed she acted within her right, as her lord Galiodien commanded. And Lamwen with Gwirwen."

"Aye," he spat, "give it enough time and we'll have the whole bloody mess of them on our side."

"And then who would we fight against?" she giggled.

"And who would we trust?" he shouted, turning to face her for the first time. His breath instantly stolen, he stared at her. Wearing the dress she had wed in, her hair hung loose to catch the rays of the moonglow as strands floated around her head.

His gaze dropping, the shoulders of the gown landed near her biceps, leaving the creamy white tops to tempt him in their nakedness. In her arms, her folded blanket lay across them, and her bag sat at her feet. "What's in the bag?" he scowled.

"Only a few things I will need in the morning. My brush and mirror… and the like," she replied quietly.

Studying her, she had the look of an angel, her beauty cutting him to the depth of his soul. "And you think this will help?" he asked more gently, indicating her with an open palm. His loins coiled, his resolved slipped dangerously close to oblivion.

"I am only happy you are home. I have missed you terribly these five days, and I do not wish to spoil our evening with a fight," she whispered.

Staring into her clear green orbs, he wanted desperately to look her over once more, her seductive attire mesmerizing. Part of him screamed he should look away and stand on his principle instead. In reality, he could do neither, as his love was too strong and his devotion too deep. Swallowing visibly, he sighed, "This isn't fair, Ami. Using my love for you against me."

Smiling, she stepped towards him, freeing her right arm and placing it around his neck. Releasing the ribbon that held back his hair, she toyed with it. "What isn't fair is leaving me alone for all these nights," she answered, her voice dripping with honey.

He had no hope of resisting. Pulling her against him, he kissed her deeply, then hissed, "Our discussion of the dragon and witch are not ended."

"As long as they are for the moment," she smiled, scooping up her bag and leading the way to their private clearing by the pond.

SIX

Blessed By Three

THE PAIR'S return to the camp the following morning felt far less painful than their first had, and Amicia hummed softly to herself when she warmed a kettle of water for tea with their breakfast. His smile equal to hers, it didn't take the others much imagination to figure out how the fight ended.

"So, I guess we have ourselves a dragon and a dark elf on our side," the Mate jabbed cruelly.

"Aye," Reynard snapped, not taking his bait. Instead, he observed, "Did you really think I would stand against her on this? If you were dead set on stopping her, you should have done so while I was gone."

"We tried," Meena joined in, "but she would not listen to reason."

"Aye," Rey replied for the second time, "but there are two sides to every coin, and I can see both of them. If you are going to follow her, then you must accept her choices, the good and the bad."

Looking at each other, the couple decided to leave it be, at least for the time being. Piers had followed Amicia's decisions often, but he could see holding blind faith in her would be foolish. In the end, he only hoped they had not come too far to be saved should her path prove to have been wrong.

"Would you like some breakfast?" Zaendra chimed in, now that it appeared safe to do so.

"Please," Rey grinned, taking a seat across from his bride and accepting his bowl of morning mash. "I thought we were going to eat better when we got here," he observed, changing the subject the best he could.

"You will once you've learned what's good here," the gnome king replied, joining them out of the forest.

"Thirac," Amicia greeted with a wide grin. "So nice of you to join us!" Toying with her meal, she hid her suspicions that he had never been far from them. She would have asked about their aid as well but didn't want him to run away too quickly.

As Thirac made his way into the camp, three shorter gnomes followed, each dressed head to toe in a shimmering grey cloak. Noticing the small staffs similar to Meena's, each perfectly suited to their height, the girl sighed in delight. "You've come to help us."

"Yes. We've been watching you for days, actually; discussing exactly what aid we should provide," Thirac explained as his three companions each stood quietly waiting for their introduction. "And the ossci have volunteered to walk among you."

"The ossci?" Piers asked, joining the discussion. Standing over the newcomers, he stared down at their miniature forms, even smaller than their siren. Dark and mysterious beneath their hoods, he pondered how much help the three could possibly be.

"Yes," Thirac agreed, "it's a name for a special group of our highest ministers. They have very distinct talents beyond those of ordinary gnomes and will be able to help you greatly on your quest, we are certain."

"I knew you were a powerful people," Ami observed, eyeing each of them in turn. "I could sense it the night I spoke before your gathering." The three before her radiated an energy that enticed her, as if she could blend with it and share in their secret circle called ossci, almost as she had basked within it the night she spoke to their gathering.

"And did you say you've been spying on us?" Hayt added, not happy at that bit of news.

"Watching, really," the old gnome shrugged. "We had to be certain who exactly we were giving aid, if you know what I mean."

"You're giving it to the rightful heir to the kingdom," Rey snapped, also put out by the subterfuge.

"Yes, as we have determined. Please, allow me to introduce the ossci," Thirac directed, his manner friendlier than it had been since they met him, which only aroused their suspicions more.

"By all means," the Mate slurred. "We have awaited their arrival with bated breath."

"Piers," Meena gasped, shaking her head at her husband's typical surliness. "Please, continue," she smoothed his words with a smile.

Giving them a brief scowl, the leader of the land seemed undaunted by their odd behavior. Indicating the first, the shorter gnome stepped forward and pulled back his hood. The same height as the other three ossci, his skin appeared a pasty white and his hair a long and shaggy dark brown, that hung to his waist. Looking up at them, beady eyes the shade of red rubies glared from beneath the locks. His beard hardly more than a few strands, he stroked the hairs a few times.

"His name is Ziyath."

"I'm a crafter," the new gnome claimed, his countenance turned by a frown.

"And what does a crafter do, exactly?" Zae asked doubtfully.

"I'm a wielder of special spells. I mean, we all can conjure them, but I'm particularly good at it, mind you," he growled, holding up a single digit as he spoke.

"What kind of special," Meena pushed, not easily taken in by such claims.

"Ah, the wan," he cackled, offering her his hand.

Taking the small appendage, she knelt next to him, waiting for his reply.

"You know of transposition?" he supplied in a low whisper.

"Of course," she agreed.

"I can take you anywhere in Eriden in the blink of an eye," he boasted.

A small gasp escaping from most of their gathering, they were all pleased at the news, despite Meena's doubtful expression.

Stepping forward, the second male also pushed back his hood to announce, "I'm Mizath, a seer." His grey hair short, it stuck out all around his smooth, round face, his bright sapphire blue orbs accenting his features.

"And what do you see?" Amicia giggled, taken with the trio already.

Producing a golden orb, he sang, "Anything you like. And we can speak through them, too."

"Bah, that's absurd," Animir whined, not believing a word of it.

"Tis true," the third vouched, also removing her hood to expose her bright blond locks that fell straight to her shoulders and framed her lovely face. Her emerald green eyes shone as she announced, "My name is Yimath, and I keep the histories of our people."

"She minds the books," the other two stated in unison.

"What an odd group of friends," Ami breathed, completely smitten. "How old are you?"

"Near on two hundred, my lady," Mizath replied with a bow.

"They are precious," Zaendra squealed, agreeing with Amicia's assessment of their new members.

"They're not children, love," Hayt rebuked, his hand waving as he turned to face her. "He just said they were born near the time of the great war."

"Yes," the Mate agreed, having picked up on that fact as well and not liking the sound of it. "You've seen a lot, I take it."

"And had a few centuries of practice," Yimath stipulated. "We will build a shelter here to be close to you and act as part of you if you wish, my queen," she continued, placing her hand on Amicia's arm.

"That would be a wonderful idea," the girl nodded, getting to her feet. Staring down at them, her mind raced, and she could see why they were chosen to help them. "If anyone can restore my dragon form, you can, I am sure of it."

"We will give it our best," Ziyath said with a wave of his hand. "For now, we should clear out our tree and prepare to get started. There will be much work ahead of us to prepare for the battle ahead."

"Well now, that's something we can agree on," the Mate observed. "Let's finish with breakfast, and then we can get on with it."

The rest sitting down to their meal, Meena offered, "Would you care for a bowl? It's a simple morning porridge, but it will see you through the day."

"We would love to try your breakfast," Yimath smiled, giving Ziyath a nudge to remove his frown. "There will be time for cottage building after the meal," she assured him.

Accepting his bowl along with the others, the first ossci they had met did not appear so easily convinced. Tasting the mixture with the tip of his tongue, his nose scrunched, and he sputtered, "It's not our typical mash."

"No, but what is the harm in sharing something new?" the female of the three observed.

"Eat it," Mizath spat, their banter earning a round of giggles from their hosts.

The three took their bowls and began settling in, listening to the conversation and learning about their new friends. Their morning planned, the ossci quickly finished their meal and left their seats. Chattering with each other in low voices, Amicia considered if they were actually kin. Observing as they scouted the nearby trees, she speculated, "Thirac, when you said the three had a talent, does that mean that is all they can do?"

"Oh, no," he shook his head, pushing back his empty dish. "They can all wield magic, use the orb, and know a great deal of our history. But each is stronger in their particular talent."

"And how did they become ossci?" Rey asked, perplexed by their tapping on trunks and examining the roots of several large specimens.

"As I said, the ossci are our highest level of priest. Not all achieve such a rank, be assured. The ossci were all but wiped out at the time of the great war, so there are really only two left who are older than those I have brought you, as these three have only recently attained their stature. Mind you, the older ossci remain hidden as age and infirmity have stolen their ability to travel and their willingness to make new friends," Thirac explained.

"Well, not to brag, but our Amicia is quite talented with magic herself," Piers boasted, giving her a wink as he patted the scar hidden beneath his shirt.

"Yes, as a dragon, she has the potential to unleash a great deal of power," the gnome agreed.

"Pfft," Rey huffed, "even raise people from the dead."

The trio at a tree close by froze in place, turning in unison to stare at him. Noting their discomfort, Thirac shook his head. "No need to embellish. We have seen the princess for who she is and recognize her potential."

Realizing his young friend had been called a liar, Piers pulled at the buttons on his shirt, opening it roughly and holding the cloth aside. The pink puckered scar exposed, he extended a single digit and pointed at it. "I assure you I was quite dead."

A heavy silence sat over the gathering for half a minute before the gnomes began to giggle and Meena hissed, "Put your clothes back on. They obviously are unmoved by your words, and there is no real proof that we may offer."

Returning to their hunt for a tree, the issue had been dropped. Changing the subject, Amicia asked, "Will we see Sevoassi while we are here? Or will you be able to take us to him for a visit?"

"Sevoassi," Thirac echoed, his eyes distant. "I do not believe I have ever heard that name."

"I'm sure that you have," Ami countered. "He's a gnome, very much like you. Red hair, beady eyes, about this tall," she described, holding up her hand to her side to gauge his height.

"I'm afraid not," the elder insisted. "Where did you meet such a character?"

"In the north woods. He helped us part from the northern pack," Piers explained, adjusting his clothing into place. "He lived in a tree, or beneath one rather, as your homes we have seen in the village."

Swallowing, the gnome shook his head slightly. "I assure you we have no such member within our ranks."

"Could he have been born elsewhere?" Hayt suggested. "Perhaps to a couple who left Falconmarsh in the past."

"There is no such couple," the leader insisted. "Gnomes do not live outside the marsh, ever. We are born here, and although we visit distant lands via transposition when the need arises, we do not travel. We do not move. And we do not mingle with those outside our kind."

"So say the trolls," Reynard mocked.

"Rey," Amicia gasped.

"Well, it's true," he laughed, cutting his eyes over at the tiny creature before he stood and strutted away.

"I'm so sorry," Ami breathed. "He must be tired after their mission," she apologized to the gnome.

"Think nothing of it," he replied. "It has been many centuries since we allowed any into our lands, much less accepted them as equals. We have shown you great honor in the forming of this alliance."

"And we appreciate the gesture," Zaendra grinned, giving him a small bow of her head.

"I only hope it is enough," Thirac agreed, getting to his feet. "For now, I will leave the ossci in your care and you in theirs. They have full use of the libraries in the village when you are ready for them, and we wish you the best of luck upon your quest."

"Libraries?" the Mate parroted, but the gnome did not reply, having turned his back and disappeared into the forest.

SEVEN

Down in the Valley

BY MIDAFTERNOON, the ossci had made their selection, a very large old oak tree that stood behind the table the Mate had constructed, but not directly as a few smaller versions hid it from their camp. Using their magic, they hollowed the space underneath, added steps, and furnished it for the three of them.

Climbing down to investigate, Amicia shook her head. "I know you have said Sevoassi could not be real, but this is too much like his dwelling. You have even hung the tiny pot next to your fire as he did," she gasped, pointing to the device.

Shaking her head, Yimath agreed, "If you think he was real, perhaps he was. This is a magical land, after all, and anything is possible."

"Rubbish," Ziyath scowled, muttering under his breath as he adjusted a hammock that hung scarcely a foot off the ground along the wall. "Gnomes do not live outside the marsh," he added, climbing in to test the bed that would be his.

Chuckling at his display, Ami offered, "I think you have just earned a nickname, my friend, and I shall call you Grumpy."

"Grumpy!" he spat, sitting up to face her squarely. "I shall not be insulted in my own home, new or otherwise," he growled.

Laughing openly, Mizath nodded at the girl. "Yes, he is! May I have a nick name as well?" the grey-haired gnome beamed.

"Well, if he is Grumpy, then you are Happy," she grinned, liking the idea of not having to recall their proper names. "Grumpy, Happy, Yimath, the three ossci of Falconmarsh," she teased. The joy she felt in their presence calmed her, as if they were old friends and their behavior perfectly expected.

Rolling his eyes, the first gnome only grumbled as he left is bed and climbed the miniature steps, exiting their quarters in a huff. Outside, he called, "Which of you shall be my first apprentice?"

"If you are referring to the transposition, I would love to hear more of it," Meena volunteered, setting her stitching aside.

"Good," he coughed. "Let us move away from these hecklers and begin our work in earnest."

Giggling at his frumpy attitude, the wan agreed with their assessment of the long-haired gnome. However, rubbing his nose in it would not suit her purpose, and she hid her smile behind a straight face. Leading him down the tree line, the pair located a spot they could practice their craft undisturbed.

Having climbed out as well, Happy nodded his agreement, "Yes, we should begin in earnest if the battle is to be won." Turning to Animir and Hayt, he added, "Would you like to hear of the orb?"

Hearing the offer, Zaendra laughed, "I shall stick to my spear."

"And I my new axe," Hayt agreed, holding up Bally's weapon, which Animir had bestowed upon him.

"Good, because you were terrible with that sword of yours," the elf grinned as well.

"Then we'll have an afternoon of training," the Mate agreed, hunting for his blade.

"I think I will learn of the orb, actually," Animir countered. "I found it doubtful when the gnome first spoke of it, but perhaps there is merit in his offer of its greater use."

"Indeed, there is," Happy nodded, producing his small, golden sphere. "Do you have your own, or shall I retrieve another?"

"No, I don't," Animir shook his long, cinnamon-colored locks.

Opening his hand, Mizath offered one to the elf. "We have plenty," he explained.

"Yes, I know they are common," his new apprentice agreed. "I have never had one of my own is all." He could have gone into detail and explained his circumstances, but he saw little point in sharing his sorrow over the past.

"Then you may keep it," the gnome grinned, indicating a path for them to follow. "Let us walk, and we shall acquaint you with its use and power."

Accepting the gift, Animir pursed his lips, glad he had kept the story of his existence hidden. "Thank you. That is most generous. I'm sure it will be of great use to me."

Watching them go, Amicia sighed, "It finally feels as if we are getting somewhere."

"The path has only begun, my queen," Yimath warned, her golden strands catching the light as she looked up at her. "Shall we visit the libraries and begin our search for your cure?"

"Yes, right we should. Which way?"

Taking her hand, the gnome transported them in an instant, and they landed in a large hollowed tree. A portion of the ground missing beneath, it formed a large cave that extended for several feet into the trunk that spanned at least twelve feet in diameter.

"Oh my," Amicia gasped, startled by the sudden travel and even more so by their destination. "Is this the library?" Large tomes lined every wall, and she could see no physical entrance or exit to the place.

"One of them, yes," the gnome agreed. "They are sealed and hidden, so only those who know of them may enter," she explained.

"Fascinating," Ami breathed, turning slowly as she took in the sheer number of volumes. "It doesn't harm the tree to remove what's in the middle?"

"Not at all, as the living part of the wood is out next to the bark," the ossci explained. "The center isn't really vital, and it makes the perfect place for storing our sacred historical texts."

Patches of light shone through holes in the top, illuminating their find in bright yellow and white. "Historical texts," Amicia repeated quietly, contemplating the notion. "So, what's in them that is so sacred?"

"These are the history of Eriden. Stories of our people and our past."

"The gnomes," the girl presumed.

"And all other creatures who have lived within our realm," Yimath beamed. "We do not interact with those of the kingdom because we are too busy watching and recording what we see," she explained, holding up her golden orb. "We can watch any and all that takes place within our world and document the cause in our great journals. We even hold the power to visit the scene should the need and desire arise."

"Can you hide within a shadow?" Amicia asked, her gaze still fixed on the texts, her eyes focusing on a few of the bindings and titles.

"Of course," the gnome agreed. "Secrecy is always vital when one wishes to observe without affecting the players upon the stage."

"How beautiful," the girl grinned down at her new friend. "But there are so many. Where shall we begin?"

"I think it would be best to start with you. I believe we will find the tome of Kaliwyn within these shelves."

"I have a book?"

"I believe that you will."

Moving to the end of the last shelf, Amicia suggested, "Perhaps I can start here on the bottom and work my way up, while you climb to the top and come down to meet me."

"That plan is sound," Yimath agreed, using a rickety ladder to reach the highest point.

A few hours later, Amicia's eyes had grown tired, but she refused to give up. They were inside their third tree, and she had just begun her second row when she gasped, "Oh my God. Could this help us?"

Sliding down the ladder, Yimath inspected the title. *The Rise and Fall of the Supreme Dragon Ziradon.*

"Well, he is your father, is he not?" Yimath observed.

"Yes," Amicia breathed, her fingers trembling as she reached for the oversized book. "Return us to the camp that we may peek inside," she commanded brusquely.

In an instant, they stood next to the table, where Meena and Zae were busy preparing their evening stew. "There you are," the older woman observed. "We had begun to wonder what kept you."

"I may have found something," the girl gasped, dropping her find on the far end of the flat surface and opening the first page, which held a picture of her father in all his glory.

Tears in her eyes, she laid her hand against the image. *He was a magnificent creature,* she observed, recalling the worn and beaten version she had met only a few days before. "We should start at the end," she said aloud, flipping the book and starting on the last page.

Finding the end blank, they continued to turn until they came to the portion containing writing. The hand a fine script, the words blurred as her drops of sorrow escaped and dripped upon the page.

"I will have to read it for you, my lady," the gnome offered. "It is in a special –"

"I read it fine," Amicia countered, turning back a few more pages while dabbing at her eyes. Her finger tracing the page, she noted a great battle between Ziradon and Gwirwen, with two of his followers helping him. Deciding more would be in order, she turned back farther, coming to a chapter titled Kaliwyn.

"This is it," she whispered.

"You can read this?" Meena asked. Her chore finished, she had joined them and glared at the strange writing in disbelief.

"Yes," Amicia nodded. "Can't you?"

"No. It's more like… scribble," the wan confessed, glancing at Yimath. "It's like a magical code."

"Yes, to prevent anyone from deciphering the words should the tome ever fall into the wrong hands," the blonde gnome explained. "It was given to our kind by the creator; a special gift only for the ossci of the gnomes. How my queen may see is a mystery."

"Not so much," Zae laughed, joining them. "We told you Amicia is a *very* powerful dragon. We saw her bring Piers back to life with our own eyes even if you do not believe."

"And so her skill would testify," Yimath agreed, her amazement at that fact evident. "What does the story say?"

"I will read and summarize," Amicia suggested, "but it will take me a while. I don't want to miss anything important."

Continuing her cursory assessment, she noted that the front held a table of contents, as the recorder outlined the great dragon's life one or two words at a time. The pages that corresponded written in a beautiful script, she traced the swooping letters with a stiff digit, admiring the beauty with which the words had been crafted.

Flipping to the end once more, she compared the two samples, noting most of the penmanship held the same features, but the last few pages stood out, as the change held abrupt and stark contrast. "Who records these, exactly?" she asked more thoughtfully. "I can tell the hand that penned them is different."

"We gnomes do get attached to our subjects," Yimath agreed with a smile. "It would appear one of us followed Ziradon's life in great detail to put this history in place. Where the writing changes, another took over in the telling, and in this fashion, there may be many who work on a particular subject over time."

"Using the orb," Meena suggested, "by looking into the past. But surely they cannot see the future."

"Yes," the gnome nodded, "that would be most likely. Futures are much harder to assess as I am sure you are aware."

"Looking into his past," Ami breathed, still drawn to the contents and his early adventures. "It would be a beautiful thing to behold, I am certain." Lifting the book, she carried it to her shelter. Lying across her blanket, with the tome flat beneath her, she propped herself on her elbows and drifted into the past.

"Ami, supper is served," Lin giggled, climbing under the shelter and lying next to her.

"Ok. I'll be right there," the girl replied, turning the page.

"You can finish tonight or tomorrow," Rey called, hoping the pair would be quietly retreating to their hidden nest among the trees soon.

"I'm almost finished," she insisted, using a stiff digit to hold her place. The light dim as the sun sank, it had become more difficult to make out the words, and she wished at the moment Kedoria had taken to the depths so she could use her hamar gem to light the passage.

A few minutes later, she had reached the end. Closing the tome, she sighed. *There's still hope.* Pushing herself up, she climbed out and saw the group at the table had moved on to eating without her. Picking up her bowl from the rock in front of her, she served her dish and joined them, taking her customary seat on the end, across from her husband.

Down the length of their setting, the long benches had become a bit crowded with the addition of the gnomes. Arriving at that moment, Lamwen landed a few yards away and ambled over to his end, where he sat up straight and glared down at them. "We have new members," he observed, his tone unreadable.

"Yes, the aid we were promised has finally arrived," Amicia smiled, scooping bites in as her hunger came on full force. "Did you discover anything new this day?"

"I have been all across the south," he reported. "The elves do indeed hold firm at Riran, but their grasp on the glen is not so formidable. They have taken over your old cabin and the meadow I used to occupy, but all south of that is still in the hands of the nymphs and satyrs. It would appear they are not giving it up without a fight."

"Good," Zaendra spat, her fists clenched as she pounded the table and shook their dinner bowls. "My people do not belong beneath the boot of the elves."

"No one does," Rey agreed, glancing at Animir.

"Did you meet any other dragons?" the Mate asked, helping himself to more water calmly.

"No. I fear they are too preoccupied with their infighting in the north to be aware that their kingdom falls in the south," he growled. "At some point, I will have to return to Adiarwen and look for my allies among them."

"Perhaps we can help with that," Happy offered. "We are practiced at blending in and often go unseen or noticed when we visit places afar."

"You can give him a shadow?" Amicia asked, surprised at the extent of their skill.

"That or a disguise," Grumpy countered. "Either would do if he needs to walk among them."

"We will discuss this further tomorrow then," the dragon agreed, lying down to rest.

Glancing at the girl, Meena could see the troubled lines in her face. "Did you find anything useful in the story of your father?" she prodded.

"I don't know," Amicia's voice quavered. "I am not certain that I am ready to speak of it."

"Tell us what you can, love," the Mate encouraged. "You can quit if it gets to be too much."

Glancing over at him, she nodded, "Ok. I'll start at the beginning, I guess. Some we have already heard, or different versions of it I think. Ziradon is near seven hundred years old. He has been the Supreme Dragon for near on five," she added, neglecting to point out that he currently did not hold that title. "He had a close friend he named to be his advisor."

"Gwirwen," Rey guessed.

"Yes. About thirty years ago, not long in the life of a dragon, he took a new mate. He had not had one since his first died, along with their sons, during the great war. His new mate was called Kilawon, and he loved her very much. They had a hatchling; me. But she was killed in what appeared to be an accident shortly after," Ami sniffed.

"It wasn't an accident," Lamwen dropped calmly.

"No," Amicia shook her head, not looking at him. "It was meant to look like one, and many believed so, including my father. But the gnomes saw everything. Kilawon was murdered. Soon after, Ziradon was cornered by Gwirwen and some of his followers. They constructed the rock prison in which he is still held and locked him away there."

Looking up, she glanced around at the members of their group, one by one. "They formed a ring around me, half a dozen of them, and forced me into this body while he watched. He was helpless to prevent it," she sobbed, her chest heaving. "One of them carried me away to Nalen, and there is no mention of me again… at least not in that book."

"We'll find another," Yimath offered.

"I don't think so," Ami sighed. "We have the story. What we need is to find the spell. You said both were recorded in the tomes of the libraries, correct?"

"Yes, there are many spells hidden in the texts," the gnome agreed.

"Then tomorrow we begin our search for those. We need a transfiguration spell. I'm certain that is how they did it, but the chant was not recorded in this record that we have found," she determined.

A heavy silence settled over the group in light of what she had discovered. Feeling the weight of it, Rey soothed, "It was a good discovery, love."

"Yes, it was a start," she agreed, stirring the remainder of her broth.

"Well, it's been a long day," Piers observed loudly. "We should clean up and get to bed. It sounds like it will be another tomorrow."

Without argument, the group disbanded, washing their dishes and putting them away. Then, the gnomes disappeared into their new home under the forest floor. The dragon curled between his giant rocks, which still felt warm after collecting the heat of the sun all day, and the rest took to their bunks under the leaned roofs that sheltered them.

"Will we sleep here tonight?" Rey asked, hoping to tempt her with their secret spot.

"Aye," she agreed in a tired voice. "Lie with me tonight and hold me as I slumber," she practically begged. Reading the words, she had lived them, and her heart ached with the love and loss her father had suffered.

Curling up behind her as she faced the wall, Rey didn't argue. His arm resting comfortably over her waist, he thought of the night he had found her in just such a position with Piers at their camp in Riran, ages ago. Shoving his nose into her hair, he breathed in the scent of her and sighed, happy to have whatever he could get.

His mind wandering, he thought about their current home such as it was, there in the valley. A beautiful place in its own way, it had turned out far safer than they could have imagined. Most of the marsh was considered a wasteland by outsiders, and the dragons seemed to have no reason to visit or even fly over it. As Lamwen had informed them, the dragons meet with the gnomes on the northern edge, between the forest and Adiarwen. If they need to go south, they fly over the mountains, leaving this one patch of land as a safe refuge for them.

Smiling into her mass of curls, he almost wished they would never find the spell she was looking for. If she never regained her dragon form, they might remain there forever, hidden in the valley between the dwarf mountain that hid Asomanee and the gnome lands of Falconmarsh, lost in their own little world.

EIGHT

Give Me Wings

LYING BETWEEN HIS ROCKS, his eyes narrow slits, Lamwen watched as Amicia and Rey returned from their secret hideaway in the first light of day. *Kaliwyn,* the dragon groaned to himself as his chest burned. The light catching her golden locks as she disappeared behind her shelter, he sighed.

"You had a pleasant evening, I trust," he reached into her thoughts.

"Shh," she rebuked, grinning to herself as they stretched out to pretend they had been there all along.

In the weeks that they had been living as husband and wife, it had almost become a game of sorts. Either the couple would stay out after everyone had turned in or lie down early and then sneak away once the others had fallen asleep. Armed with a blanket and no more most of the time, they would secrete away to the place where they had spent their first night together and slip back into their bed at the camp before anyone should notice.

Everyone knew, of course, especially the dragon, as he could observe all from his nest at their camp. In addition, he had spotted the small collection of water once while flying over it and had landed in the clearing to snoop around. Catching the scent of the lovers, he had abandoned it quickly, as the thought of them together tore his heart with rage.

The others had also observed their odd behavior, giving them clues that they enjoyed their private times together. If it helped the couple to think their love making a secret, the rest were willing to let them believe so, at any rate.

Rolling over at the sound of her giggle, Lamwen stared at the sky, watching as it grew pale before it shifted to actual blue. Part of him wanted to leap into the air and put as much distance between them as he could. The rest told him it was of no consequence; she was married to the mortal and should do her part as his wife. *Besides, if they are to be torn from each other before our war is ended, I will get my chance to claim her for my own.* And if he didn't, it was simply never meant to be.

Making it to his feet, he observed that Meena had risen, and their breakfast would soon be at hand. Lumbering around the rest of their camp to his end of their table, he growled, "We should see some progress soon, or I'm afraid all will be lost, with nothing left to fight for."

"Good morning, Lamwen," the older woman chuckled, not joining in his grumbling. "We make the progress we can," she added as she stoked the fire and filled their pot with water for mash.

A short time later, once their bellies had been filled and plans made, Amicia and Yimath set to work scouring the libraries while the others trained for the fight. Each member of their group had learned a great deal from their new masters, as the ossci were excellent teachers. Animir had become comfortable with transposition as well as the use of the orb. Meena's powers had more than doubled, and she could travel across the continent alone at will.

Even Amicia had learned the charm and disappeared as soon as the dishes were done in search of fresh texts to decipher. Arriving in a library, she paused at the dust-covered shelves, grumbling to herself, "Great. No one has been here in a while." Starting at the bottom and roaming backwards, as had become her custom, she selected a few and then transported them to their table in the morning sun. Deciding to have tea while she perused them, she set the kettle and then brushed out her hair, giving it a twist into a bun to let the air to her neck as she sat in the semi-shade that protected the table during the day.

A short time later, the gnome arrived with a few books of her own. Together, they sat turning pages in near silence, broken only by the occasional gasp or groan, until Amicia suddenly squealed, "Oh sweet Eriden, I have found it!"

"What? Let me see!" the shorter blonde commanded.

Scurrying over the top of the table, Yimath stood on the bench next to her, peering down at the passage. Pinching her bottom lip between her fingers and thumb, she squeezed it playfully as she absorbed the rendering until she gasped, "You're right. I believe this is it."

Tapping the page, the gnome looked around wildly, then suggested, "We need to bring everyone together."

"They'll be in for our dinner soon enough," Amicia advised.

"All right, I suppose it can wait a few more hours. Let's return the rest of these where we found them, but place this one somewhere safe," she advised, plucking a long blade of grass and tucking it between the pages with a small end hanging out to mark the location.

Taking the text, Ami removed as much dust as she could and hid it beneath the blanket on her bed, then returned to help with the re-shelving of the rest. She wasn't sure what order they had been stored in, but she was always careful to put them back exactly where she had found them.

Her excitement hard to contain by the time they had their stew on to boil and the group gathered, she thought she might explode. Taking seats upon the stones around their fire, Rey could see the enthusiasm in her clear green eyes when he finally observed, "I believe my wife has a story for us tonight!"

"Have I ever," she beamed. "We have found the transformation spell!" she screamed.

Lamwen had arrived early that eve and taken to his bed to rest until the meal. He didn't actually eat with them, as he hunted his kill and devoured it away from them out of courtesy. During their breakfast and dinner, he would merely sit at the end of the table and listen, giving his advice when called for. Hearing her announcement, he pivoted his ears to hear better but otherwise did not move. His heart pounding inside his chest, he dared not hope his dream might actually come true.

"What's more," the girl continued, "I believe we will be able to use it to turn anyone who wants to be into a dragon!"

Instantly, the beast's optimism sank. *Does she intend for the mortal to become a creature of the air?*

"What does that mean, exactly?" Piers asked the question, concern in his voice.

"Well, I'm only guessing from what the text says, but it does not appear that you have to have been something to become it. As I was forced to take this form, you or Rey, or any of you could be turned into a dragon," she chortled.

"For how long?" Reynard joined in, his face drawn into a scowl. "Would it be permanent, or only temporary; like Lamwen's disguises. I mean, would it be real?"

"I think he is asking if we could fly," the Mate chuckled, equally interested in the prospect. "A dragon who can't take to the air would be of little use to us."

"Surely you aren't considering this," Meena gasped in dismay. "Toying with transformations is risky, at best. What if you were to be stuck that way?"

Piers chuckled at her words, thinking of Oldrilin and her constant fears of being trapped somehow, but held his tongue, only giving her a shrug.

"I don't think that they would be," Yimath explained. "The spell is very straight forward. The original story we found of Ziradon said that it took half a dozen of them to force Kaliwyn into her human body, but I don't believe it would have taken nearly so many if she had been willing to go."

"You think she could transform on her own?" Lamwen asked, speaking for the first time. Staring at the girl, he scarcely breathed at the thought of her as a dragon once more.

Glaring at him, Reynard felt the tickle at the base of his skull. *She won't be Amicia anymore.* His lungs tight, he shifted the gaze to her, noting that her smile faded when their eyes met. "Looks like you have some decisions to make," he observed quietly. *Or we both do,* he added to himself.

"We all do," the Mate agreed, also somber. "But first, we need more details. How many of us do we need to perform the shift, and how long does it last? Those are two very good questions, and once we get past those, I have at least a dozen more."

Shaking her head, Meena stood and stirred the pot. Swallowing, she observed, hardly above a whisper, "I believe our meal is ready."

Each taking a bowl, they moved to the table, but Piers had not missed her troubled demeanor. Catching her by the arm before she could sit, he smiled down into her clear brown eyes, noting the flecks of green within them. "Ah, love. If you do not wish me to take to the skies, just say it. I will decline the offer flatly if you have any doubts."

"Have any doubts," she mimicked with a chuckle. "I'm terrified of the prospect, but the choice is not mine to make." Meeting his gaze squarely, she offered a faint smile. "What kind of wife would deny her husband the chance to fly?"

Moved by her words, he dropped his mouth to hers, tasting her sending his heart wild. "I'll be careful," he whispered, as if his choice had already been made.

Taking their seats, they joined the others as happy discussion had begun all the way around as they enjoyed their meal. Hayt and Zaendra were both pleased at the prospect of helping Amicia, but neither of them cared to join her. Animir, likewise, had no desire to find out what it would be like to take to the air or breathe fire, either one.

Oldrilin appeared frightened at the prospect of any being transformed, much less herself. "What if I get stuck that way?" she pouted, earning a chuckle from the rest and a knowing glance from the Mate.

"I think you should stick to the fish," Amicia agreed in a teasing manner. Her eyes fixed on Rey, she awaited his final choice. Part of her hoped he would choose to try it, but then again if he did, she wasn't convinced he would want to stay that way. *He is a man after all, not a dragon!*

Coming around to his normal place at the end of the table, Lamwen had gained control of his emotions and was prepared to stand as the voice of reason. "If any would care to hear my opinion, I should be happy to share," he announced, sitting back on his haunches and waiting for them to be quiet.

When they had done so, he continued, "I feel that Kaliwyn should definitely be restored. That is a given," he began. "As to the rest, I believe it would be unwise to transform any of those native to Eriden. This spell you have found is very old magic. It is not a common practice, and I fear it is something that should not be meddled with lightly."

Looks of concern passing between them, Piers asked, "What of us?"

Lifting his chin, the dragon conceded, "If you or Rey choose to come over to this side, I dare say it can't be any worse than Kaliwyn taking to yours. But you should be prepared; we may not be able to change her back, and if you become one of us, you may be trapped to it as well."

"Exactly," Meena clipped, her chin dimpled. "I could not..." she began, her voice fading as she realized it was not right for her to interfere. "I mean, I would be deeply saddened if you were to become trapped," she managed.

"No doubt," Piers laughed. "But I want to try it. I never said I wanted to live that way."

"Then we will start with Amicia. If we can return her to dragon form, we can try us," Rey agreed, his eagerness growing at the prospect.

"When?" Lamwen demanded.

"No time like the present," Piers observed, scooping his bites quickly. "Let's finish the meal and give it a try before the sun is completely gone," he commanded, glancing up at the fading light. The conversation abruptly ended, the group devoured their bowls, as each felt eager to see what would become of their efforts.

As soon as they had ended, Zaendra volunteered to do the cleanup. "I can't help, and I'm not changing, so I might as well stay out of the way," she observed.

"Right," Amicia agreed, suddenly anxious at their plans. Fetching the book out of her bed, she placed it on the end of the table and flipped to the marked page. "Ok, so the directions say we need to stand in a circle with me in the center. You will all need to know the chant, but it's short," she added, giving them the words.

When they all could repeat them easily, she moved on, "Ok, I think we are ready. We circle, we chant, and we all focus our energy on the desired outcome. That's it."

"Sounds easy enough," Rey laughed with delight, heading off into the clearing between their camp and the cave to select their location.

"I think I'll stay clear as well," Hayt interjected, accepting his wife's hand as she joined them.

"Aye," the Mate agreed, "you two and Oldrilin go sit by the fire. The rest of us will take care of this."

Standing about half way between their beds and the mouth of the cave, Amicia shivered. "I'm ready. Form the circle around me, and we can begin."

Lamwen and Meena took opposite sides from each other, as did Rey and Piers.

Happy and Grumpy also stood across, and Yimath and Animir took the last two positions, also on opposite sides. Her palms tingling, Ami turned in a slow circle, taking each of them in. Her heart racing, she could not remember the night she had been transformed before even though she had read about it.

In the back of her mind, she swore the memory should be there. *Maybe I blocked it out,* she mused. If the experience had been terrifying or traumatic, she might have.

"Maybe they erased my memory of all of it," she speculated aloud, her apprehension apparent.

"Yes, I do think they could have removed all your memories," Rey agreed, wringing his hands while anxiously awaiting the attempt.

"Relax," Piers commanded, noting the tension the couple shared.

"We are in place," Lamwen took charge, ready to see his beloved Kaliwyn returned. "Begin," he breathed, chanting the words that would do the trick.

Moving slowly, the group walked around her, each of them quietly uttering the charm. Standing perfectly still, her heart pounded within her chest. She felt light-headed and dizzy at the same time, and for a moment, she thought she might faint. Collapsing at the knees, she fell forwards, landing on her hands on all fours.

"Oh God!" she screamed, a terrible rumbling in her gut. "I feel it," she sobbed, driven to tears. "Don't stop," she warned, her eyes stinging with moisture as she began to weep.

Driven by her pleas, Rey clenched his fists and resisted the urge to run to her. He knew they must complete the ritual now that it had begun, or at least he figured they did. On the other side of her, he could see Piers clearly now that she had fallen to the ground. The other man's face formed into a heavy scowl as he shouted the words to the spell.

Matching his fervor, Rey shouted back for all the good it would do. It had suddenly occurred to him that neither he nor the Mate had any magical ability, and he doubted their participation would have any affect, one way or the other. *We're only here for moral support,* he mused just before a pure white light shot out from the center of the circle, knocking all but the dragon off their feet.

Using the back of his left hand to shade his eyes, Rey managed to sit up. Before him, he could see the outline of a shape. *Amicia.* An instant later, it was gone, and a large golden dragon with dark red accents stood before him. "Oh shit," he breathed, as if he had doubted they would succeed. "Ami?" he called in dismay.

Sitting back, the new dragon screamed, blasting flame into the air. Her chest on fire, her vision blurred as she stared at the stars above. Panting, she closed her eyes and fought to slow her inhalations. When she had control, she leaned forward, placing her front legs firmly on the ground. Turning in a slow circle, she felt ungainly, then realized her wings were throwing her off balance.

Using the muscles in her back, she pushed against them, raising them above her until they brushed against one another; then she lowered them slowly until she found a position that felt comfortable.

"Damn, these things are heavy," she said aloud.

"Ami!" Rey screamed, stumbling forward and wrapping his arms around the nearest leg. "Oh, thank God. I thought we had killed you."

"No, I'm fine –" she began, stopping when she realized her voice was different. "I don't sound like me," she observed, using her appendage to push her husband away. "Give me some room, will you? I don't even know how all of this works yet."

"Oh, Ami," he sobbed, taking a few steps back.

"She's beautiful," Lamwen huffed, crying dragon tears of his own.

His eyes roving from the ground up to take all of her in, Piers agreed, "Yes, quite lovely for a... dragon."

NINE

To Each His Own

"DEAR GOD, IT WORKED!" Reynard exclaimed, stepping back to give her some room, as requested.

Clamping him on the shoulder, Piers beamed, "Of course it worked. Did you have any doubts?"

Rubbing his face, the younger man stammered, "No, I guess not. I mean, I just didn't expect this. And what's wrong with her?"

"Nothing," Yimath explained. "She just needs to adjust to her new body."

"I'm next," Piers spoke up. "Let's reform the circle and do mine and then Rey. That way we can all be going through this recovery process at the same time."

Her eyes filled with concern, Meena didn't bother to argue. She could influence her husband about some things at some moments, but she knew when his mind was set. "Let's move over and reform then," she advised.

Taking a position to the north of the newly restored dragoness, each partner stood across from each other once again, save Rey, who stepped out and stayed behind with his wife. Daring to inch back to her, he knelt a few feet from her and asked, "Is there anything I can do for you, love?"

"I'm getting the hang of it," she growled, then raised her massive head to stare at him with her large emerald eyes. "I'm sorry. That sounded rougher than I intended. I'm not very good at any of this," she laughed, hoping to ease her words.

"It's ok. We'll all go through it," he soothed, seeing that they already had the Mate transfigured. "Wow, he's big," he observed, indicating their friend with a stiff digit.

Inside the second ring, a massive black dragon with black accents stood, lifting and lowering his wings slowly. Large enough to contend with Lamwen, the difference gave them some perspective, as Kaliwyn's form almost appeared dainty compared to the two males.

"I guess I'm up," Rey chuckled anxiously, rubbing his hands on his pants as he stood. "I'll see you on the other side," he called over his shoulder as he marched farther north and waited for them to change him as well.

Again, the circle was formed and again the chant was made. Even more quickly, as the group appeared to be gaining skill with each attempt, Reynard was transformed into a magnificent dragon of pale yellow scales and deep green trim. His size not quite the match for the others, he had a more slender and lean construction, as if he were built for speed and agility rather than raw strength.

Flapping his new wings, the younger man yelped, "Man, this feels good!" Leaping into the air, he worked the wide structures easily, hovering a few feet off the ground before he pushed for more.

Watching him take flight, Piers's smoky black eyes narrowed, and he quickly followed. Spiraling upwards, the pair met and rolled around each other midair a few hundred feet up before they turned and made a straight line for the coast.

"This is great!" Piers shouted as they flew, reaching the water in a matter of minutes. Out in the distance, he could see Dragon Rock as a mass of darkness jutting out of the rolling waves. "Let's land and get our bearings," he suggested.

"Aye," Rey agreed, pulling up and landing next to him on the small piece of land. Walking in a circle, he explored the area and got a feel for his new legs, using the back pair to do most of the work while the front balanced and kept him up.

"We'll be ready to attack the dragons in no time," the Mate predicted, fully impressed with their prowess.

"Aye," Rey said again, "but I don't understand what was taking Amicia so long to figure all this out. I mean, it all works fine to me," he laughed, despite his concern.

"I don't know," the other man-turned-dragon offered, taking a seat and staring out across the waves. His mood ebbed as his adrenaline rush subsided, and he exhaled a loud breath. "I've missed the ocean," he confessed. "As much as I love Meena, the sea was my first wife, and I have been away from her many days."

"You were a sailor for a long time," Rey agreed, also sitting to rest.

"Half my life; more than half."

"One long adventure," the younger man observed.

"Aye," the Mate breathed, his gaze into the distance unwavering. "I wish Bally could have been here for this. He would have loved to be a dragon, getting the chance to fly."

"Oh yeah," Rey laughed heartily. "That boy did love getting into things. This would have been all fun and games to him for sure."

"You miss him a great deal," Piers observed, shifting to look over the pale dragon next to him in more detail. "I wonder how it decides what color and build to make us. You're a bit scrawny if you ask me."

Grateful for the change in subject, the Rey-dragon laughed, peering down at himself. "I don't know. Maybe I'm scrawny as the real me as well. Makes me curious if we were to change back and did this again, would we get the same dragon bodies the second time around."

An instant later, they both had the same thought at the same time. His voice less than firm, Piers spoke the concern. "Do you suppose we will get our old bodies back when we transfigure back into our human forms?"

"It's a hell of a time to wonder that!" Rey snapped. His heart pounding against his ribs, he had to admit, they should have thought of it before they leapt at the chance to fly.

Heaving a deep sigh, Piers observed, "Well, it's a bit late now. We should get back to camp. We can check on Ami and plan our next move. We'll just have to worry about what we're going to look like at the end later."

"Aye," Rey agreed, leaping into the air to follow the first mate home.

After watching the pair of males disappear in the distance, Amicia sat up and stretched once more. As soon as the men had been transformed, they had taken off, leaving her behind. Returning to her side, Lamwen helped her make sense of her new body.

"That's it," he coaxed. "You're doing better with it," he praised, suppressing his laughter at her novice motions. He found it difficult to think she had ever carried wings before.

"Yes," she nodded, flapping the wide appendages and taking in the feel of them as they filled with air and pushed her off the ground. Wanting more, she fought a few more strokes, increasing the distance before she rested back on the earth. "I'll get it. I guess I'm a slow learner," she laughed, her fears lessened by the success and his presence. "Thank you for sticking by me."

"You're welcome, and you will get it soon enough," he agreed, edging closer to her and resting his head against her neck. *"I shouldn't touch you."* he informed her, switching to their telepathic connection.

"No. Why not?" she replied in kind.

"It's improper. But I must admit you are a beautiful dragon."

"Who's going to know, or care for that matter?" she giggled. *"But thank you."*

Raising his head and staring at her, he appeared lost. *"I have waited so long to have you on this side, in your true form as nature intended,"* he confessed.

"I know."

"No, you don't know," he pushed, the words tumbling before he could stop them. *"I'm in love with you, Kaliwyn. I have been for so long. Perhaps since the first time you stood before me and placed your hand upon me, so brave and without fear; the light within you so strong."*

"That was a long time ago," she agreed, taking another try at the air and flying around him in a small circle before landing once more.

"Or maybe it was the night you dared the frozen forest to join me and slept beneath my wing," he continued to reminisce.

"I'm getting better, don't you think?"

He could tell she was ignoring his observations, purposely choosing not to reply to his confession. *"Are you angry that I tell you these things?"*

Pausing, she turned to glare at him. *"Angry? No. I'm just not sure what good it would do us. My feelings for you run deep as well, but I am married to Rey. Until my issue with him is resolved, speaking of our love for one another gains us nothing,"* she rebuked.

"You feel it as well. You wish you could change your mind and be my mate."

"I didn't say that," she spat, turning once before she took a longer flight, landing at the south end of the valley.

Following her, he praised, *"That was a good run. Keep working at it, and we'll be ready to take to Adiarwen in no time."*

"Yes," she agreed, her pulse thick in her throat. *"But you are wrong about Rey. I do not regret my vow with him. I love him as deeply as I love you,"* she informed him, her green eyes glaring at him. *"Please, do not speak of these things again, as they only serve to distract us from the fight we must face."*

Swallowing, his sorrow at her words might have consumed him if she had not given him the sliver of hope; she had admitted that she loved him, even if she did love the mortal just as much. "Oh no," he grunted aloud as she took flight, leaving him for the opposite end of their training grounds.

Watching her through the darkness, his keen eyesight remained fixed on her beautiful form. *Kaliwyn is a lover of dragon and man.* The exact reality of it consumed him, the implications beyond coincidence, and not the teasing idea of it he had toyed with before. *But of course, there are those who say it is someone loved by dragon and man, not a lover of.*

The altered perspective did little to relieve his dread, as he and the mortal both loved her as surely as she loved them. *She's the one, either way.* Could the prophecy be true? *If it is, then there is no denying... the destroyer has arrived.*

TEN

Adiarwen

"MAN, THIS IS FUN!" Rey shouted as he and Piers landed next to their marshland camp.

"Aye," the Mate agreed, locating his wife and trotting around her proudly.

"Piers," she breathed, her heart racing.

"Aye," he laughed. "In the flesh, or scales as the case may be."

Swallowing, the wan put on a brave face. "You are handsome in them, love."

"You think so?" he gloated, striking a pose. "I bet you say that to all the dragons."

Laughing with him eased her concern, and she held her smile. "Only the gorgeous black ones," she agreed.

Joining them, Lamwen took charge. "I've been visiting Adiarwen using the gnome disguise, and I have identified quite a few who will support us, including Putwyn if he can be believed, and Jarrowan, who remains loyal."

"Putwyn helped us escape the dragons at Rhong," Animir pointed out as the rest of the group gathered in. "I believe we can trust him."

"How many?" Kaliwyn asked, arriving on her stronger legs.

"More than a dozen," Lamwen quickly counted. "Enough we could mount an offensive once we are ready. But they must remain hidden until then, as a few have been gleaned and killed by Gwirwen's forces since we began taking sides. The council has become divided, and full civil war rages among our kind."

"Aye," Animir agreed. "It is the fighting among the dragons that has allowed Lady Cilithrand to begin her invasion."

"Let us fly," Kaliwyn suggested. "We can form up at the dragon caves and hide inside until the colony has settled to their slumber. From there, it will be easy to take the top and free my father."

"It may be close, but I doubt it will be easy," the Mate countered. "We may need to take a few of the others with us now, before they can be discovered; perhaps this Putwyn and Jarrowan you speak of," he suggested, raising his large black chin at Lamwen.

"You could be right. They will be good in a fight should we encounter resistance. Meena and the others can transport to us when we are ready and help us bring down the cell," their resident expert on the dragon cliffs plotted.

"I believe that I can," the wan agreed, looking around at the others anxiously. "Will you be going with us?" she asked of the three ossci who had been waiting patiently for them to decide their course of action.

The three gnomes had been discussing the matter quietly to the side, but at being pressed for a decision, they appeared ready to provide one. "We should," Yimath agreed for all. "Our power is strong and may well be needed to destroy the magical bindings of such a prison. He cannot be transpositioned or even freed as long as the stones are in place."

"My father is to weak for transport, either way," Kaliwyn pointed out. "When I visited him, he is but a shell of a dragon, and I fear such a move would kill him. He will have to be removed under his own strength, if at all."

"What about us?" Hayt growled, feeling less than useful at the moment. "Is there anything a dwarf, a nymph, and a siren can do?"

"Aye," the Mate chuckled, "stay here and guard the camp. We've been safe so far, but you never know when that might change."

"You just don't want us fighting dragons," Zaendra accused, her features drawn into a small pout.

"If the fight gets ugly, you'll be glad I didn't," he countered, puffing smoke as he spoke.

Wringing her hands as she had been since the evening began, Oldrilin whined, "Rey Daye be safe to fly?"

"Absolutely," he crowed, bending over to put his head down close to her. "I am a master of the skies," he said more quietly, nudging her small frame with his snout. "Don't worry, Lin. Stay with Hayt and Zae, and we will return before first light."

"We should get a move on if that's the plan," Kaliwyn observed. "The mission must be completed before the dawn, or we will all be at risk."

"Then follow me," Lamwen suggested, leaping into the air.

The three new dragons followed while Meena, Animir, and the three ossci all watched on their orbs, waiting for the right moment to join them.

"I may need some help with the jump," Animir whispered to the female wizard when they had gone. "I'm learning to transposition, but I'm not sure if I can make the distance."

"Do not worry," she replied with a small smile. "I will see that you make it."

Arriving at their destination a short time later, the four circled a few times out over the water, then entered the southern most of the lower bachelor caves. Ambling along, they searched the side rooms until they came upon Jarrowan. Waking his ally, Lamwen growled in a low tone, "It is I, my friend; your acquaintance in our cause."

"I know who you are," Jarrowan replied evenly. "You're the only dragon who speaks to me," he laughed, "disguise or no. You have need of me this night?"

"Yes, and Putwyn if you know of his location."

Seeing the others behind him, gathered in the hall, Jarrowan gasped, "You have brought a female into our caves."

"Yes, but she won't be here long," Lamwen explained.

"It may have already been too long," Jarrowan insisted, pushing past him and leading the way out. "We should go and think of Putwyn later, when we can come for him and the others without her."

"Are you talking about me?" Kaliwyn gasped.

"Yes, very much so," their new ally hissed, arriving at the mouth of the cave. "Where are we headed."

"Up top, to free the rightful king," the Mate spoke up.

"Very well. Then let us be quick about it," Jarrowan insisted. "We'll be discovered here any second with the stench of a dragoness among us."

Taking flight, the group landed on the barren cliff above, noting nothing moved in the darkness. The point where the council held their meetings empty, they would have at least some time to enact their rescue attempt.

Leading the group to the stone fortress, Lamwen suggested, "We should circle up as we did for the transfigurations. Where are the others?"

"Here," Meena spoke, joining them from the shadows. "Let us hurry."

Staring at the odd collection, Jarrowan gasped, "Well, this is not quite what I had expected."

"Aye," the dragon-Mate growled. "Rey and I will stand watch while you magic wielders take care of this," he ordered, noting their target beneath the rocks had not stirred.

"We must wake him," Kaliwyn warned, stepping up to a gap and blowing a short burst of flame into the darkness.

Awakened by the hot blast, Ziradon stood, turning in a slow circle. Seeing his daughter, he instantly knew her. "You have returned, my sweet."

"I have," she agreed, "but there is no time for pleasantries. You must mind your head, for if we are successful, this place will soon be falling down about your ears."

"This place was built by a dark curse," he countered. "I doubt you will see success."

"I've brought friends," she laughed, backing into the shadows. "Everyone ready?" she called a bit louder.

Glancing at one another, their backs to the group, Rey and Piers kept an eye on the edge of the cliff in case any of those that slept below cared to surprise them. Behind them, the rest formed their ring and prepared to do their best.

The circle set, the group joined their magic and pulled at the stone arches. The rocks crumbled beneath their forces, and the old dragon did his best to avoid the weight of the falling stones. A moment later, he pushed himself free, standing atop the pile of rubble.

"I feared you did not hold the strength," he confessed, his large green eyes roaming over the myriad of creatures who drew near.

"Hey, we've got company!" Piers spat, hurrying towards them. "Anyone who is not a dragon needs to transport now!"

"We can't go to Falconmarsh," Kaliwyn pointed out almost angrily. "We'll be followed."

"We'll go to the northern woods," Meena advised. "We'll await your arrival at the hidden home of the gnome."

"Sevoassi?" Rey asked in surprise, seeing the bodies looming over head as they approached.

"We must fight," Lamwen urged. "Go and we will meet you there if we survive."

Unable to argue, the ossci and Animir joined hands, and Meena directed their path as she knew where they were going.

Atop the cliff, hot fire rained down.

"Father!" Kaliwyn screamed, rolling to avoid the blast. On her feet, she leapt into the air.

"Get off, damn you," the Mate squalled, slashing at a smaller beast that had latched onto one of his hind legs.

Coming to his aid, Kaliwyn blasted the creature with fire, then dove and spun. *Thank God I have recovered,* she mused as she made another pass, still looking for Ziradon. Spying him, she gasped, "Oh, no!" Reaching out to Lamwen, she begged, *"They have him pinned. We must free him, or this was all for naught!"*

Calling to the men-dragons, Lamwen advised, "We must join the princess and protect our target."

"We're with you," Rey agreed, slashing the wing of the dark brown dragon that had been tearing at his face with his teeth. The rip sufficient, it sent the attacker spiraling until it hit the rocky soil with a loud thud.

Forming a ring around their freed prisoner, the group of dragons rolled about on the earth, screeching and spewing flames amid the bite and tear of their teeth and claws. "This is no good," Kaliwyn warned, hardly able to catch her breath.

"We can't give up," Lamwen challenged, freeing her from beneath a pair of brutes. "Do you not know your queen when you see her?" he snapped, enraged at their actions toward her.

Having caught his breath, Ziradon let loose with a mighty roar, blasting flame into the sky before pulsing a wave of energy that crashed into the group and sent them reeling away from his rescuers. "We must fly," he growled.

"Yes, now, while they are stunned," the dragoness agreed.

Free, he and Kaliwyn took to the air and flew west. Flanking them on either side, Rey and Piers kept an eye out for any that might approach from the north or south, while Lamwen and Jarrowan took the rear, expecting the pack would be on them. When none came out of the darkness, they maintained the formation and the watch, but their fear ebbed as the minutes ticked by.

Her body aching, Amicia pushed, her mind fixed on her father. *He must survive.*

Not quite himself, Lamwen asked, *"Kaliwyn, are you all right?"* within her thoughts.

"I shall be fine. Tis Ziradon that I fear for," she confessed. *"He is cut very badly."*

"We have made our escape. We will hide him in the woods and tend his wounds," he assured.

"These woods aren't the best for hiding, and I can't do much for him as a dragon," she sighed. *"I'm going to transform back into Amicia, that I may be of more use in the task of nurse,"* she devised.

His chest tight, Lamwen didn't argue, as there would be little point. Instead, he thought about her willingness to go back and feared she might never carry her wings again.

Arriving near the gnome home in the northern woods, Meena looked around them cautiously. "We must be careful," she warned. "The wolves will likely attack us if they find us here."

"We parted on good terms," Animir countered, indicating the way to their destination. "Perhaps it will not come to an actual fight."

Following, the three ossci watched about them with wide eyes, using their staffs to help them climb over the roots of the trees. Arriving at the large hollowed oak, Happy stuck his head into the hole that had served as Sevoassi's entrance.

"This will make a fine gnome cottage, indeed," he observed, his voice leaking out through the small patches where the tree did not quite meet the ground.

"Let us clear the place for the fire and stairs for the door," Yimath suggested, wafting a hand at Grumpy. "You, crafter. Assemble us a table or two?"

"Might as well," he grumbled, leaving them to complete the chore.

"I'll spirit back to the marsh and bring our supplies. Our cook pot, bowls and the like," Animir suggested. "Should we bring the others here as well?"

"No," Meena countered. "They are safer where they are. Gather all a change of clothes and a blanket, though. We may have need of them before we are able to return to our own beds."

"Then I will bring our weapons," he suggested. "We may need them as well."

"God, I hope not," she mumbled as he disappeared.

Over an hour after leaving Adiarwen, the group of weary dragons arrived at the dark woods, well ahead of the dawn. Landing near the water that ran through the center of the great forest, they would get their bearing and rest.

Lapping at the cool liquid, Kaliwyn quenched her thirst, as did her father by her side. Joy overwhelmed her at his doing so, easing some of her fear at the severity of his wounds. Seeing her two oldest friends bumbling about in the tightness of the trees, she observed, "Are you ready to get back to your mortal legs?"

"Aye," dragon-Piers agreed without hesitation. "As soon as my wife arrives, I intend to ask her to fix me."

"Oh, love," Meena giggled, presenting herself before him. "We are here. Do not fret."

"We have watched your progress in our orbs and prepared a place to see to your needs," Yimath explained, directing the other ossci into their circle around his large black form. "Close your eyes, and we will have you restored in an instant."

The magical five made quick work of righting the Mate, followed by Rey, who was also ready to be his old self. They had brought cloths for them, in case they were needed, but to their surprise, they were both restored to their exact being before they were turned into dragons.

Taking a seat next to the water, Rey sighed, "What a relief. I was really afraid I would be stuck that way forever." His heart ached the instant the words had slipped from his lips, but a quick glance at Kaliwyn confirmed she had not heard; she was too busy fawning over her father.

"I wish to be transformed as well," Jarrowan announced, taking the group by surprise.

"Whatever for," Meena gasped.

"They have spent the night as a dragon," he insisted. "I wish to feel the flesh of a man. Besides, you can return me to my present state at will, or so it would appear."

"Well, be quick about it," Kaliwyn commanded. "I also wish to be restored, as I will be better equipped to care for my father."

"And I will go as well," Lamwen voiced. "These trees are tight, and I think a smaller body would be much easier to hide until we are ready for the fight." He had not said their actions had been hasty, if not foolish, taking on those in Adiarwen with so few in number, but his sentiment spoke volumes.

Taking his place inside the circle, Jarrowan was transformed into a tall, lanky young man with short, dusty blond hair, but immediately, there was a problem. Where the Mate and Rey had arrived fully clothed, the dragon arrived in human form completely naked.

"Oh my," Meena breathed, her mind clouded as her face flushed. "I did not anticipate…" she began, then cut herself off. "You were not transformed before."

"He's been naked his whole life," Kaliwyn pointed out. "Piers and Rey's attire were held as part of the spell, perhaps."

Any other time, the two men would have enjoyed the awkwardness of their new friend, but at the moment, they were exhausted either from the fight, the flight, or both. Leaned beneath a tree, Rey advised, "Give him the set you brought for me."

"Brilliant," the wan agreed, handing him the pants and shirt while they formed up to bring Lamwen over. Looking up at him doubtfully, she asked, "Are you certain you want to do this?"

"Yes, I am certain," he growled, never more sure of anything in his life. Kaliwyn intended to return to the mortals, and he would never allow her to leave him behind.

Standing before them as a man of large, burly build a few minutes later, he wore wavy, shoulder-length grey hair and nothing else. "I'll take the Mates clothes," he suggested, not bothering to cover himself before he did so.

"I'll be right back, father," Kaliwyn soothed. "I'll be able to help with your wounds then, be certain."

Stepping into the circle, the girl hoped her clothing would cross with her, as the prospect of standing before all of them naked did not suit. A moment later, she lay on the ground. She had been returned to her human form, and her clothes were intact, but the moment the change had taken place, she had felt as if the stones of her father's prison had fallen on her, crumpling her frail form and stealing her breath away.

ELEVEN

Meddle with Magic

"AMI!" Lamwen shouted, the forest echoing with his cry.

Amicia had collapsed into a lump as soon as her transformation had been completed. Standing in their ring, the group simply stared at her, stunned by her crumpled state.

Stepping over a few tree roots, Lamwen knelt beside her. The Mate's clothes felt tight, almost unbearable, as they restricted his movements, but at the moment, he held greater concerns. "Amicia?" he gasped, reaching for the wad of unruly hair that hid her delicate features.

"What's happening?" Rey demanded, struggling to gain his feet. "God this is terrible!" he shouted, unable to hold his weight.

"Aye," the Mate agreed. "Hurts a lot more coming back to the original."

"Perhaps that is why Kaliwyn had such a difficult time when she took her dragon form," Lamwen suggested, rolling her and scooping her unconscious form into his arms.

"But this isn't her original. Why is she even more slowed in her recovery?" Yimath asked, perplexed by the idea. "I should fetch the tome. Perhaps there was mention of this we had not read or understood."

"Go," Meena agreed. "Meet us at the new cottage beneath the tree."

"Cottage?" Piers grunted, fighting to stand.

"Yes. As I said, we have prepared a place for us to regroup." Looking upon Ziradon, she shook her head slowly. "I fear we cannot transfigure him; it could kill him."

"I will rest here, kind lady," he growled, indicating the stream. "I have languished too long in a prison cell, and I fear my strength has long since left me."

"I will remain here to serve him," Animir offered, "in Amicia's stead. The water will do him good, and I will hunt for nectar when I am able."

Rey glared at the mortal-Lamwen, his wife curled in his muscular arms. "How is she?" he growled.

"She lives," he replied, worry etched in his masculine features. "I wish to take her to safety. Are we ready to travel?"

"Aye," the Mate agreed, finding his way on shaky limbs. "Once we get to the hiding place, we will rest. She recovered, and so I am certain that we will as well. All we need is time."

Forming a line, the group marched through the dense trees, listening and watching about them as they made their way through to the restored gnome home. It had not taken the ossci long to install the fire, the steps, and even a pot hung over their flames so that morning mash could be prepared.

Laying Ami on the ground, Lamwen climbed down into the hole, then pulled her over using her arms to slide her in and lower her to a pallet that had been formed by her blanket. The dancing light adding a glow to her pale skin, he sighed as he brushed her hair back for a better look.

"She does not appear injured," he observed. "She merely sleeps, as if she is exhausted."

Extending and retracting his arms, Rey grimaced, "That's exactly what it feels like. I'm tapped, as if I have worked for hours and all my energy is spent."

Arriving in their midst, Yimath laid the tome on a small table Grumpy had constructed only a short time ago. Using her blade of grass, she opened to the spell and began to read over it, her lips moving as she did so. Turning the page, and then another, the silence around her held as they all waited for her verdict.

"Oh no," she gasped, coming to a few portions of concern. "This is not something we should have meddled with," she warned.

"You don't say," the Mate chuckled as he helped himself to some of the tea his wife had brewed. "What do we do now?"

"Well, it says the lethargy will pass, but each time that the transformation is made it will increase." Looking up at him, her wide green eyes grew misty. "Eventually, it will be enough to kill her."

"Kill her!" Rey screamed, on his feet before he dropped beside her. Glaring at the man-dragon across from him, he growled, "Did you know this was going to happen?"

Studying him with cool green eyes, Lamwen remained calm. "Do you think I would have taken this form if I had known it could kill me?"

"I don't think it will this time," Yimath explained in a subdued tone, "but she can't keep going back and forth. When she is stronger, we can push her back one more time, and it will tap her when we do, as it has now. But it will be the last time. When she returns to being a dragon, she will be forced to remain so for the rest of her life."

"She could choose to stay human, though, right?" Reynard asked, his mind turning. *I may still get to keep her.*

Lamwen glared at him, easily drawing the same conclusion. "Her choice will be hard to make, be assured," he growled.

Meeting his cold glare, Rey swallowed, "Indeed."

Coughing, Amicia curled, sputtering as she regained her awareness. "Where am I?" she managed.

Soothing her, Lamwen gently caressed her cheek with the backs of his fingers. "You are safe, my queen."

"Lamwen?" she breathed, hardly able to believe her eyes.

"It is I," he agreed, his lips drawn into a thin line. "You were distracted with your father when I was transformed –"

"My father!" she gasped, cutting him off as she tried to sit up. "Where is my father?" she demanded more sternly.

"He remains by the brook," Meena explained, offering her a warm cup. "Do not struggle, my child. Ziradon is safe. Animir has volunteered to nurse him, and I dare say none among us could do so well."

Turning to rest against her husband, who remained beside her, she accepted the drink. Sipping from it noisily, her thoughts remained fuzzy. "How did I get here?"

"I carried you, princess," Lamwen explained, puffing his chest with pride.

"The Mate and I were hardly able to walk," Rey countered, "or I would have."

"Please don't fight," she scowled, picking up on their posturing. "Why did this happen?"

"Meddling with magic, that's why," Meena snapped, glaring at the Mate. "I warned you transfiguration was not as easy as it might sound, and I was correct. It has a side effect that can kill you if you continue to do it."

"I see," Amicia breathed, still feeling as if her skin were not her own. "Will I recover?"

"Yes, but only in time," Lamwen informed her. "When we go back to our dragon forms, we will be forced to remain there."

Glaring at him, Rey breathed deeply. He didn't want the debate to end there, but he didn't want to upset the girl, so he kept it short. "If you go back, love."

"Of course, she'll go back," the Mate countered. "She's a dragon. But let's not argue over it right now. The meal is almost ready. We should eat and all have a rest. When our heads are clear, we will decide our next move."

Serving the bowls, the group ate in a strained silence. Nothing had gone their way in a very long time, or so it seemed. Sitting under a tree, sandwiched between troll country and dwarf mountain, they were probably surrounded by wolves; it did not appear their luck had improved.

Hours later, the group had slept away the day. The sun had moved to early evening, and Animir had come with word of their situation. Climbing down into their new quarters, he noted the beds and stools, almost as they had been when Sevoassi had resided there.

"You have restored his dwelling well," he observed as the others stirred, returning the blood flow to their limbs.

"Aye," Rey agreed, folding up his blanket to sit upon as he administered to his wife's needs. "Are you feeling better, love?"

"I am far better than I was," Amicia agreed, sitting up as well. "What news of my father?" she asked of the elf, fear quickening her pulse as she did so.

"I think he needs longer to recover," Animir explained, pacing as much as their small haven would allow. "If he were still the Supreme Dragon, he could be taken to the gardens of Jerranyth. The magic of my kin would restore his fervor in no time."

"Indeed," Lamwen agreed, leaning against an earthen wall. "I have been nursed by the elves too many times to count, but that is impossible. If they didn't turn us over to Gwirwen, they would kill him for sure."

"They might not," Amicia mused. "If he is to be the dragons' distraction while she makes her own plans, Lady Cilithrand might be more than happy to help him survive."

"Too risky," the Mate spat. "We need another place we can go. The wolves haven't noticed yet, but they will, and I do not fancy our second meeting."

"The trolls," Rey offered with a snap of his fingers. "Perhaps they would help us."

"We didn't part on very good terms," Amicia reminded him with a shake of her head, "and we certainly can't ask the dwarves."

"Our options are limited," Meena agreed, stirring the pot as she cut up the stew that would make their supper. "We must choose the one most likely to help and least likely to murder us."

"We go to the trolls," Ziradon growled through the narrow door, interrupting their chatter.

"Father!" Amicia gasped. Leaping to her feet, she forced them to climb the tiny steps to her freedom. "How did you get here?" she squealed, rushing to his side as he collapsed onto the dark earth.

The group following her out their hiding place, Piers and Animir brought their weapons, taking up guard. "Are we found?" Lamwen asked, standing behind Amicia as she fawned over her father.

"Not yet," the Mate speculated, "but it will be more dangerous with him here. How did you get here?" he demanded, facing the dragon squarely.

"I fought my way through the trees," he gasped. "I didn't dare take flight. I'm sure you have noticed we are hunted by our kin."

"I noticed," Amicia sighed, glad they had transformed and would be more difficult to locate. "You think the trolls will help us?" she asked with a tear in her eye. "They had become friends to us, but we had a falling out before we left," she lamented. Breathing deeply, she confessed, "I did something foolish, and it upset them."

"All we can do is ask," the old king gasped.

"I think I can transport him if need be," Meena speculated. "All I need to know is where we are going."

"To my cave," Lamwen supplied with wide eyes. "I had a cave that I wintered in, to the north of your cabin. He should be safe there even if only for a few days."

"Very well," Meena agreed. "Then it is settled. Once darkness has fallen, we will move to the cave."

"No," Amicia snapped. "We will go, just the three of us. I will speak with Yaodus and inform him of our plight and ask his permission to be there."

"Yaodus," Ziradon chuckled, pleased at the sound of his name. "You are quite brave to face him, my dragoness."

"I am not afraid of the troll," she replied, grinding her teeth as she recalled the day they had met; the day he had killed Piers. "I am more afraid I might lose you so soon after we have freed you."

"And if that is so, at least I die beyond the walls of my prison," he huffed, closing his eyes and drifting off to sleep.

"He's so weak," Ami whispered, stroking his head and neck in turn.

Joining her, Lamwen rested his hand upon her back, enjoying the feel of her now that he had flesh with which to do so. "Let him rest, princess. We'll take him to my cave, and he will find his strength once more."

TWELVE

Free at Last

"SEE, WHAT DID I TELL YOU," Lamwen chuckled as they arrived at his previous residence. "None will find him here." He had insisted upon accompanying the party, his protectiveness of Amicia only growing in his mortal form.

"You should have gone with the others back to the camp," Ami observed. "I could have found this place just as easily."

"Hmph. Your husband would have liked that better," he countered with a smirk.

Standing in the mouth of the cave, she looked up at his handsome new features, observing the shoulder-length grey hair and rugged chin that suited him. She had to admit, he made a handsome man, and Piers's clothing fit him perfectly.

Exhaling loudly, she mumbled, "You have always been stubborn." Turning her gaze to the cabin below, she stared at the remains with a sigh. "We have lost so much, Lamwen. But I fear it is not the end of our suffering, with the kingdom in ruins."

"There is still hope, my lady," he assured, using an arm to pull her against him. Inhaling her scent, he grinned, pleased with the tenderness the flesh of a mortal afforded him.

Leaning against him, she could feel the pull of his masculinity and drifted for a moment into the past. "I came to this cave in the darkness, snow all around me, to lie beneath your wing."

"I remember," he whispered against her scalp, his chest aching with words he dared not speak aloud. *"My fire burns for you, princess."*

Closing her eyes, she knew the profession was private, as Meena busied herself with their patient and would not have heard it even if he had not used the telepathy. Lifting her face to his, she kissed him, the feel of his lips scorching her as she lost touch with all but him for a moment, the purity of her love for him refusing denial.

Instantly, regret pulled her away from their intimate connection. *"I have spoken my vow with Rey; how dare you tempt me so?"*

"It is not I that temps you, my queen. Your heart knows the path that lies before you. You must return to your true form, and there your mortal cannot follow," he decreed, his fingers brushing her cheek tenderly as they shared.

Seeing them against the light at the mouth of the cave, the older woman stiffened. Clearing her throat, Meena gently reminded them of her presence.

Pulling herself out of Lamwen's grasp, Ami brushed her hands over her arms and torso as if removing the feel of him from her flesh. "I'll go and visit with Yaodus," she informed them quietly. "If I do not return by the dawn, you must leave this place without me."

Exchanging a glance, Meena and the man-dragon both nodded, each hoping they would not be required to do so.

Leaving them, Amicia made her way across the north ridge alone, working her way to the cave the group had climbed to the night they fled the dragons' fire. There, she made her way to the back wall, placing her hand flat against the hard surface. Pulling her merdoe free from between her breasts, she clenched it tightly in her palm. Closing her eyes, she whispered to herself, willing the cave to open to her and allow her access to the halls within.

A low rumbling breaking her trance, she stepped away as the stones bubbled and parted, presenting the entrance to the trolls hidden caverns. Taking a tentative step inside, she used the side to hold her balance while she tested the footing.

Assured it was sound, she made her way through the corridor, pausing to close the portal behind her, just as the troll king had done the night he let them in. Her pulse loud within her ears, it drowned out the sound of her feet crunching on the gravel below. Her chest tight, she breathed in shallow pants as she approached the warm glow of the great room and the fires therein.

Arriving at the central cavern, she paused at the edge to hide while she looked around. Her eyes darting over the wide space, families sat around fire pits, just as they had the last time they were there. Spying her target, gathered with his family, she swallowed anxiously. Raising her chin, she placed one foot in front of the other as she willed herself to leave the tunnel and cross the room.

Observing her before she ever got close, a silence fell across the space. All that saw only stared, motionless as they waited for her to reveal her intent.

"You came here alone?" Yaodus challenged when she stood before him.

"Not exactly," she whispered, petrified for fear of what would become of

Ziradon if she failed. "I have rescued my father, but he is injured. We have come to ask for refuge that he might heal."

"Your father," the old troll laughed loudly, then drew a deep breath. "Then you have seen the light within you."

"I have found my dragon's fire," she agreed quietly. "I'll grovel if I must," she added, daring a step towards him before sinking to her knees. "Please help him. We have nowhere else to turn."

"Desperation," he sneered. "You would not have come otherwise," he agreed.

Amicia felt hot, as if her blood boiled within her veins. "Do you wish me to beg?" she asked loudly, angered that he appeared unmoved by her plea. Swallowing the large lump in her throat, she raised her empty hands. "So be it. I beg of you, troll. Please do not let my father die."

"A dragon king," he laughed again quietly. "This I must see. Take me to him."

"He is in a cave, the one Lamwen used to oversee us when we lived on the beach below," she supplied readily, finding her feet. Standing next to him, she looked up at his towering height, a fleeting flutter of joy in her heart at the friendship they had shared. She wanted to apologize again for the rift between them, but it was not the time at that particular moment, as Ziradon's life was on the line.

Raising his hand, he indicated the direction they must travel. Following him, a few of the others fell in behind her, and she kept her body rigid, prepared for the attack that could come at any moment. Keeping her eye on the form before her, she breathed in and out deeply through her nose, making every effort to keep herself calm.

Taking a passage out of the main room, it soon parted, and he opened a fresh tunnel. A moment later, they stepped out into the back of a dark cave. Inching their way in, a small fire burned along one of the walls, casting dancing light over the deep brown of Ziradon's scales. Large gashes oozed blood over his emaciated frame. The wounds smelled of infection, and the scent of death was upon him.

His face scrunched, Yaodus inched his way forward, no longer holding his concern at bay. "Ziradon," he called, "my old friend. What has become of you?"

Turning his head in the cramped space, large glassy eyes blinked in response. A loud cough hurt her ears in the small cavern, and tears streaked her cheeks as she reached her father's head. Leaning against his neck, she wept. *Please don't die.*

Standing beside her, the troll king laid his hand upon the wide snout, only then noticing Meena and Lamwen at the mouth of the cave. "You have returned," Yaodus growled, his face wet with his own sorrow. "And you?" he asked of the unknown man before him.

"I am Lamwen, captain of the king's guard," the man-dragon announced, squaring his shoulders proudly as he did so.

"I see," the troll grimaced. Returning his gaze to the injured beast, he sighed, "He needs elves' medicine."

"The elves are raiding the kingdom as we speak," Amicia informed him, raising her chin. "We plan to stand against them now that our king is freed. If you cannot heal him, please give him a friendly place to die."

Rocking his head in an odd bobble, the troll breathed loudly again, his chest burning with unspoken pain. "He will be welcome here, princess. Do not fear."

"Then we will return in a few days to check his progress," she assured, looking over her shoulder to see the other trolls had begun to assess his needs. "Thank you, Yaodus. You are a dear friend, and I have regretted the ill will that passed between us."

"As have I, my queen," he replied, dropping his hand from Ziradon's snout and lumbering back into the Crimson Caves. Pausing at the tunnel, he placed his hand upon the wall, removing one of the bright red stones. Turning, he held it out to her.

Closing the distance between them, she accepted the gift, then looked up at him with wide green eyes. "Thank you," she said firmly, glancing at the ruby red crystal, "but what is it for?" She suspected it a talisman of some kind, but she could guess for hours without divining its purpose.

"You cannot view the inside of our mountain," he explained. "The golden orbs do not work here. If you use this stone, you will be able to see your father, even at a distance, and check his wellbeing. You may also use it to call to me if you wish."

Staring at the sparkling rock, she smiled. "This is very kind of you, Yaodus. I shall guard it with great care."

"As I will tend our Supreme Dragon with equally great care," he agreed. "You must have quite an army if you intend to stand against the elves."

"No," she grinned wryly. "We have a few dragons, and of course the lot you knew when we were here. Less Bally. He was killed by daemons beneath the dwarf mountain."

"Then you may use the stone to call us when you are ready to fight. I will hear your words, and my army will march for you when you have need."

Amicia stared at him in disbelief. "I had no idea you even had an army," she breathed.

"I use the term loosely," he shrugged. "But if what you say is true, they will be at our mountain, tearing at the walls of our caves soon enough. Only a fool would refuse to give you aid to prevent such a dark day. We are not soldiers, but we will fight if you call upon us."

Closing her hand around the stone, she nodded. "I would never mistake you for a fool. Thank you. I will check on my father often and call to you when the war has begun."

THIRTEEN

One of Them

"I FEAR you have lost sight of our cause," Jarrowan complained as he helped Lamwen construct a bunk for them, keeping his voice low as the rest of the group moved about, tending their daily chores.

Attaching the frame together, the other man-dragon laughed, "Then ask to be transfigured and return to our kind. My place is here, at least for the time being."

"You think you can win her heart," the younger dragon scowled, "but she has made a vow with the mortal. She will not break it to fall in love with you, nor will she return to her kin as long as he lives. Do you intend to kill him?"

Cutting his green orbs up at him, Lamwen growled, "I should do no such thing. Besides, you are mistaken. She loves me as dearly as the mortal; I have seen it in her eyes and tasted it in her kiss."

"Kiss," Jarrowan scoffed, hardly able to imagine such a thing. "Then you believe you can win her to your side despite her declaration to him," he laughed. "What foolishness."

"She is a dragon," Lamwen grunted. "It is only fitting she should choose me over him in time. Until then, we might as well remain here. I had made many trips to the dragon's lair before we were transformed, and I believe we have gathered all of them that we will. Our next move lies in other lands."

"Other lands," Jarrowan groaned, flopping his hands over his face and pulling them down in angst. "As dragons we ruled them all, and now we are weak as any human. Look at us, donning their cloths to hide our nakedness and wearing their boots to protect our tender feet." He held up one of them, thinking of the trip

Meena had made to the wizard markets to acquire them. "That wan is quite smart, though, even I must admit."

"Yes, intelligent and powerful, she casts and wields as well as any male wizard I have encountered in my day," Lamwen chuckled. "We are among a talented group here, Jarrowan. Amicia is a strong and fierce dragoness, and she has been gifted with the sight of what is to come, as well as what must be done."

Turning to the mattress Zae and Lin had constructed for them, he dragged it over and laid it on the floor of his structure. He then spread his new blanket across it, again thinking of the wan. She had made the trip to the plaza of stalls with him to stock his bed as if he were one of them. *I am one of them,* he silently cursed. "I have been among these people for many moons. My choosing the flesh was not simply a whim. In my heart, I needed to see and feel what it was like to be one of them."

"And it has changed your perspective," the other dragon growled, flopping down on the ground next to him and toying with the grass.

"Aye," Lamwen mimicked the Mate with a short laugh. "I feel I have become wiser in the few days I have walked on two legs than the many years that I flew the skies."

"Have you, now," Piers interrupted, inspecting their work. Lamwen had constructed his leaning shelter behind that of Rey and Ami, between it and the rocks that had once served as his lair. "If you are finished here, there are chores to attend to before the evening meal is served."

Getting to his feet, Jarrowan sulked at the prospect. Life had been much simpler as a dragon. When he wanted a meal, he hunted a kill, and having been ostracized by the others, he had little else to occupy his time beyond sleeping. It had only been since Lamwen had befriended him that his days held any real purpose.

"I will tend to the hunt," he offered. "Has the elf already begun?"

"I'm on the way out," Animir offered, holding up a bow. "Your weapon is finished, complete with a few arrows."

Accepting the gift, he stared at it, the craftsmanship of it unmistakable. He and Lamwen may have been beasts of the air only a few days ago, but the mortals had accepted them whole-heartedly upon their introduction to the group. "Thank you," he mumbled, thinking of the girl. *She's the one who compels them to be so open.* That and Lamwen had truly been a part of them long before he took to their flesh and blood.

Looking up to study the elf, he again considered the dilemma. "If or when I return to my true form, do you think we should still be friends?"

"I believe that we would," Animir grinned. "My life has changed so drastically since the mortals were brought into the city. Having a dragon companion might once have seemed odd, but now I can hardly imagine my life without it," he boasted, glancing at Lamwen as he spoke. "Come. Let us supply the meat for our supper."

Leaving the camp in search of the food, Animir and Jarrowan talked and joked with one another, as if it were Bally who would join him on the hunt.

Watching them go, Amicia sighed, then announced, "We will discuss our plans over the dinner. I have formulated a few, and we should get started on them as soon as we are able."

"Then Lamwen and I will bring in the wood and set the fire," the Mate agreed. "Where are Hayt and Zaendra?"

"They've gone for a walk," she laughed. "He has taken a notion he can find that garden of statues he spoke of when they first arrived here, as if doing so might help us in some way."

"Stranger things have happened," Piers shrugged as he hoisted the axe and beckoned for Lamwen to follow as they headed into the woods.

Little did Amicia know, Hayt had achieved his goal almost at the moment she mocked him with her words. On the far end of the valley, he and Zae had found a section of brush growing against the side of the mountain with a peculiar path winding through it. Using his sword, he cleared a bit of the growth before he gasped, "Oh sweet Eriden, this is it, love! These are the statues of my line."

Looking up at the height of them, she teased, "Are you quite certain? They appear quite tall for dwarves." Seeing the scowl cross his features, she laughed boisterously as she began pulling at the vines. "They are stubborn," she observed at how difficult the foliage was to remove. Managing to free a few of the stones, she gasped, "Oh, Hayt! These are magnificent!"

"Yes," he agreed with pride, forgetting her poking fun. "There should be a dozen or so of them. And over behind is the entrance to Asomanee."

First clearing some of the statues, the couple worked in unison to restore them to the sun. Some being very old, their faces had been worn away over time, but a couple still stood up to the weather and could be recognized.

"This one strongly resembles you," she observed, indicating one close to the slope of the mountain.

Studying the inscription at the base, he gulped, "Oh my. Yes, this was the last king of Asomanee. Asyng and Baeweth's father, to be exact. He was the ruler when the dark elf came, and they made their escape to the north."

"He laid the plans for Rhong?" she surmised.

"Yes," he nodded, fighting tears. Overcome with emotion, he breathed, "I never thought I would lay eyes upon this place."

"Oh, Hayt," she sighed, placing her arm over his shoulder to comfort him. Guilt twisting her gut, she wished she had not belittled him or his kin in her teasing manner. "Perhaps now that the witch has been removed, your people may reclaim what once was theirs," she offered.

"Maybe someday," he sniffed. "But it will not be I that leads them. I gave up my throne for this cause."

"And you regret that choice?" she asked, feeling his sorrow.

"Oh, no, love," he chuckled anxiously. "I know we lie low and prepare for the fight. I do this as much for my own kind as I do for our small group of friends. All of Eriden needs us to prevail. I fear all will be lost if we do not."

Shaking off the somber mood, he pulled himself free. "I'm all right. And we must hurry, as the day is all but spent."

"We found the statues. Was there something more?" she asked, wafting her hand to indicate their treasure basking in the sun.

"The entrance," he pointed with his sword. "It should be this way."

Fighting through more brush, they pushed their way towards the rock, soon finding the side of the mountain where it had crumbled and covered any opening that had once stood.

"Well, that's that I suppose," he growled, examining the length and height of the slide. "It's almost as if someone brought the mountain down upon it with purpose."

"Could the previous king have done so for fear the creatures within would escape?" Zaendra speculated.

"Perhaps," he shrugged. "I'm more inclined to think it was the elves in an effort to ensure we would be trapped below with it forever."

"I guess that's why the other cave remains," she deduced. "They didn't know about it and therefore did not destroy it."

"Agreed," he nodded, clapping his hands together as if to dust them. "Well, our mystery is solved, and my kin are found," he announced, indicating their likenesses. "We might as well return to the camp for our supper. We can come back and clear a few more of them if we ever have the time."

Offering her his arm, she wrapped hers around his, and they ambled back to the others, eager to share the news of their discovery for the evening's tale.

FOURTEEN

Desperate Times

"THESE ARE DESPERATE TIMES," Amicia declared as she stood at the end of their table while the others enjoyed their stew. She had worked all day on the speech and felt confident in the words she would speak. "Things have not often gone as we have planned, and yet we push on."

"What else can we do?" Reynard laughed, raising his cup to her in a mock toast from his place at their end of the table.

On the far end, a second length had been added to accommodate their growing numbers. Seated across from one another, Jarrowan and Lamwen exchanged a glance before the older man-dragon scowled, "But you think you can outrun your bad luck on the next one?"

Giggling at his rough demeanor, her mind wandered for a moment as she recalled his attitude had always been gruff. "No, my dearest Lamwen," she sighed. "I have no illusions that what is to come will be easy. But I have prepared a list of targets, if you will. Goals I feel will be important if the war is to be won."

"We will be taking on the dragons and the elves simultaneously, I fear," the Mate observed. "I do not believe we hold sufficient numbers to be much of a threat to either one."

"Ah, well, that could be true," she replied mysteriously. "I also believe we do not hold the force it would require to attack them head on, and therein lies the beauty of my plan."

Unrolling her list, she had prepared an outline and began at the top. "First, we must provide relief for the sirens. I have watched them in my orb, and they suffer greatly at the hands of the elves who occupy Riran. We will send a small force if necessary, but I think they may be able to escape on their own if they simply had somewhere to go."

"Where will we go?" Oldrilin sniffed, her eyes filled with tears at the thought of how her kind had been hurt in their ordeal.

"They will leave one morning as usual and not return," Amicia proposed. "Instead, the entire lot of them will swim for the marshes."

"The marshes," Grumpy gasped. "What madness is this? It was difficult enough allowing you lot to invade our lands, much less a group of wailing vagabonds."

"We are not wailing vagabonds," Lin cried, surprised by his attack.

"There is plenty of room here in the marsh," the girl assured. "They will be keeping to the eastern coast, as they still need access to the water. And do not fear. They will only be here until the war is ended and they can return to their warm and happy lives within the lagoon of Riran."

"Do Thirac and the elders know of this plan?" Yimath asked, also concerned.

"Yes. I have spoken with him and received their blessing," Amicia assured. Swallowing, she held her resolve, not wanting to come down on the others harshly but feeling as if they thought they might dissuade her from this course. *They will not.* Everything she had planned would happen, no matter what it cost her to see it through. "When we are ready to begin, that will be our first step."

Clearing her throat, she pushed to her next point. "Once the sirens are on the move, we will send reinforcements to the glen, as the elves have not gained a foothold there, but the nymphs and satyrs are weakening."

"And where do you propose these reinforcements will come from?" Piers ask, glancing around at their small party. "We are not an army, love."

"I intend to send the dragons. Those who have pledged themselves to Lamwen will be dispatched to take up the fight in the glen. Since Gwirwen and the council members who wish to overthrow him are at odds, I dare say they will not be missed. It is imperative that the elves be denied those lands, and if they can be kept busy there trying to take them, all the better."

At her words, the group stopped eating and glanced from person to person. Eventually, Lamwen observed, "I can no longer fly to the caves at Adiarwen, and if I went in this form, I would certainly be killed." He swallowed as he glared at her, hoping she would not command him to take this task.

Not meeting his gaze, Ami stared at her list, her eyes growing misty. "Tough choices will have to be made," she whispered, mostly to herself.

"I'll go," Jarrowan spoke up, wriggling in his seat.

Raising her chin, Amicia blinked at the young dragon-man as if she had forgotten he had become a part of them. "You know how dangerous the transfiguration is," she replied, her bottom lip quivering.

Swallowing, he could hear the concern in her voice. "I have only undergone the shift once. Surely going back will do no permanent harm. Besides, I have no intention of remaining a mortal of the rim," he laughed anxiously. "I will take this assignment. You may transfigure me back to my original form, and I will carry your orders to our brothers within the caves."

Their eyes locked, the girl imagined his doing so. "It might work," she confessed. "I thought they would need to hear the order from Lamwen."

"Why?" Jarrowan shrugged. "I helped to recruit a fair number of them myself. They know he and I stand together on this," he added, giving the man across from him a smile. "It would be my honor to take this assignment."

"Then you shall have it, my captain," she sighed. "Rally our queen's guard and fly them to Esterbrook when the time arrives."

Flicking his eyes between them, Lamwen curled his tongue. Had she intended to bestow the title upon him? Not daring to ask, he waited to hear the rest of her list, as he would never contradict her before the others.

Smiling to herself, Amicia bolstered her nerve. She had made it through the first few items unscathed, but it would only become more difficult as she went.

"Now, I must admit those first two acts will be the easy part, and it will only become trickier from there. We will return to the trolls and raise their army. Together, we will march on the dwarves and deal with them accordingly," she suggested firmly.

"Deal with them," Hayt spoke up, pushing back his empty bowl. "What does that mean exactly? My people usually hide under their mountain. I doubt they are willing to stand against us in our plans. Why must we attack them?"

"It is not their loyalty that I question," Amicia sighed, tapping her page. "I believe they will need to take a side on this, as we will need their forces. If they do not join us, they will fall to the elves, and we cannot allow that to happen."

"Oh ho ho," the dwarf laughed, pushing his hands out in a halting motion. "My kin will never side with the elves."

"That would not stop Cilithrand from attempting to annihilate them," Animir pointed out. "It would be better if they joined our cause."

"Agreed," Amicia replied sharply, hoping to minimize the banter. "It will be your job to convince them of this," she informed their heir. "You may not ever sit upon your throne, but you hold rank among your kind. You could convince them of our cause and the necessity of their actions."

"I doubt that," Hayt grumbled, shaking his head as he leaned against his hands, elbows on the table. "I left them behind, and I am certain they would rather hang me than listen to my reason."

"We will convince them," Zaendra spoke up, slipping her hand through the loop of his arm and laying her cheek on his shoulder.

"Are you taking her side on this?" he whispered to his wife, surprised by her willingness to do so against him.

Shocked, she rubbed her face against him and cooed, "I believe we should follow her, yes. We agreed we would accept her choices, good or bad."

Hayt opened his mouth as if he were going to argue further, but seeing his bride's wide ebony orbs blinking up at him stole the argument from his lips. Instead, he grumbled, "I'll agree but under duress. Mark my words, the dwarves will not take such a path without some sort of motivations."

"And you, or we, will provide them," Zaendra beamed.

"I see where this is going," Meena spoke up, glancing around their group. "When do we get to the wizards?"

"Uh, now actually," Amicia replied airily, hoping to hide her trepidation. "They are the strongest of all the groups, both in number and land, if not magical prowess. So far, the elves have left them be, but I daresay that will not keep."

"You've got that right," Rey grunted. "Bloody elves would control half the continent if they succeeded in turning the wizards."

"And that is why we must get to them first, and the quicker the better," Ami agreed. "As soon as we secure the dwarf mountain, we turn to the desert and the communities that lie along its borders."

"I doubt they will follow you," Meena observed. "They are very patriarchal. The fact you are a woman will win you no followers there."

Leaning against his hands, Piers tapped his extended index fingers against his lips. He had remained silent as she listed her plan, or the main points of it in the least, and allowed the others to debate the merits of it, but it appeared they needed a little help with their designs. "I'm certain there are details in all of this you have failed to mention," he pointed out quietly.

"Yes, of course there will be parts that will need to be resolved," she agreed, fear twisting her gut. "Do you doubt my plan?"

"Did you come up with this on your own? Who have you consulted on all of this?" he asked, avoiding her question and her gaze.

"Do I need to consult anyone? As I understand, I am to be the queen of all of Eriden. I assure you my strategy is sound!"

"Well, you may be headed to the throne, but there are many bumps in the road to get there," he grunted, dropping his arms and climbing out of the bench. "Let us think on this."

"I won't," Ami shouted, her gaze flicking around at the others for help. "You may help with the particulars, but I assure you this is the path we must take."

Pausing, his back to her, Piers pushed, "And this was your idea, thought of all by yourself?"

"I have spoken with my father on this matter," she replied, raising her chin.

The admission brought a smile to his lips, and the Mate turned to face her. "Good. I'm glad to hear this isn't some child's folly. Does he think we can pull this off?"

"Child's folly?" she seethed. "It wasn't a good plan until it wasn't mine."

"I never said that," he chuckled. "I just feel better knowing you had a bit of guidance in the making of it. Your father was a powerful leader in this land for not just years, but for centuries. If he has approved of this course, it only adds weight to the chances of our success."

Not wanting to argue, the Mate turned and walked away, not waiting to see if that was all she had to say.

FIFTEEN

Private Moments

"IT SOUNDED like a great plan to me," Reynard soothed with a shrug, still seated to her right as he grinned up at her.

"Leave me be," she growled in return. Turning on her heel, she marched between the shelters and into the opposite side of the woods.

Watching her go, the group stared in awe.

"I thought it a good plan as well," Animir agreed quietly.

"Yes, well, the Mate is accustomed to being in charge," Lamwen offered, getting to his feet and heading after her.

"She said to let her be," Rey called after him.

"She was speaking to you," the man-dragon grunted as he disappeared into the line of trees. Trailing her path, he reached out to her. *"Amicia."*

"Why do you follow?"

"Because I must. Stop and wait for me or tell me where you are going."

Stopping, Ami stood perfectly still, not intending to help him find her. *"That arrogant ass. My plan is a good one, regardless of who did or did not help."*

"Piers is afraid for his people," Lamwen countered. *"The war is getting very real, and once we begin the fight, it is likely some of us will die."* Seeing her ahead of him, he paused, admiring her blond hair in the moonglow.

Realizing his presence, she turned slightly, able to see his hazy form behind her. "And he thinks I am not afraid of that as well?" she spat aloud.

Taking gentle strides, he arrived next to her, his hand resting on her back. "It is a good plan," he soothed. "Do not allow Piers's fears to dissuade you from your cause." Looking around, he held up his other hand to indicate the forest. "Think of this place. Our lives have been good here; quiet. If you chose, we might hide here forever."

"And let the elves have the rest of Eriden," she spat angrily. Turning to face him squarely, he did not drop his hold on her, sliding the hand around to her arm where he gripped her firmly. "I could never allow that, Lamwen," she breathed. "Every creature here is important to me, from the mighty dragons to the lowly desert fairies. They all have their place in the grand scheme of things, and I should never want to sacrifice one for another."

"Even the elves?" he asked with a crooked grin.

Calmer, she studied his changed appearance. "You look so different as a man," she observed, raising her hand to toy with his shocks of grey hair. "Your eyes are still green, but your features reflect your years."

"It is not only my appearance that has changed," he confessed, catching her hand to fold it between his. "I have walked as a mortal a mere ten days, and yet I feel as if my whole life has been altered."

"How so?"

Releasing her palm, he brushed her cheek. "I feel so different in this form. As a powerful dragon, there was much less to concern myself with. Now, I feel so much a part of things."

"Will you go back to Adiarwen?" she snapped, disturbed by his words.

"When the time is right, I will retake my dragon form," he laughed. "Do not fear, my queen. But until then, I enjoy the feel of this body. It has changed me in a way that I am certain cannot be undone, and I wish to taste all that it might offer." Leaning forward, he kissed her.

Pulling away, Ami broke the connection, but his hand shot from a gentle caress of her face to holding the back of her neck, preventing her from running away. "I am spoken for," she whispered. "I have asked you not to tempt me."

"Amicia may have been claimed, but Kaliwyn is another story," he growled, pushing his body against her. "I told you. This form has changed me and left me delirious with desire. To know a mate as a dragon is to own her, to possess her that she might bear my young, and I have never had the means," he confessed, his eyes flicking to her lush lips. "But this flesh knows of other pleasures a dragon may never have. Share them with me, Kaliwyn."

"You're mad," she spat, pulling against his grasp.

"Am I?" he laughed. "You said once that you loved me. I only ask for one night that you might show me."

Ending her struggle, she glared at him. "Do you know what this would mean? If Rey were to learn of what we had done."

"Tell him the truth if you must, for it is the dragon part of you that is mine. Release her to me. I swear upon my life I will not speak of it to anyone," he growled, brushing her lips with his, pushing his mouth across her flesh in search of her neck as his fingers pulled at her hair.

Staring into the trees with clear green orbs, her pulse raced, and she could almost hear the two arguing her course within her mind; Amicia and Kaliwyn. She was both of them, but they were not each other. "There is logic in it," she whispered, the feel of his teeth on her jaw destroying her clarity of thought.

Transporting them in an instant, they stood in a dark part of the forest far from their camp. Pulling at his clothing, the beast within her broke free, and Kaliwyn growled, "Have me then on this night as you desire, but we shall never share another."

"I only need the one," he agreed, returning her fervor within the darkness.

It did not take Rey long to decipher what had become of the pair, as neither of them returned during the night. Instead, they made their appearance as breakfast was served so that no one could have missed their tryst. Glaring at her with a cold stare from his rock before their bed, he grated his teeth against one another.

"Man up or forget it," Piers growled in his ear as he served his mash into his bowl.

"Would your advice be the same if it had been your wife?" the younger man spat.

"My wife does not have a dragon inside her," the Mate replied. "You must remember she has chosen to walk by your side. Be careful you do not drive her from it. It is in our nature to be possessive of that which belongs to us, but a woman's heart is far more complicated and must be treated as such."

"And you are an expert on such matters," Rey replied, filling his bowl and turning his back to walk away, wishing to eat undisturbed.

Taking his seat at the table, the Mate observed, "I assume you have resolved your anger at my observations for your plan."

"Resolved," the girl giggled, her mouth screwed into a twisted growl. "Unless you have a concrete objection, it is the path we will follow," she dismissed his concerns coolly.

"Then I will be transformed soon?" Jarrowan spoke up.

"When we are ready to implement our actions, in a few days at most," she agreed.

Meena's orb on the table between them, Piers glanced at it as he listened to the discussion. Seeing an image of Rey within it, he shook his head at the younger man as he leaned against a tree and ate his mush alone. A moment later, he reached over and picked up the orb, glaring at the glossy surface.

"Would you like to check on something?" his wife asked, holding out her hand to take the magical device and adjust the scene for him.

"I already see something," he breathed, confusion in his voice. Offering it to her, he showed her the image of the boy. "Do you see Rey?"

Glaring at it, an eerie silence fell over the group.

"Is it because you were a dragon for a few hours?" Amicia postulated.

"I doubt it," Meena denied. "Even in dragon form, it would not give him any more power than was previously his, just as the power within you belongs to Kaliwyn."

Turning the orb, the Mate changed the scene, observing one of the markets they had visited a few days before. "Well, I'm definitely controlling it. I've never tried before, and I wasn't really trying now; it just sort of happened."

Lifting his gaze, his large brown eyes stared into those of his wife. "What could cause this?"

"It could be the marsh," Happy spoke up. "This is a magical place. Perhaps you have absorbed some of the radiant energy collected here."

"Oh, like the rings in Esterbrook," Amicia gasped. "Remember when we all were infused with the power of translation? It hasn't worn off, either, so maybe this is a similar manifestation."

Their conversation paused as Rey came out of the woods. Hearing the silence as he washed his bowl and spoon, he placed them in their gear and snapped, "Well, don't stop on my account." Not turning to face them, he felt certain he had been the topic before he interrupted, and his ears burned with silent rage.

"Actually, it's not on your account really," Piers countered, getting to his feet, "but since you're here, there is something you can do." Standing before him, he offered the orb. "Take this," he commanded.

Snatching it, Rey scowled, "And?" He squeezed it as if it would crush beneath his angry grasp.

"What do you see in it?" the Mate asked calmly.

"I don't see…" he began, cutting himself off. "I see Adiarwen," he breathed. "They're having some kind of meeting up on the rocks where we tore down the prison." Turning to the others, his voice grew loud, "What's going on?"

"We think you are absorbing some of the energy from the marsh. You are picking up some of the magic of the land," Ami explained softly, then added, "I wonder if it will affect all of us."

"If it does, maybe the sirens be healed," Oldrilin added with excitement in her voice.

"Healed?" Animir asked.

"They were burned by the dragons," she recalled. "They are scarred, but when they come, they might be healed."

"Maybe," Amicia agreed, joining the two men so she could see the orb more clearly. Watching the dragon meeting with him, she sighed, "We will have to act soon. Whatever they are discussing, it can't be good."

"Maybe they are going to attack the elves," Zae suggested.

"Unlikely," the Mate grunted.

"And why not?" the girl insisted.

"Because the elves didn't steal their prisoner," he clipped. "This is getting out of hand quickly," he observed, glaring at Amicia. "You want to implement your plan, then let's do it. No time like the present."

"We can't," she sighed. "I still have a few preparations to make, maybe two or three days to complete."

"Then maybe you should be focused on that instead of –" Rey snapped, stopping short of saying the words, but the cut of his eyes at Lamwen spoke volumes.

"He is part of us and as valuable as any," she countered, turning to stomp off into the trees. "I need to pull a few tomes from the libraries, and I will begin right away. I will need a change of clothes for each of us and a set of stones; again, one for each of us. They need to be small and fit comfortably in your hand."

Not bothering to explain why, she disappeared, leaving them to their own preparations as she had asked.

SIXTEEN

Old Friends

LEAVING the group to gather the items she had requested, Amicia transported herself to the eastern entrance to the Crimson Caves. She had been visiting her father regularly, but her heart ached as she prepared to meet him on this particular day.

Lifting her chin, she drew a deep breath. Pushing her doubts aside, she opened the tunnel and made her way into the inner chambers.

"Ami!" Traok squealed in greeting.

"Hello," she grinned, accepting his hug. "You're getting taller," she observed, noting she needed to look up at him these days.

"Yes," he nodded, pleased with his height.

"I've come to visit my father," she announced. "Does he still slumber?"

"He is down on the beach," the troll replied. "Shall I walk with you?"

"No. I'll find my way," she nodded, laying her hand over the merdoe out of habit as she made the jump.

The sun instantly bright around her, Amicia shaded her eyes as she scanned the shore. At the edge of the water stood the charred remains of an unfinished boat; the one the group had been constructing under the pretense of leaving Eriden. Turning in a slow circle, the cabin also stood in ruins at the edge of the woods.

Sighing heavily, she completed the scan, not seeing any sign of Ziradon. Facing the sea once more, she stared out over the calm waters that gently lapped the shore. "How I have missed this place," she sighed, distracted for a moment by the past.

While her thoughts churned, a large shadow swept over her, its presence fleeting as it skimmed out over the surf. Looking up, the large beast turned, and she grinned in recognition. Waiting patiently, he landed on the sand a few paces away a few minutes later.

"You're looking well," she observed, his figure fuller than her last visit. "All muscle, I hope."

"Indeed," he laughed, swishing his tail in delight. "I have regained much in my time here, but I'm afraid I'm still an old dragon in the end. Have the others been informed of your plan?"

Walking past him, she hesitated, and he fell into step beside her. When she was ready, she admitted quietly, "The Mate is afraid. He didn't even want to talk about it until he learned you had helped in its formation."

"That's too bad," Ziradon winced. "His faith in you is lacking, my princess."

"I am not a great warrior," she giggled, "despite the blood of our line. I understand his hesitance to follow on my word alone."

"Then tell him the plan is mine. It does not make it any more or less sound," the old dragon laughed, turning to catch more of the wind in his great wings. "I fear I will not see the end of this, Kaliwyn. You must be strong and not let the words of others dissuade you in your cause."

His use of her dragon name stirred within her chest, and she sniffed, "I do not feel I deserve to be followed so blindly."

"And why is that?" he prodded, folding the appendages and ambling along once more.

"Lamwen and I were intimate," she confessed, her chin dimpled. "I have broken my vow to Reynard, and I feel less than worthy of any such devotions."

"Ah, the mortal," Ziradon grumbled lightly. "I'm surprised it has lasted as long as it did."

Her eyes snapping to glare at him, she growled, "You feel I am weak in my resolve?"

"Not at all, my child," he insisted. "Rey is a human; a mortal of the rim. You may walk in the flesh beside him, but within your chest beats the heart of a dragon."

"You are saying we are different. Too different to make it work," she cried, tears wetting her cheeks.

"I know that you love him," the old dragon proposed, "but in time, your paths would drift apart. Even if you were to choose to forgo your wings, his blood would never burn with the heat of our kind."

Thinking of the single night she had spent in Lamwen's arms, she had to admit it had been nothing like the tender love of the mortal. There had been a magic to it the other man could not match, or so it would seem. "You do not think I should feel guilt at breaking my vow," she concluded.

"It was inevitable, as is the war between us and the elves," he agreed. "Do not let the words of the one called Mate dissuade you. You must act quickly in the steps we have discussed. If, and only if, you are able to spread the resources of the elves thin enough will you be able to defeat them."

"Is that how you beat them last time? In the great war?"

"Oh, the great war," Ziradon moaned, his eyes distant as he thought of it. "I lost your brothers then," he sighed.

"Yes, I have read the telling of your story as recorded by the gnomes. I'm sure it was painful to endure." The wind whipping her hair, she paused to study him, noting the large tears that formed in his glistening orbs. "I once wondered if dragons had tears."

"We do," he agreed, returning from the past. "You are all that I have left, Kaliwyn. And yet, I am willing to risk you to this cause. We must protect Eriden from the forces that threaten to crush it."

"I know, father," she agreed with a firm nod. "And I am willing to see to the cause, no matter the cost. I hope you are wrong about yourself, though. I wouldn't mind allowing you to rule a few more years," she laughed.

"Are you not ready to be queen?" he queried. "Tell me of your strength."

"I can transport anywhere in Eriden," she bragged. "I hardly use the merdoe and no longer miss the hamar gem. I feel strong and can defend against attacks, as well as cast against others easily."

"And you feel those are your strengths," he mumbled.

"What else would they be?"

"Your heart, sweet princess. Your love for those around you, even to the smallest of our inhabitants. The care and regard you have for others, even those who would be your enemy. Those are the things that will make you great," he professed.

Nodding, she sighed, "I cannot deny them although I would not call them strengths. I will take your word on the matter," she laughed, holding the smile for a moment before it fell away. "I guess you know I am undecided about my physical form."

"I sense your indecision," he agreed.

"I feel the urge to return to my dragon body, but I know when I do, it will be the last."

"You are reluctant to part with that which holds you bound to your husband," he observed calmly.

"Yes. I fear our marriage will die when the choice is made."

"Then cherish it while you may, princess. For he will live but one life and not a long one at that. There will be time for you to have both if fate wills it."

She grinned at the thought of it. "If he isn't too angry over Lamwen. He went off by himself this morning, probably because of it."

"You did not hide your indiscretion?"

"No," she admitted quietly. "I thought that I would, but in the end, I chose to let it stand. I love Lamwen, and they all are aware. What would be the point in pretending?"

"What would be the point, indeed," her father replied in his gravelly tones. "Then you have no need of my advice on the matter." Staring at her, he reached to her mind. *"Do you hear my words, Kaliwyn?"*

Picking up on his thoughts in an instant, she turned to face him. "Are you reaching out to me?"

"Our time grows short, my daughter. Your visits to this place will end, and we should practice our telepathy if we are to have it," he agreed.

Her heart beating faster, she pursed her lips. *"I am too easy to contact, I fear."*

"Many share your thoughts," he observed.

"Yes. Meena is afraid of it, I think. Should she be?"

"Does her fear change anything?"

"Not really."

"Then stop letting fear guide you, my queen."

Grinning brightly, she walked for a while in silence, observing the sun had reached the top of the sky. Eventually, she paused to announce, "I need to go. They should have everything gathered for me to infuse."

"Infuse?" he asked, his curiosity clear.

"Yes. I've found some interesting spells in the tomes of the gnomes. Things that will help us greatly. But somehow, I think you already knew that I would."

"The gnomes are old friends, as are the trolls."

"You have been well loved by many in Eriden," she observed.

"As I have loved all of my kingdom," he agreed.

"Then when it comes my time to reign, I will remember that," she smiled, reaching to lay her hand against his scales briefly before she disappeared.

SEVENTEEN

Of the Power

AMI RETURNED to the camp to find the others had done as she requested. On the table lay a pile of clothing, one change for each of them, and a small stack of rocks.

Glaring at her when she arrived, Rey spit in a surly tone, "I assume you don't care whose rock is whose."

"Not at all," she grinned, happy he was at least speaking to her. Inhaling deeply, she wanted to apologize to him, but the words caught in her throat, and she released the breath without uttering a word. Instead, she pulled out the tome she needed from under their bed and opened it on the table.

Staying to watch her as she thumbed through the pages, Rey scowled at her profile as she located the spell she wanted to use. She could feel the anger radiating from him and hoped it would soon wane.

The others curious as well, the camp soon filled with onlookers. "Do you not have better things to do?" she growled, not addressing anyone in particular.

"We're only watching," Hayt explained, indicating the neat line of rocks that she had been fiddling with. "What good are rocks going to do us?"

"Well, hopefully a great deal," she grinned. "When I'm ready, I'll show you how to use them."

Leaving, she transported to one of the libraries to retrieve another text. Taking it back to her workspace, she located the proper spell and enchanted the clothing one piece at a time.

By the time she had finished, the sun hung low in the sky. Meena put on the pot, as Jarrowan and Lamwen provided the meat for the stew.

Seeing the way her dearest dragon friend glared at her, she recognized the hunger in his eyes. *"I knew once would not be enough,"* she teased.

"Does that mean we will share another night?" he replied, glancing in the direction of the mortal who claimed her.

Shaking her head, she didn't say yes, but she didn't say no. Instead, she held up one of the stones and announced, "I'm ready to show you how these things work if anyone cares to listen."

The ring formed around her almost instantly, as all had been hanging close by in wait.

Poking the pile of shirts and pants, Piers noted, "They don't look any different to me."

"I have found a special spell," she smiled, wondering if she should tell them what they did, or simply demonstrate. Opting for the latter, she lifted one of the garments and sauntered over to the fire, where she tossed it in, or mostly in as it landed with one of the arms laying over the ring of large stones and onto the ground around their pit.

"What the hell!" Rey spat, watching as his second shirt lay within the flames. "I realize you're pissed at me, but that doesn't mean you should burn my clothes!"

Her jaw dropping, she gasped, "Pissed at you? Why would I be?" she began, stopping when she noted his eyes flick to glare at Lamwen. "Oh, I see," she finished. Reaching down, she caught the arm of the article that had survived the tossing and used it to lift the rest out of the fire.

Staring at the pristine material, gasps and whispers rippled through them.

"Cloth that doesn't burn," Piers surmised.

"Exactly," she nodded. "It will offer you some protection against the dragons, like armor only lighter."

Her eyes wide, Meena glared at her. "I have never seen such magic."

"Well, it was there in the tomes," Amicia informed her tartly.

The trio of ossci huddled together, they spoke in low tones to one another, adding a seditious air to the proceedings. When they continued, Amicia demanded, "Is something wrong?"

Breaking their conversation, Grumpy observed, "It would be unwise to have too much faith in such things," he warned.

"We'll keep that in mind," the girl smiled.

"What he means is," Yimath tried again, "this spell is impressive, and your powers have obviously grown since our arrival here. We are only concerned of the false confidence they might inspire. Dragons are dangerous creatures, and caution should always be taken."

Nodding, Ami agreed, "I understand. Everyone will have time to practice and learn about these things before we use them in actual combat."

"What about the stones? Are they for water?" Animir asked, thinking of the wan's previous trick.

"No, but I suppose we could make some if we needed to," the girl agreed, "now that I know how. No, these are a shield," she explained, indicating the row with a flattened palm. "Choose yours," she commanded.

Snatching the rock he had added to the pile, the elf adjusted it in his hand until it fit comfortably. "What do I do with it?" he asked, gripping it tightly within his fist.

"Close your eyes and imagine that your body is covered with a thick layer, like you are wrapped in a blanket head to toe."

"All right," he replied, conjuring the image in his mind.

"Now, imagine that the blanket is so strong that nothing can pass through it. Nothing can reach you."

"Ok."

Reaching out, her fingers fell short of his arm, and a small blue spark arced when she got close, forcing her to withdraw the appendage. Opening his eyes, he gasped, "Did that hurt? I felt it, like a little shock between us."

"A little," she grimaced, flicking her fingers playfully.

"How does it work?" the Mate asked, pinching his lip as he studied the elf. Before she could respond, he reached out to receive his own shock. Withdrawing the digits quickly, he shook them as well. "That does hurt. Will it stop a sword?"

"We'll have to test it," she nodded, "but from the spell book, it acts with exactly the opposite of the force used against it. If you push a little, it pushes back a little."

"If you whack it hard, it's going to hurt like hell," Reynard concluded, lifting his own stone to play with. "Did you bother to read the fine print? Last time we tried out one of your spells, it nearly killed us."

Ami shook her head at his tone. "I read the whole thing if that's what you mean," she sneered. "They are perfectly safe to use, but I caution the magic within the stones is finite, as it was with the water stone. Once you have used it all up, it won't work anymore."

"Ah, nothing is infinite, not even magic stones," the Mate muttered, also taking his. "This is actually pretty clever, but it will take practice turning them on when we need to so we aren't wasting them. And I am curious if we receive part of the blow or if it is all returned to the attacker."

"How did you know Piers and I would be able to use them?" Rey demanded, also taking his. "We only found out this morning that we were being infused with the use of power."

"I didn't, and I wasn't going to make one for you until we realized you were able to use the orb," she confessed with a shrug. "I'm glad it has worked out."

Glancing at one another before they snatched up their stones as well, Zaendra and Hayt laughed with obvious glee.

"You seem happy, at least," Amicia smiled.

"I am quite pleased," Zae replied, gripping her stone and urging Hayt to reach for her. When he jerked the appendage back, she roiled with peals of laughter. "It does shock a bit when he tries, but the fact he can't get through is amazing."

"Aye," Piers agreed, "but everyone take care while we are testing them. We need to know exactly what they protect against and what we need to do to produce the charm before we are ready to use them."

"I'm sure we will figure it out," Zaendra beamed. She had always known she had magical blood, but now it was more than that, and she felt as if she had fulfilled some great destiny by being there. "Somehow, I think this is why I left the glen. I'm supposed to be a part of this battle and here to help my friends."

"I'm glad you think so," Ami agreed with a pat on her arm. Then she announced, "I have one more enchantment to make, but I can do that tomorrow while you practice with these."

"What does it do?" Animir asked, impressed by the girl's growing talents. "It seems you have found your knack; enchanting objects."

"Perhaps," Amicia shrugged. "If the next one works, your blades will be unbreakable and, even better, able to penetrate the scales of the dragons," she explained, closing her tomes and disappearing to return them to the library.

"What," Rey sputtered. "Did she just say penetrate dragon scales?" He glared at Lamwen as he spoke, thinking how handy such a tool would be.

"Yes, and I'm doubtful it will work," the dragon-man growled. "Of course, it is of little consequence, as after having tested your mortal bodies, I feel you would still be no match for a dragon, even with these toys."

"Oh, I think this evens the odds pretty well," the Mate countered, finding his clothing in the pile to retrieve it. "Besides, dragons aren't the only things we will be fighting, and over all, these definitely give us an edge."

Not bothering to argue, Lamwen's thoughts churned. He had to agree with the mortal; enchanting objects had become Ami's specialty, which in itself was impressive. However, it frightened him as well. *Her skills are growing, and she is far ahead of the others in our group in power and ability,* he silently mused.

Studying his stone, he knew he would keep his fears to himself. *No dragon has ever been this powerful, not even the great Ziradon.* He would have to keep himself sharp for trouble, as her talents could hold great consequences for them in the future.

EIGHTEEN

Allies Among the Stones

THE MORNING BRIGHT, Amicia completed her work on the weapons as soon as breakfast was over. Then donning one of Meena's wizard robes, she left the group to their testing and practice. Her night had not been restful, as she had declined Lamwen's offer for a second night of vigorous copulation. However, she had not been in the mood for Rey's tender love-making either, and that had left her nothing to do but lie beneath her blanket and consider what lay ahead.

Deciding to put some distance between them, she first ventured to the market in the northern wizard city of Heewan, where she explored the shops in search of things that might catch her eye. Her disguise in place, she relaxed as she moved among their people, as if she had nothing more pressing to occupy her time then magical trinkets and household wares. Locating the stall where they had purchased their cloth, she smiled at the red-haired merchant and his scruffy beard when he appeared to greet her.

"Ah, you have returned," he grinned, spreading his arms wide in salutation.

"You recall my previous visit?" she asked, wandering around the tables of cloth with her fingers trailing over a few of the fine threads.

"But of course," he chuckled. "One never forgets one whose fire burns so brightly."

His words gave her pause, and she slowly turned her head enough to catch sight of him. Seeing that his gaze was fixed upon her, she swallowed, then asked, "You are a wizard, yes?"

"I am," he nodded. "Does that frighten you?"

"Only if you wish me harm," she stalled, wondering if returning there had been a bad idea. Drawing her robe closer around her, she considered using the transposition to disappear on the spot.

"Only a fool would stand against you," he assured with a sparkle in his eyes, "wizard or otherwise. Now, have you come to shop for something special, or are you here for a simple visit?"

"I'm afraid nothing I do is simple these days," she sighed, the weight of her life heavy at the moment. "I just came to roam the plaza and while a few hours," she confessed. "It feels good to wander without purpose at times."

"Let us have a stroll then," he proposed, turning before she could reply. At the back of the shop, he called into the smaller, adjacent room, "Come and mind the front!"

A second man of medium build quickly presented himself, and the shopkeeper moved to the door, indicating the exit with an open palm. Joining him there, she noticed the smell of him as she drew near; *sweet, pleasant, like spice.* Images of her home across the sea filled her mind, and she sat again at her mother's funeral. A young man stood before her, handing her a simple rose before he disappeared. *A boy with red hair.* The image filled her with dread she could not explain.

When they entered the square, he leaned closer to her, so their words could be heard over the crowd. "You are a mortal of the rim?" he asked.

"Yes," she nodded, then glanced at him. He knew of her deception, she was sure of it. "Do you make the cloth that you sell?" she asked, steering their conversation away from herself but not daring to ask the question that burned in the back of her mind.

"I make very little of it," he explained. "Our looms are there in the back, and we have weavers who run them. They are quite skilled, actually."

"Ah," she sighed, her eyes roaming over the throng. Tense, she realized the walk with the stranger wasn't helping her nerves. "Thank you for the visit, but I think I should go."

"Still searching," he offered.

"Searching?" she asked, thinking it an odd thing to say, her mind again on Arely.

Pausing, he stared down at her, and she faced him, the shoppers around parting to the left or right. "You seem familiar," she whispered.

"Certainly, I am familiar," he chuckled. "We had a very good day the last time you visited," he informed her. "Our till was quite full after you left."

"Yes, all the cloth," she mumbled, still taking him in. "That isn't it. Are you sure you are a wizard?"

His voice deeper, his smile dropped, and a wrinkle creased his forehead. "You are not ready, Amicia Spicer. If you were, you would not ask," he replied, then turned his back on her and walked away.

Hearing her name fall from his lips, she gasped, "Oh God!" Pushing through the crowd, she tried to catch up, but he had disappeared. Arriving back at the shop, he wasn't there. Deciding not to wait, she left via the street, by the opposite way of the bazaar, and transported herself as soon as she felt safe to do so.

Arriving at the Crimson Caves, she felt relieved to be there, as the strange shopkeeper had disturbed her to the core. Placing her hand on the ruby red wall, she smiled as if she were home.

Following the path, she arrived in the central room as usual and grinned at the activities of her largest friends.

"Amicia," Yaodus greeted with arms stretched wide. "Another visit so soon!"

"Yes," she grinned. "Time is close, and I may not get to come again once we take the fight to the elves."

His features grew tight, and the troll nodded. "We have heard of the sorrows and watched with our magical fires. It is truly a shame," he lamented with a shake of his head.

"I'm glad you understand," she sighed, pondering the day's visit. "Is my father around?"

"He is asleep in his pod, but I will send for him," the king offered.

"No, please don't bother him," she interjected. "I need a word with you as well, and perhaps this would be a good time to have it."

"Very well," he agreed, taking a seat on his rock before the flames of his pit.

Taking hers close at hand, she observed, "Remember when you gave me the stone and offered to stand with us when the time came to fight?"

"Yes, very well," he agreed.

"The time is close, Yaodus. A few days at most and we will be ready to march against the dwarves," she explained.

"And you wish us to join you in this fight," he inhaled deeply. Seeing the tension in her jaw, he nodded, "I have promised our support, and you shall have it, my queen."

"Thank you," she breathed in relief. "At least something has come easily." Seeing his features crumple, she realized she might have spoken too soon. "Will there be a problem with our cause?"

"Only the wolves," he groaned.

"The root of our dispute," she frowned. "Surely they have given up trying to reach you."

"No. They are stubborn creatures," he pointed out. "If we intend to march against the dwarves, they will have to be reckoned with beforehand."

An angry twist in her gut, Amicia fumed, "They have no right to stand in our way. Why are they not our allies, as the southern pack has been?"

"I know not what twists a wolf's mind," the sovereign cackled. "I only know they will stand against us when we leave this place."

"Not if I can help it," she growled. "Be ready in three days, as we will make our move. And do not worry about the wolves. They will not resist our movements on that day."

"This is getting easier," Rey observed, shielding himself expertly when Piers swung his blade, the magic absorbing nearly all of the blow. "It does still sting, but not at all as if I were cut or stabbed."

"Aye," the Mate chuckled, "but my hands ring like I have whacked this blade against a large rock. A few of those, and we will have anyone's attention."

"I wish there were a way to know how much power is left in the stone," Hayt observed, watching covertly as his wife took large chunks out of a tree with her enchanted weapon. "I can't believe you made her a spear."

"Why wouldn't I?" the taller man sneered. "She's been feisty ever since I met her and damn good with a club, let me tell you. I simply gave her an upgrade, putting the blade on the end."

Placing his stone in his pocket, Rey poured a glass of water for each of them from their elvish wine bottle. "I think we have a fighting chance. Amicia did well with her enchantments."

"Obviously, she did well," Lamwen began, stopping short when she appeared next to her husband.

"How was the training?" she huffed without preamble.

"Fine," Piers toasted with his cooling drink. "You have improved our odds for certain."

"Then let's make a little test run, shall we?" she suggested, pulling off her robe and hunting for her bow.

"Test run?" Jarrowan asked as he joined them. "I thought this was the test."

"No, I mean against a real enemy. The northern pack will stand against us when we march with the trolls for the dwarf mountain," she clipped, her voice holding undertones of anger.

"And how do you know this?" Piers frowned.

"I saw Yaodus today. I asked them to be ready to go in three days, and he said the wolves have been hanging around more than ever, causing problems," she explained. "I think we should attack them now, when it will be a surprise, and get them out of the way."

"Ok," Rey agreed, fidgeting with his sword. "Where do we find them?"

"Search the woods with our orbs," Meena suggested. "We all are adept at them by now."

Each pulling out their device, or at least all who owned one, they combed the forest until Edeill had been located.

"He's close to Sevoassi's cottage," Animir observed. "Do you think they know we have been there?" The thought of the pack hanging around and waiting for their return was disturbing, in the least.

"I fear that they might. We should transport there, since they are close, and we can move from that location," Amicia suggested. "Everyone bring your stone and your weapon for a proper fight."

Grouping together, each of those practiced at transporting claimed the hand or arm of one who could not, and together they traveled the distance in the blink of an eye. Arriving next to the gnome home they had hidden within after Amicia's unfortunate transfiguration, they formed a ring and looked around.

"See anything?" Piers whispered loudly.

Using her orb, Ami pointed. "I believe they are this way."

"As do I," Meena agreed.

Moving towards them, they found the pack moving along the trail they had used back when they had ridden upon their backs. "Good. We can follow them until they make camp for the night," Rey suggested.

"I think we should transport ahead, or at least part of us, and get on with the fight," Amicia grunted.

"I'm with Ami," Zaendra hissed. "I do not wish to wait in case something should go wrong."

"All right. Ami, Rey, Hayt, and Zaendra all jump ahead of them. Stop for a chat if you like, and we will push in from behind," Piers suggested.

"Sounds good," Amicia agreed, offering her hand to her husband for the transport.

A moment later, the four of them stood upon the trail as the wolves came into view. Reaching out to the wolf, Amicia announced her presence. *"Edeill."*

"Amicia Spicer?" he replied in surprise.

"Wonderful. You haven't forgotten me. We're on the path ahead of you, and would like to talk," she suggested.

"You are here – now?" he growled, unsure what they could possibly need to discuss.

"Yes, straight ahead of you," she repeated.

"And how do you know of our location?"

"Much has changed since we last met," she hinted. *"Perhaps we should come to you. Take a rest, and we will be right there."*

"I wouldn't advise that," he spat. *"As you said, much has changed."*

Her face growing tense, she placed an arrow on her string as she announced, "He doesn't sound happy to hear from me."

"Then we won't worry about the chatter," the dwarf laughed, hoisting his new axe and preparing to swing it.

"Don't forget your shield," Zae said with a grin, equally anxious for the fight.

The wolves were on them before he could reply, the first leaping and landing on him squarely. To everyone's surprise, the creature bounced, flying backwards and landing against a tree with a loud thud, followed by a series of yelps.

"It works!" Amicia shouted with glee, sending her arrow flying, then another.

The rest of their group close behind, they filtered into the small clearing from all sides, their swords singing as they swung them through the air.

With the aid of their enchanted stones, the wolves were prevented from landing a single blow, and their tough hides were no match for the special blades and arrows. Within a few minutes, two of the giant wolves lay dead and several more severely injured.

"What trickery is this!" Edeill growled as Ami and Rey held him cornered by a large trunk.

"I have become friends with the gnomes," she grinned, raising her chin to indicate the ossci. "They have taught me much since we last met."

His yellow eyes burning, he glared at Lamwen, the aura of the dragon unmistakable. "So, you have learned of your true nature."

"Yes," she hissed. "I have even carried my wings. One day soon, I will reclaim them forever."

"If that is true, why do you still stand before me as a mortal of the rim?" the wolf growled in disgust.

"Because it suits me," Amicia laughed. "I am Kaliwyn, heir to the throne of Eriden," she proclaimed. "I do as I please."

Edeill lowered his head, but he did not appear to be groveling. He looked as if he were plotting.

"Hear my words, wolf. I intend to let you go if you tell me what I want to know, on a given condition," she insisted.

"Name your terms," the alpha spat.

"Why do you torment the trolls?"

"Because Queen Cilithrand demands it," he sneered.

"You take orders from the elf?" Amicia gasped in surprise, cutting her eyes over at Animir as she did so.

"She sent a party to meet with me long ago," he explained. "We came to an agreement, and she has been sharing with me telepathically ever since."

"When she has a job for you," Animir speculated.

"You could say that," the wolf agreed. "Anything else you feel entitled to know?"

"If I let you leave this place, we shall not meet again," Amicia threatened. "If we do, I'll take it upon myself to rid the forest of your existence. And be sure you don't go anywhere near the trolls as well."

Laughing at her, Edeill barked orders to his pack. "Leave the bodies and meet at the base of the waterfall." Bowing to the girl, he howled, then leapt past her as he trotted down the trail.

NINETEEN

Sides to be Won

"WHY DIDN'T WE KILL THEM?" Reynard growled when they had returned to their camp at Falconmarsh.

"What?" Amicia replied, taken off guard by his anger.

"The wolves," he snapped. "We had them dead to rights. We could have left their bodies where they lay and been rid of the whole pack. But instead, you let them go."

"We're not murderers, Rey," she sighed. "We made our point and learned a bit in the process. I don't think they will be any more trouble."

"Trouble," the Mate grumbled, not eager to join the argument.

"If you have something to say, lets hear it," Ami stated more forcefully. "You used to trust my choices."

"Aye, but I fear your judgment has become clouded," their leader snarled, glaring at Lamwen.

Drawn to her defense, the man-dragon replied, "It is not our place to wipe out the northern pack because they do not agree with our cause. Kaliwyn knows what she is doing."

"Ah, back to her dragon name, I see," Rey spat, sharing his foul gaze between them. Turning his back, he marched into the forest, Lamwen in close pursuit.

"Is that how it is?" the newcomer snapped when he caught him. Grabbing his arm, he forced the other man around.

"How what is?" Rey replied tartly, glaring at him through narrow slits.

"You pick a fight with her and then run away."

Rey clenched his jaw, causing the veins in his neck to ripple below the flesh. "Mind your own, dragon."

"Kaliwyn is my own, or have you forgotten?"

"Amicia is my wife in name and practice. She does not belong to you in any way."

"So, that's what this is about, is it?" Lamwen observed, his eyes flicking down to take in the other man's clenched teeth. Still toe to toe with him, he laughed boisterously, "You are angry that we share her."

His fists clenched, Rey bit, "We do not share Amicia. I'm not sure how you convinced her to spend the night –"

"Watch your tongue," Lamwen cut him off. "She may look like a mortal of the rim, but I assure you she is as dragon as I am."

"That's why you took human form, isn't it?" Rey accused, stabbing him in the chest with a stiff digit. "You think you can steal her away from me. But you won't."

"I didn't need to take this body for that," Lamwen snarled. "She has loved me of her own accord. I have tasted her of her own free will," he scoffed, "and will do so again."

"Not if I can help it," Rey pushed back.

Glaring at him, Lamwen's mind raced. "You know, I have learned much since I took this form, living in the flesh and blood of a mortal. To be given a mate as a dragon is an honor. Most males live their lives alone, without the company of a female. You have been lucky, Reynard Daye, but somehow I doubt you have seen it."

"What, so you want me to feel sorry for you?" Rey quipped.

"Not at all," Lamwen replied, much calmer. "My eyes have been opened, if you will. I understand her choice and what lies before her. Kaliwyn is the queen of Eriden, or good as. It is not her place to extinguish the inhabitants of her kingdom. The war will end, and there is all that comes after that must be considered." Taking a step back, he grew thoughtful, his gaze distant. "Perhaps I should rethink my primal desires and the pressure I have placed upon her."

"That makes a lot of sense," Rey grumbled, certain the other man was toying with him. "Do you have any idea how long I have waited for her?"

"I know exactly how long," Lamwen coughed. "You forget I have hunted you for most of it. But I have no need to press her to abandon you so harshly. The time will come with or without my insistence."

"Hardly," Rey sniffed, angry tears forming in his eyes. "We have spoken our vows, and if you leave her alone, they will hold."

"Oh, Rey," the man-dragon's voice fell as he shook his head. The human before him had become his friend, and his candor should be tempered with caring;

Amicia had taught him that. "What do you think will happen when she retakes her dragon form? Your bond will be broken. Unless you intend to live the rest of your days as a dragon, but I daresay you would be disappointed."

"Why would that disappoint me? To have my life with her, I can think of nothing sweeter."

"Dragons are not like men," Lamwen informed him, his anger purged. "Our rituals are quite different. No making love beneath the stars. As fantastic as it was to be with her, I know it will not be so when we have returned to Adiarwen. Even if she becomes my mate, our procreation is far less..." His voice drifted away as he searched for the right word.

His face shifting to a bright red, Rey accused, "I suppose your animalistic barbarism suits her better." Lifting his fists, he stepped towards him as if to pummel him. Holding to a single punch, he split the other man's lip and waited for the return blow, ready for an all-out brawl should he get one.

"I'm sure she enjoyed it," Lamwen grinned, stepping back from the challenge. Dabbing the drops of blood, then licking at the flow, he held up open palms of surrender. He deserved the beating and would have enjoyed the fight, but there was far more at stake that they had to resolve. "But that is not the point, my friend. You may love her in your own way until her choice is made, but you cannot let your limited view of the world trick your heart, or hers. Do not berate her for her duties as our leader. She must act as our sovereign and the Supreme Dragoness without fear of reprisal from you."

Wiping at his face, Rey's rage slowly ebbed. "The wolves will tell Cilithrand what happened. They will stand against us at every turn, and our element of surprise will be gone."

"We will adapt and deal with what comes," Lamwen assured, indicating the camp. "Let us return to the others and decide calmly what course we should take. Do not let this disagreement between us cloud what we must accomplish."

Noticing their gruff demeanors and Lamwen's swollen injury when they returned, Amicia reached out to the dragon anxiously. *"What did you say to him?"* Her eyes roving over Rey, she could see no harm had come to him, at least nothing physical.

"I only shared the truth," he grinned. Flicking his eyes over at her and brushing his lip gently, he praised his restraint inwardly. Aloud, he announced, "We should move up our timetable. Rey is right, our element of surprise will be lost, and we should adjust our intentions."

"I'm still not certain this hopping around will work," Piers growled, having brooded over the matter while the other two men quarreled in the trees.

Standing taller, Lamwen defended, "You are short-sighted, I believe. Yes, we want to win, but it cannot be at all cost."

"Exactly," Amicia agreed, stirring the pot that had begun to simmer. "I know you want to crush our enemies, but what good does it do to win if all that we hold dear has been destroyed? We cannot allow that to happen, and we certainly cannot be the force that brings such annihilation."

"We should go to Riran and retrieve the sirens as quickly as possible," Lamwen suggested, his gazed fixed on Oldrilin's hunched form. "They have suffered greatly in these decades of uncertainty, and I fear their rescue is critical if they are to survive."

"Agreed," Amicia smiled at their small friend.

"If you're going after the mermaids, then I should lead our troops to the glen," Jarrowan suggested. "If the dragons are divided to search for the sirens, it will be more difficult for me to complete my task. I need to do this before they can be split."

"Then we should perform your transformation this evening, that you may be recovered through the night and take your flight before dawn," Amicia suggested.

His frown in place, the Mate grumbled, "All these plans."

"It will be all right, love," Meena interjected. "I see the logic in wishing to preserve as much of our kingdom as we can."

"What about the trolls?" Piers insisted. "Will they be ready to march against the dwarves?"

"I told them three days," Amicia nodded. "They will be ready to leave when we get there. Until then, I will recharge the shield stones and ready our weapons. Rey and Animir can see that the sirens are settled along the shore, with the ossci's help if they would like."

"It won't take three days to recharge the stones," Rey challenged.

"I know. I have one other place I wish to visit, and I think I need to go alone," she replied, hardly above a whisper.

"Then our plans are set," Lamwen announced, ending the discussion. "Should we perform the transformation now or after the meal?"

"After," Jarrowan grinned. "I have come to appreciate their evening stew."

Laughter rippled around the group at his observation as they dispersed to enjoy what they could of what would be their last evening before the storm.

TWENTY

Return to Riran

"THIS IS the place where I made camp," Rey informed her, showing Ami the location with her golden orb.

"It looks nice," she agreed. "Will they have access to the water?"

"Yes. It's not the sandy beach they enjoy now, but none of the shoreline on this side appears to be," he sighed. "I think they can get by, though."

"Then you and Animir will go and see that it is ready. A throne-stone for Olirassa and anything else you can think of to make them comfortable in their exile."

Listening to her speak, Reynard could hear the sadness in her voice. Lamwen's words had weighed heavily upon him during the night. "I'm sorry I doubted your judgment," he whispered.

Cutting her eyes up at him, she scowled, "I don't have time to worry about us right now."

"I know, and that's not what I meant," he insisted. "I know you have a lot on your shoulders, and I certainly don't mean to add to your burden."

"Then do as I ask and don't say anything else," she clipped, inhaling deeply to clear her thoughts.

"Aye," he grumbled, leaving her to locate Animir. Finding him and Oldrilin together on the north end of the valley, he spat, "You ready?"

"Yes. I have gathered what I can from the siren about their needs. We should be able to prepare a suitable place for them," he grinned.

"Great. Then let's get to it. They will be arriving between midday and early evening at the latest." Turning to the siren, he asked, "Are you sure you don't want to come with us? We don't mind you being there," he assured. "You won't be in the way."

Looking up with large blue eyes, she smiled, "Rey Daye make Lin's new home?"

"Temporary home, yes. Come on. You can come back here with us when we return," he offered.

Reaching for his hand, she accepted the invitation. Taking his other arm, the elf transported the trio to their destination, and they set to work on their task.

After they had gone, Amicia sat on a rock next to the fire and adjusted her orb so she could see Riran. Piers, Meena, and Oldrilin had made their visit early, before the sun rose over the lagoon. After informing Olirassa of their plan, they had returned a short time later to share their success, at least in the preliminary portion. The actual outcome remained to be seen.

Her focus with the device greatly improved, Ami could visit virtually any place in Eriden that she desired. Currently, she stared at the trees that marked the entrance to the lagoon. There, a handful of elves had gathered, possibly to stand watch. They had built a camp up the shore, near the previous location of their flat. Looking closer, into the forest, it appeared they intended to construct more permanent residences upon the shore.

"They're really branching out," she muttered.

"Any change?" Lamwen asked as he joined her on the massive stone.

"The elves are still there," she sighed. "They don't appear to have realized anything has happened. I don't see any sirens left on the beach, so they have all at least swum out to sea."

"Then they will be headed north," he surmised.

"Hopefully. I wish we had been able to transport them. It's a long swim, and I worry not all of them will make it."

Staring at her with tender eyes, he reached for her elbow and gave it a squeeze. "They are accustomed to long swims."

"And sharks?" she asked pointedly.

"Fair enough," he shrugged. "A few may be lost, but most will be saved. We have to take the victories we can get."

"Has Jarrowan made it out of Adiarwen?"

"I don't know; he's not telepathic," the man-dragon informed her. "Perhaps you can see what's going on there," he suggested, indicating her small sphere.

"Right," she grunted, ready to move on from the sad sands of Riran.

Turning the orb between her fingers, she focused on the dragons' cliffs. Nothing seemed out of the ordinary as a few large forms flew in and out of the caves. The waves crashing on the rocks below, she could almost hear them, drawing comfort from their unending motion.

Switching to the glen, nothing stirred. The elves had taken over their cabin and a few other meadows, but for the most part, the nymphs and satyrs still held the area. Skimming over the great rings, she sighed, "I can't see that anything is happening."

"I believe all is well, then," he grinned, still holding her arm.

"The calm before the storm," she countered, thinking of home, or at least the place she had grown up. "I recall more times than I can count when a squall formed out on the horizon. I would be working on the spice farm and see the clouds off in the distance. We would scramble to secure everything before it rolled in with howling wind and driven rain."

"We have the same on the dragon cliffs," he nodded. "But you know that the storm is our strength."

Looking up to meet his gaze, she grinned, "That's true. You brought the storm when you attacked, several times in fact."

"Did it frighten you?"

"A little," she giggled, toying with her darkened sphere. "We suspected it was part of your scare tactics."

"A frightened enemy is much easier to defeat," he confessed, licking his lips. Sitting so close, the scent of her surrounded him, drawing him in. Without warning, she raised her mouth to his. His heart pounding, he shared the moment with her, grinning when she pulled away. "I'll always remember this," he whispered.

"What?" she demanded, her voice weak in the aftermath.

"The tenderness of mortals," he laughed. "Dragons are more... brusque... in their courtships."

Nodding, she understood. "You realize I have not yet decided what I will do when all of this is over."

"I know," he agreed, "but my days as a man are numbered. Soon, I will return to my kind, a wiser dragon to be certain. If there was ever meant to be a future for us, you will join me there."

Catching motion from the corner of her eye, Ami realized they were not alone. "I'm glad we had the chance to educate you," she snorted, turning to find Piers inspecting their stones and weapons at the table.

"All is in order," she informed the Mate, leaving Lamwen seated at the fire as she ambled towards him.

"If you say so," he shrugged. "I'm still not convinced all this will work or protect us."

"You have a better plan?" she offered.

"Nope. So, we'll give it our best shot. Any word from down south?"

"I've been watching in my orb," she confessed, holding it up to evidence her claim. "All appears calm, at least for the moment. I'll be leaving on my quest shortly. Hopefully I will return tonight, but I will be back by tomorrow at the latest."

"Still not telling us where you're going," he grunted, not that it mattered. There were only a few that could be her target. Besides, she was a big girl and could take care of herself.

"You and Lamwen can reach me if you need to," she grinned, cutting her eyes over to see the dragon still watched her from across the camp.

"Aye," Piers scowled, troubled by that fact. "Did you ever wonder why you and I use the telepathy, but you and Rey don't?"

"Well, I never tried," she lied, saddened that her attempts had only ever met with silence. "Perhaps he and I could as well if we were both of a mind to."

Also glaring at the man across the way, he said no more. She had been speaking with him in the covert manner since he hunted them, so there would be little point in worrying over it now. "Be safe," he urged instead, placing his stone in his pocket as he left the camp in search of his bride.

He had liked Amicia Spicer once; now he wasn't so sure. She had become secretive, her behavior erratic. She toyed with Rey and the dragon openly, pitting them against one another at a time they needed to be firm in their resolve. "She'll get us all killed," he muttered as he spied Meena and the ossci gathered away from the camp, on the far north end of their valley.

"What's going on?" he asked gruffly as he approached. Pausing when he drew near, he looked up at the oversized statues. Noticing Hayt and Zaendra there among them, his spirits lifted. "Are these your kin?"

"Indeed, they are," the dwarf beamed. "I was just showing everyone we had found them. Getting rid of some of the coverings and all."

"They're splendid," Zae observed, touching one of them fondly.

Glancing down at the three gnomes, he ventured, "You wouldn't happen to know how any of this is going to turn out?"

"As it should," Grumpy replied.

"Yeah, that's what I figured," Piers chuckled, joining in the clearing of brush for a moment before he announced, "Amicia is leaving shortly to go on her secret mission. If she doesn't come back tonight, I have one of my own that I could use a little help on."

"What do you have in mind?" Meena asked doubtfully, still watching the work in a motherly fashion.

Cutting his eyes over at her, he pursed his lips, considering his choice to include the others. "I want to return to Riran at dusk."

"Whatever for?" she gasped, the others pausing in their cleaning to stare at him.

"Look, I know that Ami wants to be gentle about all of this and not hurt

118

anyone she doesn't have to. Me, I know how all this works. I want to go back with a show of force," he explained. "First, make sure all the sirens made it out. Second, I want to leave a bit of a body count; give Lady Cilithrand something to think about."

"Do you think that is wise?" Yimath asked in surprise.

"I believe it would be prudent. They need to know we mean business, and you don't make that kind of statement without spilling a little blood," he replied curtly.

"I'm in," Hayt announced without batting an eye.

"What?" Zaendra gasped. "I thought we were following Ami."

"We are," the dwarf shrugged, indicating his frozen kin, "but these guys didn't get to stand here by playing it safe. The Mate's right; we need to bash some heads along the way, or this war won't ever end. We have to give them a reason to come to the bargaining table, and that only happens if they have something to gain, or fear of something to lose."

"And sneaking out and handing over the lagoon without a fight is not making a statement," Piers agreed.

"We aren't giving them the glen," Zaendra countered, still at odds with her husband's choice. "Are you going to tell Amicia what you're planning?"

"No, and neither are you," the Mate growled, taking a step towards her, then glaring at her husband. "Hayt and I will take care of this if no one else wants to go."

"I'll go," Lamwen spoke up, interrupting their plotting.

"You?" Piers snapped, turning to gape at their uninvited guest.

"I said so, didn't I?" he clipped. "Amicia has gone, and we have free reign until she returns tomorrow."

"Then she had no intention of coming back tonight," the Mate grunted, raising his chin. "You won't feel bad about going against her wishes? She might not like you stepping out of line."

"I'm not her pet if that's what you mean," the dragon denied with a scowl. "Besides, I feel the urge to shed a little blood myself. Just because I agreed with her choice not to slaughter the wolves doesn't mean we shouldn't kill some of them when the time is right."

"And the time is right," Piers growled.

"I believe that it is," Lamwen agreed with a sly grin. "Will it just be the three of us, or is the whole group going?"

"Animir and Rey will be tied up with the sirens," the Mate pointed out. "I figure the three of us should be able to handle it."

"I'll go as well," Zaendra volunteered, earning a dark scowl from Meena. Seeing the look, she mocked, "Stand aside if you want. If the Mate feels this will help our cause, I'm willing to give aid."

Shaking her head, the wan sighed. Looking down on the ossci, she whispered, "Forgive us. We are not always as civilized as we would like to be."

"We understand," Happy agreed. "We would come as well, but someone needs to remain here in case Amicia were to return or something go wrong with the mermaids."

"Or the glen," Yimath added, sadness in her voice.

"Good. Then it's settled. We leave at dusk," Piers announced before resuming the clearing of Hayt's kin. Mounting one of the statues, he fought a thicker vine, working to remove it without damaging the surface beneath.

Watching him for a few minutes, Lamwen gathered his nerve. "Actually, there was another reason for my visit," he informed them. "I came to ask you... for a favor."

"Well, looks like we're all helping each other out today," Piers laughed sarcastically, his hands still tearing at the vines.

"I want you to return my dragon form."

The words hung in the air, like a dark cloud, freezing all of them in their places. Cutting his eyes over at him, Piers grunted, "When?"

"Tonight. Now. Before we return to Riran," Lamwen replied, then swallowed. "I'm going to rain down fire on the elves the likes they have never seen," he bragged.

"Ami isn't going to like that," the Mate pushed, dropping his fist full of vegetation and climbing off the statue to face him squarely.

"I know," the dragon agreed. "But I have told her I intended to return to my true form. I am not a man, and as much as I have learned living as one, it is time I returned to my own kind."

"But you will remain with us, here?" Zae asked doubtfully, saddened that he might leave.

"Certainly," he grinned. "You are my friends, which is something I have never boasted before. If luck shall have it, you will remain so all the rest of our days. And Amicia will forgive me, if it upsets her."

"Then we will return you to your former self," Yimath agreed for them, bowing her head. "We should do it now, though, so you can recover before your visit to Riran when darkness falls."

"That's a good idea," Piers agreed, beckoning the others to follow. "Do you think we will be able to achieve it with our small group?"

"All we can do is try," Meena sighed, standing across from him as they formed the circle.

Glancing at Lamwen, the Mate added, "Well, can I have my clothes back?"

"Your clothes?" Hayt laughed.

"Well, he isn't going to need them. Would save my wife a bit of sewing," he pointed out.

"Sure," Lamwen agreed, stripping them off and tossing them aside. Covering himself, he gave Meena a wink. "I don't mind being naked, but I can see our female companions are a bit troubled by it."

"Yes, please," Meena coughed, her face flushed at the display. "Are we set now?"

Seeing everyone in place, they focused their magic. Each muttered the chant as they marched around Lamwen's naked frame. At the critical moment, light flashed, knocking them back as he was transformed into his old familiar self.

TWENTY-ONE

Troubled Waters

"HELLO?" Amicia called, lowering her hood as she looked around. She had donned one of the wizard's robes again on this mission, as it made her feel stealthy. Nothing moved in the cool darkness, and she drew the material more tightly around her chest, thankful in her choice to wear it.

Her gaze swinging around the clearing, she was certain she had found the spot. Closing her eyes, she reached out, *"Uscan?"*

She had seen them on the trail using her orb only moments before she traveled. His failure to reply troublesome, she shrugged with a heavy sigh.

"I know you're here," she tried again.

Silence.

Up ahead, she would find the clearing where they had first encountered the protectors of the Shadowlands. Still holding her robe around her against the damp air of the trees, she marched towards it, hoping she would make contact.

"Uscan, I need to speak with you." They had not conversed since they had left the northern pack after meeting Sevoassi. *So long ago,* she mused. *"I know it's been a while,"* she sighed.

Arriving in the circle where they first met, her steps slowed. The air felt different, as it had the day they had passed through it as they fled Jerranyth. Licking her lips, she shivered, the light dim despite it being midday. Looking around, the trees held an ominous vibe, reminding her of the foreboding forest and its little goblins.

"Uscan, I have so much to tell you."

"I'm sure you do," came a cryptic reply.

From the ring of trees, the wolves crept forward, presenting themselves with their typical posturing. Uscan's head held high, he came to stand before her. "By all means, speak."

"Uscan," she whispered, a faint smile on her lips. "I have discovered myself," she confessed, adjusting her robe anxiously. "I am Kaliwyn –"

"Of course you are," he growled, his previous devotion to her nowhere to be seen. "You have been busy as of late from what I hear."

"Yes," she nodded. "We are preparing for the war."

"And is that why you are here? More preparations to be made?" he snarled.

"Uscan, I'm here alone. I only came to talk. I guess you have heard from Edeill."

"Indeed."

"What did he tell you?" she asked, standing straighter as she held her ground.

"Two of his pack dead by your hand. More injured. How have you betrayed us so?"

"Me?" she gasped. "They have been harassing the trolls, who are under my protection. Trying to break into their mountain. We only wanted them to stop. I asked him to speak with me, but they wanted to fight," she gushed.

His eyes narrowed, the great grey wolf studied her. His massive jaw clenched, and his lips receded, exposing his white teeth in a silent snarl.

"Do you also serve Cilithrand?" she asked in a timid voice, afraid of what he might say, uncertain of what she expected to gain from the knowledge.

Growling at her, Uscan barked, "You should speak to me with treachery in your heart! I know you have attacked our brothers to the north, then secreted away to hide while Eriden burns. Is this why they call you destroyer?" he accused, narrowing the distance between them.

"It was the northern pack who drew first blood," she insisted quietly. "I swear to you we had no intention of harming them, as I have no weapon and mean no harm to you, either."

"You have come to stand before me unarmed?" he laughed in a low rumble. "How foolish. I know of your powers, Kaliwyn. I am not impressed by your bravery."

"We are friends, Uscan. I trust you with my life."

"What evidence do you have that my kin transgress against the trolls?" he snapped, causing her to jump.

The tension mounting around them, her eyes flicked to the wolves who flanked him. "I don't need evidence. I will soon be the Supreme Dragoness, and my word is my strength."

"You will only be so if you survive the coming war," he growled, "and it isn't looking very likely."

"So, you have sided with Lady Cilithrand as well," she sniffed, unable to hide the hurt his betrayal brought her.

His body stiff, Uscan appeared equally disturbed that she would insinuate such a thing. "Allow me to clarify. I merely meant that the rightful Supreme Dragon will take the throne once the elf rebellion has been squashed and Gwirwen removed."

Glaring at each other, the seconds ticked by in silence. Sweat formed on her upper lip despite the coolness of the air.

"Uscan," she breathed, her voice trembling.

Resuming the quarrel, he asked, "Are you also responsible for the attack on Esterbrook, after all that the nymphs have done for you?"

"What attack?" she gasped, perplexed by the shift in the conversation.

"Do you deny that your dragons are there now?" he countered.

"Of course they're there. I sent them to fortify our position against the elves!" she defended.

Not waiting for her to finish speaking, Uscan leapt through the air, his massive frame knocking her to the ground as his teeth sank into her soft flesh.

Remembering her shield, she called the magic forth, blocking him from injuring her further. Her shoulder torn and bleeding, she lay on the path in a crumpled heap. Leaping against her and bearing their teeth, the wolves couldn't get to her, but she had no strength to fight back, much less teleport home. Holding the shield in place, she waited for them to give up.

At that moment, the scout Uscan had dispatched earlier in the day reached into his mind to give his report. "Stand," he ordered, calling off the pack while he listened.

"The dragons are here, as suspected, but they have turned on the elves," Mirean informed him.

"And what's happening?" Uscan growled.

"Things are rough. The satyrs are using their weapons against the elves as well, and with the dragons' help, it looks like they are pushing them back."

Glaring at the girl, Uscan's mind raced. "You sent dragons to protect the nymphs."

"That's what I said," she breathed, her pulse weak. "All of Eriden is under my care, and I must not fail in this cause," she whispered before slumping further, the stone dropping from her grasp.

Bouncing around the group, Lamwen flapped his massive wings, then leapt into the sky for a quick loop around the marsh. Landing, he pranced on his four legs as he growled, "God, it feels good to be me again."

"Silly dragon," Hayt chuckled. "Are we ready to depart for Riran?"

"I believe that we are," the Mate agreed, smiling at his wife. "Are you sure you can transport him?"

"I can manage the four of us and one dragon," she grinned at his concern. "Everyone gather in close. Put your hand on Lamwen, and I will transposition us as a group."

Following her command, Hayt, Zae, and the Mate all squeezed in, a moment later standing at the waterfall behind the mermaids' lagoon.

"Nice work, love," Piers praised, his eyes darting around to see if they were alone. "From here, we branch out; no quarter."

"I'll fly over and start the party," Lamwen laughed, flames dancing between his teeth.

"Aye, you have missed burning things down, I think," the Mate mused, oddly pleased at the havoc they would soon reek.

Giving no reply, the dragon took to the air, flying west over the forest until he located the new structures of the elves. With a fierce stream of fire, he sent a few of them scattering as their buildings burst into flames, but their number appeared small compared to the report they had previously been given. Satisfied with the destruction, he searched for more, looping around towards the lagoon.

When none of the sirens had returned with the coming darkness, many of the elves had gathered on the beach, near Olirassa's stone. They stood in small groups discussing what to do about the situation when their new forest took on a bright glow against the dim sky, and their calm discussions quickly fell into fear-driven jabber. Diving over the sand, the dragon screamed above them, sending the elves running in terror.

Following his assault, Meena stunned the gathering with a blast from her staff. On them in an instant, Zaendra stabbed at one of them as if it were the tree she had been practicing on.

Grinning at her brutality, Hayt swung his axe, using it to dismember the elves that were within range. Their shields almost an unfair advantage, the four slaughtered all they could catch, with any return blows bouncing off of them with flashes of blue light.

Fleeing up the sandy shore, only a few of the elves managed to escape. Headed west, they dove into the forest, just as the group of friends had done the night they themselves had run from the dragon's fire.

Once the area had been cleared, the group assembled on the beach in front of Olirassa's stone. Turning in a slow circle, they examined the carnage.

"We have done well this night," Piers praised. "This is a message they won't soon forget."

"It bloody well is," Hayt agreed, using a scrap of material torn from one of his victim's robes to clean his blade. "I am also certain we have earned their attention."

"Shall we go?" Meena asked, less enthusiastic about their success.

"Aye," the Mate grinned as Lamwen landed beside them. "Everyone grab on."

When each had placed a hand upon his scales, the wan carried them back to the camp with a single burst of power. As soon as they landed, they could sense something was wrong.

Everything was exactly the same as they had left it, which it should not have been. No fire burned in their pit and no stew in their pot.

Looking around, the ossci who were supposed to be awaiting their return were nowhere to be found.

Her eyes fluttering, Amicia sensed heavy darkness around her. Forcing them open, a thin slit was all she could achieve. The night air cold despite her wrap, she wanted to pull it in around her, but moving sent sharp, stabbing pain through her body.

Blinking, the fog within her mind began to clear. *Uscan.* She recalled the argument and the flying accusations. They had both been angry, distrust heavy between them. *Stupid girl,* she rebuked herself. *What the hell were you thinking coming here alone?*

Aware of her conscious state, the wolves gathered around her. Next to her, Uscan's body pressed against her frame; his breath rose and fell, gently pushing against her as his fur helped to keep her warm.

Seeing them grouped before her, she breathed deeply, expecting to be torn to shreds. "I'm not afraid of you."

"We have word on the glen," Uscan huffed.

Forcing herself up with her good arm despite the pain, she replied, "And?"

"The dragons have forced the elves back, and they are now at a stalemate once more, but their position is stronger," he informed her evenly.

"Good. Then the elves will be occupied there a while longer," she surmised, holding her wounded arm with her other hand. Jolts of pain stealing her air, she cried in a sharp yelp.

"Why would you come here alone and stand before me?" Uscan demanded bitterly.

"Why wouldn't I? We were friends; allies. Or at least I thought we were," she replied, unable to prevent the tear from spilling over and wetting her cheek.

Spying the drop of sadness, he growled, "I could have killed you. In fact, I still may."

"Go ahead," she bit back. "I think it would hurt less." She coughed a short laugh, but the accompanying spasm of agony squelched it. Drawing a deep breath, she said more evenly, "Lamwen will lead us in my stead. My father is too weak and aged."

"You have freed your father," Uscan assumed. "I had not heard of this."

"Yeah, well, we weren't exactly staying in touch as of late, now were we," she replied, doing her best to hold still. "Yes, we figured out how to transfigure, and I took my dragon form to make it happen. The Mate and Rey also were dragons, but when we changed back, we found out that going back and forth could kill us."

"If that is the case, why do you sit before me as a mortal now?"

"Because I had some things I needed to finish before I turned over for good," she snapped, the torture wearing on her gentle nature. Looking around, she sighed. "I'm going to contact Piers. Let him know where I am and what has become of me. Then you can finish the job," she informed him, closing her eyes as she made her attempt.

"Princess," Uscan called, his breath warm on her face.

"Uscan, please," she sobbed quietly, squinting her eyes tighter. "Using my power is far more difficult when I am injured."

Calling into the darkness, she could feel nothing in return. *Damn.* "So, this is what it was like for Oldrilin, the night we carried her from Riran. She couldn't transform into her fish self to swim away."

More tears fell as she thought of the siren. Exhausted, she stretched her good arm up to lay on, curling the oozing shoulder to keep it still. Staring across the ground at the odd angle, she watched the massive paws of the southern pack as they paced around her until she lost consciousness.

"What are we going to do with her?" the pack beta asked.

"I don't know yet," Uscan replied. "I am inclined to believe her story, but to take her word over that of our kin could be disastrous. We are mere wolves; our magic is limited."

"She will die here," his beta pointed out. "If she does, her friends may kill more than just a few of us."

"If she does, her friends will not be our worry, as all of Eriden may be lost," he replied.

TWENTY-TWO

Raging Battle

"YOU NEVER SHOULD HAVE LET her go," Rey muttered, pacing back and forth between the tables and the fire, wearing a path around Animir and Lin's shelter. "Why did you let her leave, especially alone?"

Glaring at Piers, he waited for the reply. He and Animir had been busy with the sirens when the girl had gone on her mission, and they arrived home only minutes ago to find she had not returned. What's worse, the ossci were gone, and he had missed the attack on the elves at Riran. Getting no reply, he grunted, "Some leader you are." *I'm gone for a day, and everything falls apart,* he lamented silently.

"This is not my fault," the older man replied tartly, also pacing a patch of grass and moss between the table and trees. "You know how uncontrollable she has become, if she ever was controllable." Turning to face him, the Mate scowled, "She would not have listened to you any more than she did to me."

"Maybe, but at least I would have discovered where she was going!" he shouted.

"She wouldn't say," Lamwen defended, stretching around his giant rocks. "Don't think we didn't try."

Still glaring at the other man, Rey grinned in spite of himself, glad the dragon had given up his human form. "You should go look for her," he suggested.

"There is no where he can fly we can't see by magical means," Meena pointed out, setting their pot for stew. "And we can see much quicker, I might add."

"Am I interrupting?" Thirac asked, stepping from the shadows of the trees.

"Well, not exactly," Piers scowled, glancing between the others, suspicious of the timely arrival.

Walking into the clearing, his hands behind his back, the gnome inspected the group and noting their long faces. "I heard you had quite a night."

"You could say that," the Mate continued the banter. "We got the sirens settled on the coast." Swallowing, he remembered his manners. "Thank you again for the use of your lands."

Raising his brow, the elder clicked his tongue. "I assume they will be removed as soon as possible?"

"When the elves have been defeated," Rey replied crisply. "But as you know, that would have been easier if the ossci hadn't disappeared."

"We have done all that we can for you," the elder replied. "We are not warriors, as we have said." Looking around again, he observed, "Your queen is not among you?"

Noting his choice of words, Piers studied him, then shook his head, "No. She had to be away on a mission." Curling his tongue, he added, "Do you know something of her whereabouts?"

"Only that she is in a dark place, where she cannot be seen," he provided. "I fear she may have been injured, even near death."

"So, you pointed out she was missing to see what we would say," the Mate grunted, unimpressed by the tactic. The gnomes never had been overly cooperative. "How do we know you haven't had a hand in her disappearance?" he accused.

"Piers," Meena gasped, shaking her head at his insolence.

"If you tell us where, we'll go help her," Rey interjected, eager for the knowledge.

"As I have said, we will no longer interfere," Thirac countered. "We have perhaps already done too much, and I honestly do not know the whereabouts of the princess."

"Really," the Mate scowled. "You did promise us aid. Why do you now withdraw it? Doing so on the same night of her disappearance is damn suspicious, I don't care what my wife thinks."

"Our conscience will not allow it," the small creature explained, flicking his gaze between Meena and the Mate. "That is how it has always been. We are watchers and historians, recording the affairs of the lands, not shaping them. You are welcome to the valley, and the sirens to the coast, for the time being; but we hope to have our lands back soon enough."

"If the battle is lost, your lands will be as well," Animir pointed out stiffly, joining the conversation abruptly.

"We do not fear the elves," Thirac replied coolly, glaring up at the one in his presence. "I should go. I'll leave you to your evening and your plans." Disappearing the way that he came, the group let him go.

"You think he knows where Ami is?" Rey asked, cutting his eyes over at the Mate.

"Their words are often enigmatic," Meena pointed out. "If one of them was watching Ami, since they are watchers in their words, they know exactly where she is. Not sharing the detail is what gives me pause."

"It gives me more than pause," the Mate spat, clenching his fists. Seated at the table, Hayt and Zae both used orbs to scour the continent. Glancing at them, he pushed, "I think the gnomes have always known more than they let on. However, they are a secretive and powerful race, and we can at least count ourselves lucky they allow us to remain here."

"So, what do we do now? I think if we were going to find her, we would have," Reynard sulked, indicating the pair of searchers with an open palm.

"We sleep on it," the Mate advised. "She may still turn up between now and the dawn."

The silence over their dinner stifling, each turned in with much to consider. Lying in the darkness of their leaning tent, Rey's head filled with what had taken place between Amicia and Lamwen. *Or Kaliwyn.* He had thought of little else while caring for the sirens as they were relocated, and his heart had softened on the subject.

If the girl and the dragon were two different beings, as a few of the others had suggested, it would explain a great deal about her behavior, as if two individuals existed within her and were forced to share the single caporal form. Glaring through the thatch wall, as if he could see Lamwen among his rocks, he sighed. *It's good that the dragon is no longer direct competition. But could he have something to do with her disappearance?*

Surely not. If anything, he knew the beast held as much concern for her as he did and probably loved her just as much. *A sad thought, indeed.*

His eyes heavy, Rey finally drifted towards sleep, his final realization being how difficult his wife's choice was going to be, if she lived to make it.

"Red sun at morning, sailor take warning," Piers grumbled, sitting with his bowl of mash.

"What?" Meena replied, assuming the seat next to him.

Glancing at the horizon, he indicated the blood-red ball of fire with his spoon.

Blinking at it, she stammered, "And what does the sun have to do with Amicia?"

"It doesn't," Rey sighed. "It's a warning about the weather. A storm is coming."

"Yes," Lamwen agreed, lumbering to his spot at the end of the table, "a storm is definitely on the horizon. She has not returned to us, and we have arrived at the morning of our move against the dwarves."

His back hunched as he stirred his meal, Hayt exhaled loudly. Sensing his unease, Zae looped her arm through his and laid her head against his shoulder. "I don't think any of them will be harmed," she reassured. "You will speak to your uncle and persuade them to join our cause."

"We hope," he retorted, spilling a spoonful of mush back into the bowl.

"Well, we cannot wait here forever," Piers observed, "storm or no storm. We need to gather with the trolls and begin our march through the forest, towards the mountain."

"It will take us days to get there," Rey observed. "Without Ami and the ossci, we have no hope of transporting everyone to save the time."

"Aye," the Mate growled, lifting his cup for a drink. It was a bad omen on the horizon, but they hadn't had any good ones in a while, if ever. "We must keep to the plan, either way."

Finishing their meal, the group packed their gear and weapons for the battle that loomed ahead. Forming two groups, Meena took the dragon, Piers, Hayt, and Zae, while Animir transported himself and Rey, as Lin had remained with the sirens and would not be joining them.

Arriving at the entrance to the Crimson Caves, Traok greeted them. "You have come to see us to the battle?" he asked, almost sounding eager. He carried a long spear in his hand, obviously ready to join the fight.

"Well, some of you," Piers agreed, following the king's oldest son into the shaft that opened for them. Doubts forming in his mind already, he would not have anticipated using men so young.

Inside the great room, they found more of the same. Looking across the wide space, it appeared any male of at least five feet in height was preparing to go. "Some of your warriors are awfully young," he pointed out as Yaodus joined them.

"They know the risks," their leader grunted, waving his long arm to indicate the lot. "Each family is sending the father and oldest son. All the rest will remain here to protect the women and children."

"We appreciate your sacrifice," Meena sighed, her gut tight at the realization some of them would never return.

Watching them, the war seemed more real, causing Reynard's heart to race. Suddenly feeling like an outsider, he wondered what he, a mortal of the rim, was even doing there.

"Where's my daughter?" Ziradon asked as he slithered up behind them.

"She..." Piers began, drawing out the word as he considered his response. "She went on a mission and has not returned."

"A mission," the older dragon parroted. "And she didn't come back to lead our forces?" Silence hung in the air as his massive head took in each one in turn. Coming to Lamwen, he prodded, "Well?"

Addressing his king, Lamwen provided the truth, "She did not tell us where she was going or exactly when she would return. We expected her back by last night, but that did not happen. Thirac, the gnome, says she is in a dark place and cannot be seen, which stands to reason since all our attempts to locate her have been unsuccessful. The plan was to come and transport the forces here to confront the dwarves, and so we have come in accordance with those directives. If she returns to the empty camp, she will know where we have gone."

"And you will lead us in her stead," Ziradon clipped.

"I will lead them, yes," he accepted the position. "But there must be some adjustments. The ossci have not come, as they have withdrawn their aid. That means we do not have enough who can transposition to carry this many people if that is what she had intended. That is one detail she failed to share, and as it stands we have no other option. We will have to go on foot."

Hearing the news, Yaodus appeared grave as he observed, "It's five days march to Rhong from here, at a hard pace."

"Aye," the Mate confirmed. "But we have no other choice. Meena and Animir could take us over in groups, but with only the two of them, it would take too long."

"It wouldn't take five days," Yaodus snapped.

"I think we should walk," Meena whispered, the thought of making the jump so many times disheartening. "It is not as easy as you might think. Even if Zaendra could join us and take a few at a time, it would be more difficult than simply walking."

His eyes shifting again across the faces of the group, the sovereign replied, "Then we will walk." Turning to his troops, he called them to attention and ordered that they would form up outside the eastern cave. Leaving the group, he located his son so they could make their way out together.

"Since you walk, I think I will remain behind," Ziradon informed them. "I can join you at Rhong in five days just as easily."

"I'll take to the air and watch for trouble," Lamwen agreed. "I can land to join the troops as the sun sets for camp."

"Then all is agreed," Piers growled. "Let's get out front with the others and be on our way."

Making their way through the tunnels, Rey confessed, "Ami and I never had connected telepathically, but I've been reaching out and hoping we might."

"Aye," the Mate nodded. "I have as well, since yesterday. I have heard nothing back as yet either."

The two men glanced over their shoulders simultaneously at the dragon who followed a few steps behind. "Nor I," the beast confirmed. "I have not spoken of it so as not to add to our worry."

"We're already worried," Meena sniffed from the head of the group. "I have reached out as well and used my orb but also get nothing."

Trailing at the back of the pack, Ziradon made a few calls into the darkness, his heart heavy that she did not reply to any of them. He had volunteered to remain behind, but he had no intention of doing so; he would hunt for her until time to meet at Rhong with or without the group's blessing.

Coming out into the early sun, the group gathered as Lamwen took charge. Giving commands, he divided them into groups so that they could cross the forest efficiently and not lose anyone. Once they were set, they headed out, moving in three columns about fifty feet apart as the trees would allow.

Staying with the center group, Piers and the others walked in silence while the trolls chatted and called to each other almost eagerly.

"Do you think they've ever been to the dwarf mountain?" Rey asked curiously.

"I doubt they have ever been anywhere," the Mate grunted.

"We stay close to our mountain," Yaodus agreed. "We have only ventured south a few times in my reign and only when the search for food demanded it."

"Well then, keep your eyes open, and let's hope your first trip out isn't your last," Piers snorted, not at all amused by the situation.

As soon as the last of the group members had disappeared into the trees, Ziradon leapt into the air. Flying west, he feigned a visit to the beach. Making a turn above it, he headed south, deciding to start with the wizards along the coast as he made his way towards the Shadowlands, as that was the darkest place he knew.

TWENTY-THREE

Dwarves in the Trees

THE RED SUN rising had been a bad omen, and the rain started before midday. Walking in the deluge, Piers grumbled, "Man, I hate being right about these things."

Wearing her robe, Meena adjusted the hood and snickered, "I hate you being right as well. How long do you think it will last?"

"Until it stops," he grunted in return, glancing around at the trolls, who didn't seem to mind the damp.

Keeping his head down, he tried to hold a positive attitude as he had once suggested on their raft, but it had gotten harder as their time in Eriden progressed. By late afternoon, he was exhausted, and there was no sign the shower would end before nightfall. The view ahead had steadily declined until only a few trees could be seen in the distance. The sound of the drops on the leaves a steady buzz, he couldn't imagine their march getting any more miserable.

"Is that yelling?" Rey asked, pulling his hood back to listen.

Pausing his step, Piers joined him. "Son of a bitch!" he shouted, tearing off through the trees. "We've got trouble!" he warned at the top of his lungs.

The path between hindered by the thick foliage and puddles of mud, the center column reached the western one as quickly as they could, but the wolves had already exacted a heavy toll. Remembering his shield, the Mate protected himself with his left hand while his sword in the right lashed out through the rain.

Leaping to him, one of the beasts attempted a few chomps before giving up and returning to the softer targets of the trolls. Knocking one of the younger bodies down, it tore at the flesh, while bright red blood mixed with the water collecting on the earth.

"No!" Piers shouted, jumping at the furry back and sinking his sword into the dense mass.

Yelping in pain, the beast released his lifeless victim, turning to snarl at the defender before limping into the trees and disappearing into the darkness. "God, help us," the Mate groaned, his broad chest heaving as he looked around him at the slaughter.

The wolves had been purposeful in their attack, taking the trailing edge of the column by surprise. More than a dozen of the trolls were killed by the time their reinforcements arrived, and the pack fled as soon as they did so, disappearing back into the trees.

"Do not follow!" Piers shouted, hoping to minimize their casualties. "We need a runner to bring the southern group over."

A pair of the younger trolls took the assignment and darted through the forest to warn and gather the others.

"Damnit," the Mate continued to curse, Meena joining him as they inspected the damage.

One of their allies lay on the ground, holding a gaping wound in his side. Kneeling beside him, Rey asked, "What do we do?"

They had known there would be injuries and even deaths, but they had not expected them so soon. Taking the other side, Piers knelt as well. In a quick jerking motion, the blue-skinned creature clamped his arm with a firm grasp. Through gritted teeth, he gasped, "Do not walk. They will pick you all off if you do."

"Aye," the Mate agreed, patting the back of his digits. "We'll find a way to transport us even if it takes all night."

"I'll take him back to the caves," Animir offered.

"Good idea," Piers agreed. "Be quick about it while they may still be able to save him."

Leaning over, the elf placed his hand upon his shoulder, and the two of them disappeared.

Staring into the eyes of his bride, Piers frowned, "We have no choice, love. Either we go back, or we figure out how to transport all of them to the mountain and leave the wolves behind."

"Yes," she agreed somberly, staring at the blood-coated leaves they had left in their wake. Standing, she turned in a slow circle. "We will be vulnerable on both ends and must have some strategy about the move." It was one of those puzzles that give people a headache to figure out.

Deciding her plan, she said more loudly. "We need to reform the groups. We need a strong group who can go first and be protection at the new location while we bring in the rest. We also need a strong group who will remain here and go last in case they come back before we are all away."

"You can't take us in three waves," Rey pointed out. "There's way too many for that."

"No. It will take many trips," she agreed. Her eyes meeting Zaendra's, she lowered her chin. "Will you be able to carry?"

"I can try," the girl replied, shifting from one foot to the other anxiously. "I have taken Hayt with me a few times but not for such long distances."

"Then you will only carry two or three," the wan agreed. "I could possibly push six or eight, and Animir will be able to take some when he is finished with the wounded and the dead," she calculated, seeing him return and leave again with another group of injured.

Breathing heavily, the rain ran down Piers's face as he turned in a slow circle, his eyes roving over their troops. "Yaodus, select a dozen of your men who will go ahead, the strongest preferably. Then set aside another dozen who will remain here as guard to those who await transport."

"Agreed," the king nodded, turning to give the command.

The first group quickly divined, Meena and Zaendra transpositioned them and the Mate ahead. Scouting the area, they selected a clearing that still held sparse trees in the center; enough to offer a good deal of protection from the air. As it was large enough to accommodate their over-sized group, the twelve guards remained while the three returned to the others.

Taking over the waves, Piers grouped them, sending Yaodus to handle the receiving end while the girls bounced back and forth, making their deliveries. As soon as he had finished the trips to the Crimson Caves, Animir joined them, taking group after group until they were down to the last who had stood watch over the process.

Fortunately, the wolves had not come back, and the last group landed to find the rain had stopped on the southern end of the woods, where their camp was located. Fires had been lit, and pots of stew and skewers of small game roasted in the growing darkness.

"How many did we lose?" Lamwen growled when he joined them.

"Seventeen," Animir sighed. "Only two of them will make it. The rest were cold by the time I got them home."

"Damn," Piers muttered. "Well, at least they didn't return."

"I made sure of that," Lamwen coughed.

"I saw," the Mate agreed. "Your fire is strong even in the rain," he recalled having seen it first hand the night the dragon had sunk the Sea Serpent.

"Yes, and the northern pack knows it. But we are only a few hours walk from Rhong. I think we can make it easily enough," the dragon suggested.

"I should go ahead of you," Hayt warned. "I can speak with my uncle and offer our bargain."

"And give them a chance to fortify themselves against us?" Piers protested.

"Surely you don't intend to attack them," the dwarf gasped. "I thought we had come to recruit them."

"Aye," Rey nodded, "but as we said before, we can't leave them to the elves. If they won't accept our terms and join the ranks, we'll have to take measures to ensure they can't be of use to Cilithrand and her troops."

His eyes wide, the dwarf wiped at his nose, sniffing loudly as he considered the methods of persuasion the group would use. "I'll convince them," he announced.

"How?" the Mate clipped.

"I don't know yet, but I don't really have a choice, now do I?" Hayt scowled. Turning his back, he left them in search of his wife and a good meal. Letting him go, the rest took their leave for rest and comfort as well.

Piers located Meena, seeing her sitting on a large stone with her feet pulled up beneath her long skirt as she shivered, and his heart ached. He could have lost her that day, and it was only the beginning. Picking through the sea of pink and blue bodies, he ambled over and took a seat beside her. "You ok, love?"

"Exhausted," she mumbled, her face resting in an open palm. "I don't think we can do that again."

"Let's hope we don't have to," he agreed, running a hand over her shoulders. His eyes skimming their weathered troops, he could see the day had taken its toll. Wet, tired, and hungry, the jovial demeanor of the trolls had been wiped away.

The camp in near silence, second thoughts seemed to float in the air as they ate and took to their blankets for what rest they could get.

"Piers," Meena whispered, giving her husband a shove.

"What?" he grunted, his mind clouded by sleep, as they had scarcely laid down an hour before.

"I think we've been discovered," she replied, her heart racing as she listened. Turning over, she reached into her bag around her waist, searching for her orb and pulling it out. Skimming the woods around them, she quickly located the source of the sounds that had awakened her.

Half sitting up beside her, his head slowly cleared. "It's dark. How do you know something's out there?"

"I heard something," she replied, pushing the glowing orb towards him. "It's a patrol, I think, and they know we are here."

"Probably saw the lights or smoke from our fires," he agreed, sitting up a little more. Spying Hayt through the dim light only a few feet away, he crawled over and gave him a shake. "Hey. You're up," he grunted.

"Up? For what?" the dwarf barked.

"Your kin have come out to meet us or to kill us," the Mate replied tartly. "You should go find out which and present our offer."

Her eyes wide, Zaendra inhaled deeply, sitting up next to him. "Be careful, husband," she implored as he stood and gathered his weapon.

"I have my shield," he agreed, suddenly very glad Amicia had become so proficient at enchantments.

Picking his way through the slumbering trolls, he exited by the south end of their camp and called into the hazy mist that hung between the trees, "Hello?"

Shoving a long spear in his face, a dwarf of about four feet presented himself as he grunted, "Hold still!"

"I am still," Hayt replied, his tone dripping with sass. Seeing the party was small, of only four dwarves, he growled, "You out hunting?"

"We are investigating this group of trolls," a second spoke up, pointing at his slumbering comrades across the way.

"Ah, wasn't sure you had noticed them," Hayt chuckled. "They're friends of mine. We're on our way to speak to Baeweth." He didn't recognize any of the small group, which felt odd considering he hadn't been gone from the city that long; a few months at most.

"What makes you think he'll see you?" the first dwarf spat.

Glaring at him, Hayt's mind raced. "You're not with the guard," he observed aloud. "What are you guys really doing out here?"

"We'll ask the questions," a third intruder growled bravely, shoving his weapon at him before dropping it when the blue jolt hit him. "Ow," the dwarf moaned, shaking his hands vigorously, then began to cry quietly to himself.

"Smarts, don't it?" Hayt chuckled, realizing the group was just youngsters. An instant later, an idea sprang to mind. "You're not supposed to be out here," he accused.

"We're hunting," the fourth finally revealed.

"Hunting," Hayt, repeated, rubbing his blond beard. "Well, I take it you don't have permission, so I'll make you a deal. You get me in to see Baeweth, and I won't tell anyone you were out here."

"We don't need you for that," the first and obvious leader of the quartet snapped.

"Ok, fine," Hayt countered. "I'll just have my friends detain you while I'm inside," he offered, indicating the Mate and Rey as they presented themselves from behind, weapons drawn.

Reaching out with a quick stab, the first youth also met with blue sparks. "Hey!" he shouted at the jolt, the weapon deflected from penetrating Rey's defenses.

"Ok, we'll take you," the second offered. "Just don't tell them where we were."

"That's more like it," the Mate grinned, stepping aside so they could pass.

Picking up his spear, the third youth sobbed, "What do you want with King Baeweth anyway?"

"Oh, a family reunion of sorts," Hayt chuckled, following as they led the way.

Arriving at the front gate shortly before the dawn, the four young dwarves waved to their accomplice as they approached, presenting him with a small pouch as they ambled by.

"Who's this?" the guard grunted when Hayt stood before him. "There were only four of you when you left."

Pulling himself to his full height, the extra dwarf growled, "Mind your tongue, or I'll have you hauled to the cells for taking bribes."

"Hayt?" the sentry gasped.

"Shh," he replied, clasping him by the arm. "I've come with an urgent message for my uncle. Let us in, and there won't be any trouble, I assure you."

"Hayt," the dwarf replied, shaken at his appearance. "You're dead."

"Do I look dead?" He spread his arms to present himself.

Perplexed, the guard stiffened as he shifted his gaze between the four young hunters and the king's nephew. "If I let you in, they'll know."

"Bah," Hayt grunted. "Don't worry about that. Once my uncle hears my news, he won't care how I got in," he assured, marching on and shooing his new young friends ahead of him.

Climbing the walkway, they took a tunnel into the halls, the sounds and smell of the cave washing over him like a drug. Inhaling deeply, Hayt sighed, "It's good to be home."

"We'll see you around," one of the boys called before he disappeared, two of the others close behind.

"Cowards," their leader muttered, raising his hand to indicate the hall to the palace. "Need me to show you the way?" he asked, doubting they would ever get past the guard.

"I know the way," Hayt grinned, his eyes roaming over the familiar path. "Get yourself home, and stay out of the forest," he warned, giving him a firm smack on the shoulder as he sent him on his way.

His feet crunching on the gravel, a spring formed in his step as he approached the great hall. Crossing to the left, he took the tunnel that would see him straight to his target, only hesitating for a moment as he approached the main entrance.

"I must see my uncle," he announced firmly with a small wave of his hand, not stopping as he marched by the stunned dwarf.

"HEY!"

"Look, I don't have time to argue," Hayt insisted, shaking his fist at him. "I assume he's still in bed?" he supplied, pointing the direction he intended to go as he kept walking.

Staring after him, the guard blinked rapidly, unsure if what he had seen was real. Looking around as he licked his lips, he was still considering his options when their previous heir to the throne disappeared into the palace halls.

Glancing over his shoulder as he arrived at the king's chamber, Hayt chuckled at his success. "Poor bugger thinks I'm a ghost," he presumed. Giving the entrance a firm knock, he pushed against the door and announced, "Are you asleep?"

"What?" Baeweth grumbled, rolling over and fighting to sit up on the pliable surface. "What's going on?" he shouted, assuming there had been some kind of trouble.

Joining him as he removed his covers and stood by the bed, Hayt grinned, "Tis I, uncle. Hayt, in the flesh." Pushing his chest out, he stood tall and waited to be recognized.

The light of the single candle dim, Baeweth growled, "Who ever came up with this trickery is going to regret it."

"It's no trick, uncle," the blond replied, losing a bit of his confidence. "Here, light the lamps and have a good look," he offered, marching across to start the small fires. The illumination growing with each one, he had lit four before he paused to see his kin staring at him.

"Uncle?"

"Hayt," the old man breathed.

Looking him up and down in the dancing light, his nephew faced him. "Yes, it's me. I've come with a message I must deliver; I'm afraid it can't wait until morning."

His hand shaking, Baeweth raised the appendage and rested it against the intruder's chin. "Hayt," he repeated.

Grasping his palm, his heir snickered, "It's been a while. Perhaps you thought I would never return."

"Are you a ghost?" the king gasped.

"No, I'm not a ghost," he snapped. "I told you we don't have much time. Please, get dressed, and let's go to the throne chamber, or the meeting hall, or somewhere we can talk."

"Hayt?" Asyng gasped, standing at the door.

His back to her, the younger dwarf froze. Turning slowly, he met her gaze, his eyes drifting top to bottom as he took her in. "Hello, grandmother," he managed in a weak voice. He hadn't expected to see the woman who had raised him, at least not this soon after his arrival.

"How did you get here?" she breathed, pulling her nightgown around her to hold out the draft.

"That is a long story," he replied with a smile. "If the two of you would like to get dressed, I'll wait for you in the garden and I can tell you all about it."

TWENTY-FOUR

Unlikely Comrades

STANDING NEXT to the glowing pond, Hayt's mind drifted back to the day he had explained it to Zaendra. *The day we moved into the palace,* he sighed. Things had moved pretty quickly between them, being married after only knowing each other five days.

His eyes darting around the open chamber, he recalled her reaction vividly. *So much has changed, and yet so much is the same.*

"Hayt," Baeweth interrupted his thoughts. Entering the room, he pulled his favorite robe around him. "It's really you."

"Yes, uncle," the younger dwarf replied with a sheepish grin. "I was not devoured by the daemons of Asomanee," he offered, his arms wide to present his evidence of the claim. "Although we did lose one member of our group in the crossing," he confessed.

Joining them at that moment, Asyng swept into the room, her robe flowing around her as she met him, throwing her arms around him as she gasped, "I knew you would return."

Accepting the hug, he smiled, glad their greeting had at least been civil. "I must speak with you," he assured. "We have a party in the woods. An army, really. I have come to ask you to join it," he informed them, getting right to the point.

"An army," Baeweth rasped, still taken with the notion they had survived their escape. "You break away with our prisoners and flee into the darkness only to return and ask such a thing?"

"Yes, uncle. All of Eriden is at stake, and we have need of your assistance."

"Eriden seldom concerns itself with our affairs here under the mountain," Baeweth denied.

"But this is different," Hayt insisted, pulling a golden orb from his pocket. "You recognize this?" he asked pointedly.

"Oh," the king breathed, "where did you get that?" His hand trembling at the thought of touching it, he waited for the reply.

"The gnomes. Once our allies," Hayt explained. "We came out of the far tunnel to Asomanee and have resided there in the marshes since our escape. They have awakened the use of magic within me and taught me how to use it."

Swallowing, Asyng recalled their decision to allow magic back into their kingdom, second guessing their choice. "Where is your wife, Hayt?"

"With the others," he assured, lighting the globe to search for her. "See? There she is," he grinned, the morning sun on her ebony skin as she and the others walked towards the mountain. "They will be here soon to hear your reply." He cut his eyes over at the king, his pause pregnant with expectation.

Glaring at the image of the girl, trolls could be seen in her company. "You bring the beasts to our door."

"They're not beasts," his heir denied. "They are not so different from us, actually. The wolves on the other hand," he chuckled. "And the elves. If we don't pick a side and make some friends, they will tear us apart," he predicted.

"Rubbish," Baeweth snapped, turning his back on the scene. "We are safe within the mountain. No harm will come to us here!"

"Yeah, I'm sure your father thought the same thing," Hayt sneered. "The elves sent the daemon. One in our company knew of the treachery and told us how she was sent to destroy us." He inhaled deeply, his argument growing momentum along with his tone. "If we stay here, they will send another. And another. Until there are no dwarves left to hide beneath the mountain."

"This is madness," Asyng countered. "They steal you from us, and what have they done? Your mind is cursed to believe such things!"

Shifting his search, Hayt hunted the elves. "I can prove it to you," he promised. "Oh God," he gasped. "Shit!" Looking around wildly, like a trapped animal, he practically shouted, "I have to go."

"You're not going anywhere!" Baeweth bellowed. "Guard!"

"No, uncle, you don't understand," Hayt stammered, holding out the orb. "Look. The elves are coming. They are so close they may beat my friends here. Oh no," he paused, licking his lips. "How is the new vista?"

"The vista?" Baeweth snapped. "You have more pressing matters to worry about." Turning to the guard, he instructed, "See my nephew to a cell."

"No, uncle. Listen to me!" Hayt shouted, shaking the orb in desperation. "If the vista isn't finished or well-guarded, they may use it to get inside!"

"We have guards there watching the forest. That's what it was designed for, after all," the king snapped.

"What about the cliffs above? Do they watch those as well?"

"None could come that way," the king's sister laughed. "It would be suicide."

"Oh, I wouldn't put it past them," Hayt sighed. "Take me to a cell if you like. These are your people, and you do what you see fit with them. I came and said my piece; the rest is up to you."

His eye dropping to the warm glow of morning sun in the palm of his hand, his uncle followed the motion. On the smooth surface, the image of elves crossing an expanse of stones and jagged rocks was clearly displayed.

"Have you conjured this scene?" Baeweth growled.

"No, uncle," Hayt breathed, shaking his head. "I'm not that clever with my powers. Otherwise, I would simply transposition and be gone at this point. And even if I was, I would never deceive you."

"You did deceive me," the older dwarf spat. "You married that girl and then ran away with her!"

"I'm sorry," Hayt sighed. "We had to. We couldn't let the dragons get their hands on Amicia. And," he paused, shame coloring his cheeks, "I really didn't want to take your place as king."

Staring at him, Baeweth considered the confession while his sister focused on the previous statement.

"She's a dragon," Asyng gasped. "I knew it!"

"Well, yes," her grandson shrugged. "She even took her form back for a few hours, but she's a human again," he paused, rolling his eyes, "and actually missing right now. The point is, we have to do something about these elves!" he stated emphatically, shaking the orb.

"What do you think, dear sister?" the king asked in a subdued tone, hurt that the boy had run away rather than accept his place as heir.

"I think we have had our share of hard times, dear brother," she replied. "Prudence dictates we at least listen to what his friends have to say. They made it through Asomanee after all. They have some knowledge, or a bit of luck about them; we could use either of those things at this point."

"Very well," he groaned, turning to his guard. "Forget the cell. We are going to have some visitors at the gate shortly. See them inside. I want the ones in charge brought to the dining room for breakfast," he added, heading out the door and mumbling to himself as he went.

"Well, it took you long enough," Hayt chided as he met Piers and Yaodus at the front gate. Tilting his head back, he searched the sky, spotting Lamwen's massive form circling to the south. "Is he coming in or staying outside?"

"Coming in?" Meena question, joining them. "Are we invited?"

"Yes. As unlikely comrades as we seem, my uncle has agreed to an audience," the dwarf explained, producing his orb. "He took a bit of persuading, but these guys did the trick."

"Oh, that's not good," Rey observed, pulling at his hand for a better look. "Where are they?"

"Somewhere over the mountains, above us perhaps. We've added extra guards at the vista to keep an eye out in case they decide to come over the top and down the face of the cliffs," he assured. "But they are too close for comfort, and that is all that matters." Glancing at Animir, he sighed, "I'm sure he realizes you're still with us, but please don't be offended if I ask you to remain outside."

"No," Piers snapped. "Last time we were here, Baeweth was a complete ass. Animir is one of us, and he stays with us."

"My uncle is the king of the dwarves," Hayt retorted. "He's allowed to be an ass. But if you insist, then he can come; just don't say I didn't warn you." Beckoning them with a wave of his hand, he added, "Yaodus, you should as well."

"I wish to bring my son," the troll clipped.

"Yeah, him too. There are plenty of chairs," the dwarf agreed, turning his back and leading the way inside.

The gravel crunching noisily beneath their feet, they soon arrived at the dining hall, where a large spread had been placed upon the table.

"Well, this looks familiar," Piers growled. "I believe all dwarves do is eat."

"Come and sit," Baeweth invited gruffly, noting the trolls and the elf with a shake of his head. "We are keeping odd company as of late."

"What's that supposed to mean?" the Mate paused.

"Nothing," the old king sighed, still shaking his head. "We used to keep to ourselves, that is all. Trolls, elves, wizards. Where's the siren?" he demanded, noticing Zaendra had returned without her.

"We have helped them escape Riran, and she is with her kind, for now," Zae explained, greeting her new kin with a bow.

"The elves have taken Riran?" Asyng asked doubtfully. "How could the dragons allow such a thing?"

"The dragons are caught up in a civil war, or so it seems," Rey explained, taking a seat to her left and serving his plate. "We thought it would be us fighting to get Ami's place back as queen, but some others on the council want the seat for themselves. While Gwirwen is squabbling with them, the elves took Riran and have a contingent battling for the glen."

"Plus the ones coming here," Meena observed, also taking a plate.

"How does she have so many troops?" asked Yaodus, standing behind the chair at the king's right hand.

Looking up at him, Baeweth sighed, "You might as well sit. I assume you are the sovereign?"

"I am," the old troll agreed, offering the chair next to him to his boy. "This is my eldest son, Traok."

Nodding slightly, Baeweth turned to Animir, certain he would know. "How did she come by such an army?"

"Well," the elf offered, taking his seat next to Traok, "Cilithrand has been on the throne for two centuries. Over that time, we have filled the armory at Jerranyth to the brim with weapons, and I dare say it is not the only one. The villages higher up in the mountains are sure to house a few more, and the people there could have produced a sizable population, perhaps fit for an army of thousands."

"I thought you said you only had a few children even if you lived hundreds of years," Piers recalled.

"Normally, I would say that is the case, but as we have seen, the queen has been planning this for a while. Who knows how or when it started, but obviously our population has been growing in secret for some time."

"The smaller elves," Rey recalled. "Not the ruling class such as yourself. That's who were at Riran when we paid them the visit."

"Exactly. Village elves... servants, soldiers, merchants, and the like. The mountains behind Jerranyth are full of them. Overfilled with them, would be my guess," Animir explained.

"Ok, we know where they came from. How do we stop them from overrunning the dwarves?" Zaendra asked, her concern genuine.

"Did you say they are above us? Up on the mountain?" Piers asked.

"From what we can tell," Hayt agreed.

"Oh, that's beautiful," Piers grinned. "We push in behind, through Asomanee."

"Through Asomanee!" Asyng gasped. "Are you mad? The daemon would have you all!"

"The dark elf has been removed," Animir informed them calmly. "When I realized what she was, I knew I could trap her, and we did. Amicia even convinced her to help us if the need arises. The only problem is, they can't be exposed to the sunlight, or moonlight for that matter. It would have to be in the caves or a moonless night for them to do us any good."

"But still," the Mate insisted, "we could go through the tunnels and surprise the elves from behind."

"What about all the minions?" Zae countered. "The halls were filled with them even with the ones we destroyed."

"They can't reproduce without their queen," Animir stated thoughtfully. "If we moved through, wiping them out, they would be eradicated. In theory, you could even reclaim the halls once it was done," he offered as incentive to the king.

Pushing his empty plate back, their host looked at each in turn, recalling the first time they had eaten at his table. "Call me an old fool, but you've beaten them once. I believe you could do it again. We'll gather our forces and prepare for the battle at once. Let's hope we're not too late."

TWENTY-FIVE

Honor of Old

"IF WE ARE GOING to go through Asomanee, we should go right away," Meena observed. "It is quite a distance to the barrier, and even farther to the exit on the other side, even without stopping to clear the halls."

"I'll prepare my forces," the king agreed, pushing his chair back to stand. "Finish your breakfast and meet me in the great hall," he called over his shoulder to the rest.

Looking down the long table, Yaodus asked, "Are you the queen?"

"No," Asyng coughed. "Baeweth is my brother. I'm his advisor, I guess you would say."

"Our family has suffered for many generations," Hayt offered.

"Your family?" the troll asked in surprise. "I was not aware you were of royal blood."

"I'm Baeweth's nephew. I was heir to the throne before I chose to run away," he sighed.

"I wouldn't put it like that," Zae defended. "He didn't give you a lot of choice, now did he?"

"It broke his heart that you left," Asyng informed him.

"I still don't want to be king," Hayt replied, getting to his feet. "We need to bring our forces inside and join with the others," he suggested, hoping to change the subject.

"Agreed." The Mate also stood.

Reluctantly, the rest of the group followed, calling in the trolls and marching through the halls to the giant chamber where Hayt and Zaendra had exchanged their vows. Taking his hand as they entered, the girl smiled, tilting her head back to admire the high ceiling. "I'm glad that I chose to be your bride," she breathed.

"As am I," he agreed, giving her a kiss on the cheek.

"Later," Piers grunted, pushing his way past to get to the front.

The room already filled with dwarves, the trolls lined the walls as they came in. Up on the small platform, Baeweth was addressing his troops.

"And so, we are going to cleanse Asomanee as we push our way out to flank them and take them by surprise," he finished.

"Are we all set?" the Mate asked when he reached him.

"I've just finished briefing the troops, and my captains have each been assigned a section of the old halls to sweep with their teams."

"Good. Might I suggest long clothing and plenty of light," Piers added, rubbing his hands together anxiously. "Honestly, I'm not looking forward to being down there –" He stopped abruptly. "We will come upon Bally's body."

"Oh," the king scowled, aware of the implication. "Where will we find it?"

"He's in the great hall. We had almost made it out when he was bitten," the group's leader explained.

"Well, I'll see to it a few of our men are assigned to take care of him. Gather his remains so he can be given a proper memorial," Baeweth offered.

Studying him, Piers rubbed his chin. "Thank you. I didn't think it would matter to you."

"Of course it matters," the king scoffed, offended at the jab. "We dwarves are not beyond honoring the dead." Realizing a moment later he hadn't been very hospitable the last time they were there, part of the blame for the boy's death lay on his head. "I guess things could have gone differently…"

"Don't trouble yourself," Piers grunted. "We all make choices. Sometimes they turn out to be more important than we thought they were, that's all." His eyes misty, he knew all about that.

A short time later, the barrier to Asomanee had been torn down. Lighting torches, each group of dwarves were given a section of the halls to search. The trolls and their friends would come in behind, along with a few more soldiers from the king's garrison. From there, they would push their way through to the marshes and prepare to make their way up the mountain to engage the elves.

All going surprisingly well, considering they were hunting down venom filled daemons, the caverns and chambers had been swept in a matter of hours. True to his word, a special trio of dwarves had been assigned to collect Baldwin's body, and he was placed in a plain wooden box before the rest of his party were allowed to enter. Carrying the crate back the way they came, they assured it would be placed in a private place for safe keeping until it was decided when and where he would be laid to rest.

Tears in his eyes as they walked past, his best friend swinging between them, Rey thought of Amicia. *God, I hope we haven't lost her as well.* He had reached out in random intervals, still hoping at some point she would reply, but he had not heard anything.

"Thinking of Bally?" Animir asked, clamping him on the shoulder.

"Ami, actually," he sighed.

"Don't worry," the elf grimaced. "There's still hope. For now, we have a battle to win."

Making their way through the last section of tunnels, Animir paused at the final slope. Kneeling, he rested his hand upon the magical markings that had preserved his life. A cynical grin on his lips, he stood and marched to the surface above.

In the daylight, the sun had passed overhead and hung in the west, darkness only a few hours away. "I think we should camp here tonight and march over at first light," Animir observed, "but I don't think the gnomes will like it."

"Why not?" Piers sneered. "They said we could stay."

Coughing a laugh, Rey pointed out, "I'm sure they didn't mean for us to invite friends over while we did, especially trolls and dwarves."

Rolling his eyes, the Mate didn't care. He had had about all the gnome logic he could stand. Locating Baeweth, he offered, "Our camp is over there against the tree line. This valley runs for quite a ways in both directions, and I think it would make a good place to call it a night. We get a good night's sleep and climb the mountain tomorrow."

"I agree," the old king sighed. "Somewhere along here is the original entrance to Asomanee."

"Oh," Hayt gasped, "it's this way." He curled his fingers for him to follow. Leading the way to the north end of the valley, he presented the statues with an open hand. "We cleaned them after we found them. They were covered in growth. The entrance is over behind, but it's in rubble, probably caved in by the elves ages ago."

Making his way through the stone garden, tears touched the old king's eyes as his fingers traced the feel of the rocks. "You have honored our heroes, restoring them to the light."

"Aye," the Mate agreed, joining them. "Perhaps it's fate that we get this second chance to know each other," he grinned.

"Even in these dark circumstances, I have to agree. For now, I'm going to go see the gnomes and alert them to our presence. You have the men make camp so we can get some rest. We want to be fresh for the fight," he instructed his nephew before he headed across the clearing and into the woods.

"Well, this feels strange," Piers mumbled to his wife as they took to their bed.

"What, being back here after leaving only yesterday?" she deduced, lying against the back wall with him between her and the opening.

"Aye," he chuckled. "I'm surprised the gnomes allowed the trolls and dwarves to stay."

"They were allies, or at least the dwarves were," she pointed out.

"That was a long time ago," he grunted. "Still, I'm glad they will honor it. Tomorrow is going to be one hell of a fight."

"Goodnight, love," she whispered, turning on her side and drifting off to sleep.

"I find it odd as well," Animir spoke up, sitting on the rock in front of their shelter.

"Good night, Animir," Piers replied, dismissing him to his own bunk.

Shaking his head, Rey joined him, indicating the dragon curled around his rocks with a wave of his hand, "Lamwen says the elves are grouped for the night as we are. I don't think they have any idea what we have planned, or that we know they are there."

"How could they?" Animir snorted. "They think access to this side is blocked." Thinking of the trapped dark elf, he stood, searching for Ami's bag. "Good. She didn't take it with her."

"Take what with her?" Zae asked, joining them in front of the fire.

"Her pack. She put the hamar gem in here."

"So? You can't let that thing out," Rey scowled.

"I don't plan to," the elf agreed, "but it wouldn't hurt to have her handy in case we needed her in a pinch."

"We don't plan to be that desperate," Piers groaned, his face pressing into an open palm.

"I thought you were going to sleep," Animir observed, locating the stone and holding it up to admire it.

"Who can sleep with all your chatter?" the Mate countered, noting that Meena actually did. Gently extricating himself, he climbed off the mattress and joined them on their oversized seats. Holding out his hand, he waited for the stone to be placed in it.

Handing it over, Animir coerced, "I promise I won't pull her out unless we need to."

"Aye," he growled, still studying the gem. "I worry she won't attack her own kind and would probably turn on us."

"Well, let's hope we don't have to find out," Rey observed.

Hearing loud voices carrying from the north end of the valley, Piers sighed, "They are a rowdy bunch. Even the trolls don't make so much noise."

"Yes," Animir agreed, accepting the trinket and adding it to his collection in the pouch at his waist. "Let us hope they fight as well as they play."

"We should really get some sleep," Piers concluded, shooing each to their beds. Retaking his, he closed his eyes, willing his mind to relax. *"Amicia,"* he reached.

Silence.

"Amicia, love; we're looking for you." They weren't really, but they were still hoping at any rate. *"We take on the elves on the morrow, as you wanted. We've brought the trolls and recruited the dwarves. It was a good plan, love,"* he sighed, tears touching his eyes.

No reply came to him.

Breathing deeply, he went over what he hoped would happen with the coming of the sun as he drifted off to sleep.

TWENTY-SIX

Awakening

AS SOON AS the group of warriors left the Crimson Caves, Ziradon had set out on his own private endeavor. Hardly content to lie in the darkness and call out to his missing heiress, the old dragon intended to find her.

She's the only possession I have in the world, he lamented as he reached the beach on which they had walked hardly a few days before. Flying over the burned cabin and boat, tears filled his tired eyes.

They had built a home there next to the waves. *Loving and kind,* he fumed. *That's all she has ever been.*

Turning south, he trailed the edge of the coast. Reaching Abolia, he paused, landing on the edge of a vast graveyard. The mortals of the rim had been banished from their kingdom long before he was hatched, but he knew of their story.

His eyes sharp, he scanned the waving grass, picking out the markers that stood taller than the rest. "Heads of families," he grumbled. The mortals were weaker than Eriden's magical inhabitants, but that did not make them any less important. *My daughter understands this,* he recalled with pride. *I taught her well in the short time I held her in my care.*

His mind drawn to the night she was cursed into mortal form, he sighed. *Where would she go?* There had to be a clue. "She is in a dark place," he repeated. *That's what they were told by Thirac.* He knew the old gnome, one of the few inhabitants of Eriden older than himself. *A trickster, to be certain.*

It had bothered him that his daughter and her friends had chosen to trust the gnomes, but he had not spoken of it. Any advice he could have offered would have been in hindsight, as the alliance had already been formed by the time she came to him, winning his freedom.

Somewhere dark. Thinking again of the Shadowlands, he flapped his massive wings and took to the air, once more trailing the western edge of the continent. Woods and coastline stretched for miles, until he came to the northern wizard village of Heewan.

"If only I could walk among them, as she does," he considered, making a few passes to observe their streets and courtyards. Spying a large plaza in the center, he flew low so that his shadow would be detected, turning their worried faces up to him. "Fear me," he growled, puffing bits of flame and smoke into the air, scattering the weakest of the lot.

Spying none that resembled his target, he moved on.

Again, moving south, he felt less drawn to the next village, and then the next. *She would have no cause to visit such a place,* he surmised. Turning east, he took to the sands of the desert, the waves of hot air rising to scorch the bottom of his wings as he skimmed the surface. He approached Whitefair, flying low in hopes of avoiding detection.

"This is a dark place beneath the brightest of suns," he observed, recalling the trade that thrived there. "Murderers and thieves, a den of inequity in the heart of the desert."

Looming over the adobe walls, he scoured the narrow streets and passages, those who walked them paying him no mind. These were accustomed to dragons flying overhead and thought nothing of it. Sorely tempted to vent his frustration upon them as flame, he took to the sky, beating his wings fast and hard as he climbed.

Reaching the thin, cooler air, he leveled out and turned a slow circle, taking in the wide desert sands for miles around the oasis. To the south, a dark blanket lay across the sand, and his heart raced. His distance above sufficient, he knew he could observe the object unseen and flew in its direction to have a closer look.

"Elves," he muttered to himself, noting they made camp on the edge of the shifting sands. The mountain met the empty void there on the eastern side, and a grassland had formed. On one side, rivulets fed small springs where the snow melted and ran down to the sparse foliage below. On the other, the sun burned away nearly all that lived, leaving only bright yellow sand.

In the line along the two, a garrison of Lady Cilithrand's finest made camp, perhaps awaiting their orders. Squinting against the glare, the old dragon estimated their numbers. *Thousands of wretched souls.*

It burned his heart that the elf queen had such grand visions. She would depose the dragons if it were within her grasp, and from their sheer numbers, it most likely was within her grasp.

"I have no time for this," he scowled, noting the group of minions were not marching and simply lay in wait. Deciding he would return and investigate them further, he continued south, flying over the foreboding forest, aware that the place was filled with goblins and haunted trees.

He knew instantly she was not inside. It might have been a dark place, but his daughter would have no reason to visit such a cursed land, for the creatures therein would serve no master; not even the Supreme Dragoness.

More forest and trees passed below him, but of the normal variety, and he could see the glen in the distance to the right. Thinking of the nymphs and the satyrs who protected them, he felt certain that was not her location either. *Ester-brook is neither dark nor would its inhabitents be blinded by the tricks of the Lady Cilithrand.*

To the left, he glared at the deeper, darker woods of the Shadowlands. *The place I have suspected all along.* Taking to the upper atmosphere once more, he circled in the failing light, slowly descending for closer inspection. Each opening in the trees a clearing on the ground, he would search them all until he found that which he was looking for.

Her eyes flickering, Amicia stared up into the light. Her body stiff, she moved with great care. Remembering her torn shoulder, her fingers snaked across her clothing, drawing them to inspect the wound.

Finding her shirt torn, the blood had dried into a crust embedded in the material. The flesh beneath it did not ooze and felt firm to her prodding.

Tracing the puckered flesh with the tips of her fingers, she thought of the scar that forever marked the Mate's chest. A healed wound touched by a special magic that would forever remain a part of him.

Uscan's large head brushing against her, she turned her gaze to find him lying next to her, his massive body stretched as she languished in its warmth. "How long have I been here?" she croaked, her mouth dry.

"A day or two," he replied evenly.

"And yet I still live," she chuckled softly. "Or did you want me conscious when you tore my soul away from my flesh?"

"There will be no tearing, my queen," he growled, raising his eyes to indicate their visitor.

Turning slowly, as the ache persisted, she focused on a large dark form. The edges taking shape, she gasped, "Oh, father!"

"Rest, my daughter," Ziradon commanded.

"But how did I –"

"We are sworn to secrecy," Uscan informed her, "so you needn't bother to ask. You are healed, for the most part, but your strength will only return over time."

Nodding, she didn't argue. Her eyes leaping around her, she noted she remained in the same location as the attack, in the clearing where they had first met. "Can I get a drink?" she asked, fumbling to sit up.

Next to her, a flask of water had been provided. Lifting it, she drank greedily from the cool liquid. On a flat rock that acted as a table, a selection of dried meat, bread, and cheese also awaited her. *Food. They couldn't have done this.*

"Who's been here?" she demanded, a little more forcefully.

"We are disinclined to share," Ziradon replied in a toying manner. "Eat and regain your strength."

Her empty belly rumbling, she tasted the meat, noting it to be tender and deliciously spiced. The cheese reminded her of Rey, and her head swam. "Where are my friends? Can you tell me that?" she asked, her fingers trembling as she searched for her orb in her pocket.

Emptying the contents, she found it, along with her shield stone and the crystal from the Crimson Caves. Snatching the red rock first, she clenched it and peeked inside the home of the trolls.

"Oh, no," she gasped. "They went without me."

In the great hall, the trolls that remained in their mountain mourned. She could see the bodies being prepared for their rituals, as they would be burned and returned to the cycle of life there among the inhabitants of the northern forest.

Dropping the crimson glass, she switched to the orb and scoured the land, coming to the dwarf mountain. Many were still inside the maze of halls and chambers, but mostly women and children. "The dwarves joined the fight," she assumed with a small grin.

Expanding her vision, she located her friends atop the mountain, their swords singing as they were whipped through the air and flung against the elves. At their side, the trolls used long spears to extract their own blows, and the dwarf swords and axes glinted with sunlight that appeared to be fading with the dusk.

"A great battle," she breathed. "I must get to them!"

"You must rest, Kaliwyn," Ziradon replied. "You are in no condition for travel."

"You don't understand," she argued. "I am their leader. It is my duty to be there, to guide them, and to fight with them."

"Lamwen has taken on the charge of leading the battle," the old dragon explained.

"It's not the same!" she spat, leaving the remainder of her meal and forcing her shaky legs to stand.

"Ami, listen to me," Uscan agreed with the dragon. "You are in no condition to leave. Sit and finish your rations. If you can walk afterwards, perhaps your father will agree to spirit you to the north, but you must be rested and ready before you face the dangers of combat."

Scowling, she sank to her knees. Taking the food in eager bites, she hardly chewed it, then washed it down with large gulps of water. When she had made it all disappear, she snapped, "Satisfied?"

"Sleep, my dragoness," Ziradon implored. "I promise I will take you to them at first light, but for now you must rest."

Blowing flame into a collection of wood, he lit the fire that would keep her warm as she lay beneath the stars and followed his command.

TWENTY-SEVEN

Shadow Warriors

"THIS IS INSANE!" Reynard shouted, Animir and Piers both close enough to hear. "We've been slaughtering them all day, and yet they still come!"

"Not all day," the Mate chuckled wryly. "Only since noon," he teased, his shield holding as an unwary elf took a swing and was smacked down by blue light. "I love Amicia," he quipped. "Her charms are exquisite." Sinking his blade into the throat of the attacker, he pulled the steel free, and the elf's bright red blood gurgled from the wound, coating his flesh and the ground beneath him.

"Let us hope they hold into the darkness," Animir agreed.

Most of the elves who came in contact with them recognized their protections quickly and moved on, preferring the soft, delicate blue and lavender skin of the trolls. Many of the Crimson Cave's inhabitants had fallen, but they had not lost their heart or the desire to rid the land of the elven hoard that threatened them all.

The dwarves a much tougher breed, they had quickly adapted to the fight, and the clanging of sword and axe echoed across the top of their mountain. The group had risen with the sun, taking a small breakfast before they climbed the incline behind the statues that heralded their past kings, and they were eager for the fight with blood-lust in their eyes.

Almost at the precise moment the ball of fire hung directly above, they ran into the back of the elf forces as they pushed their way across the rocky mountains. Slamming into them from behind, they began cutting them down with haste. The elves fell quickly, but those ahead were alerted to their presence, and the battle was begun.

The soldiers of Cilithrand were not the tall, magnificent elves that had been abundant in Jerranyth. Instead, they were smaller, only matching the height and build of Rey and Piers on occasion, as most were a few inches shorter and lighter. The trolls killed them easily, as did the dwarves, and it was only by sheer numbers that they had held out this long.

Pausing his swing, Animir stared at the last sliver of the sun as it disappeared in the west. His gaze swinging the arch of the sky, he gasped, "The dark moon. We can still win this."

Holding his sword as well, Rey wasn't looking at the sky. Below them, the side of the mountain was covered with bodies, corpses of the fallen, as well as the writhing masses as both sides engaged their battle. "How," he grunted. "There are so many, and our numbers will be exhausted before the moon rises."

"There is no moon," Animir repeated. "It is the night of the new moon, and the world will lie in darkness until the sun appears again on the other side of the sky. It is a sign, Reynard. We must unleash the dark elf."

"Are you mad?" Piers joined them. "I told you we have no guarantee she will kill them. She would destroy our forces in a matter of minutes."

"Amicia has secured this ally for us," Animir pushed, his chest heaving. Wiping at the side of his mouth with the back of his hand, his mind raced. "If you ever believed in her ability to be our queen," he panted, licking his lips. "If you ever believed in her, then you must trust that Kedoria will be our savior."

Staring at him with cold brown orbs, the Mate breathed in heavy strokes. His chest ached, and his lungs burned from the fight. They had been at it for hours, and in the last light of day, it appeared all hope was lost. "Then do it, and may God have mercy upon us."

Pulling the hamar gem from his pouch, the elf did not hesitate in the task. Holding the stone before him, he waited until the last of the light had gone and pure darkness remained. His lips moving slightly, he whispered the charm that would free their prisoner, and she sprang from the dark crystal to stand before him.

Turning slowly, her black gown hung around her, limp against her frame. Her gaze wandering, she looked across the field of bodies, her vision better in the darkness than most have in the brightest of lights. "This is no fireside," she growled, her glare reaching the three friends. "Where is the dragoness who commands me?"

"Amicia has been detained," Animir informed her curtly, "but you recall who I am, I am certain."

"I know you," she replied in a gravelly voice, tilting her head as if to consider the choice before her. Deciding to let him live, at least for the moment, she awaited his explanation as to the reason for her release.

"Good," the elf spat, his tone one of authority. "Then we have need of your dark arts. Call forth your minions and take up your vow of service."

A fierce wind slammed against them, carrying the stench of blood and carnage.

Her grey eyes shifting between the three who stood before her, she recognized the other two as mortals of the rim. "Do you fear me?" she hissed.

"No," Piers clipped, his eyes squinted against the haze and dust. "My mistress, Kaliwyn, has assured me of your loyalty, and my faith in her is strong. You will remove the elves from this battlefield before this night is ended, I am certain."

Her smile an evil twist to her lips, she agreed, "The dragoness has chosen her company well. We will complete the task before us." Spreading her arms, smoke billowed from her slender form, and the four minions who served her fell off of her. Landing on the ground, they writhed as if in agony before finding their feet and standing next to her.

Their bodies short and black, as if they were small children charred by the fires of hell, their limbs burned with faint yellow and orange flame. Her command a subtle hiss, she swung her arm to indicate the sea of elves before them and the feast that awaited her servants.

Running across the loose stones, the creatures squealed and shrieked in terrifying voices. The sound echoing through the night, many paused in mid swing, their weapons suspended in the air as they listened to the noises of the daemons.

Reaching their first victims, they laid not a hand or mouth upon the dwarves and trolls; their intent set upon their former masters. Catching them, even those who tried to flee, they pulled at their robes and searched out the soft, pale flesh underneath.

Their mouths gaping holes in their smoldering forms, they sank invisible teeth into their prey, the venom within them coursing into their trembling forms. Within minutes of being bitten, the elf would be paralyzed, soon to draw his last breath.

Standing atop the mountain with the three of them, Kedoria never moved. Her beady eyes watching the carnage, she breathed deeply, enjoying the power she wielded through her miniature servants.

Next to her, the trio did not resume the fight. Engulfed in the horror that transpired before them, they could not tear their eyes away. The four daemons parted the sea of soldiers, the battle on both sides still roiling; oblivious to their presence. Their victims claimed, they moved on to the next, on and on in a narrow path of devastation that weaved back and forth, a spindle of destruction across the wide living cloth.

The trolls and dwarves, though amazed at the removal of their enemies, were not thwarted from the fight. Instead, they turned from their suffering adversary to find another elf in need of butchering.

The field of their carnage long and wide, the spectacle continued until the hours had passed and the sun had made the journey around the world to peek at the field of battle from the other side. As soon as the golden rays broke the surface,

Kedoria and her four minions vanished into ashen nothingness, and what remained of the elves were left to the defending army to dispose of.

Amicia awoke with the sun, her strength more than it was but far short of what she had hoped for. Rolling away from Uscan's slumbering form, she pushed herself onto her knees, sitting up to have a look around.

Still in the clearing, she sighed, weary of being there. The magical luster of the place had grown stale, and she longed to flee that she might return to her friends.

Thinking of the group, she located her orb. Opening her hand, she stared into it, seeing that the battle continued but on a much smaller scale. "They didn't give up," she croaked, happy in the knowledge they still might prevail.

Darkening the orb, she forced her legs beneath her, stumbling the few feet to her father's side. He awoke the moment she touched him, lifting his massive head as he groaned, "Kaliwyn, you should be resting."

"I have rested," she countered, indicating the ball of fire to the east. "The sun is rising, and you have promised to carry me to my friends."

"You still lack the strength to go by transposition?"

"I have not tried," she confessed. "I shall if you refuse to take me, but if I may ride upon the strength of your wings, I can preserve mine in case it is needed when we arrive."

"Then I shall carry you, my dragoness," he agreed, lumbering to his feet. "Uscan!" he bellowed, awakening the pack.

Rolling over to stretch, the alpha detected the missing lump of human flesh that he had cradled through the night. Placing his paws flat on the ground, he stood, ready to follow her command. "What would you have of us, my queen?"

"I'm glad to see your allegiance has returned," she scowled, snatching up the flask and finishing off the water. "I want you to go to the glen as quickly as you are able. The elves there must be crushed, and perhaps with you and the dragons I have sent, the nymphs and satyrs can finally turn the tide."

"As you wish, princess," he replied, barking to the others to follow.

Watching them disappear through the trail at the southern end of the clearing, she sighed. "What really happened after I was bitten?" she asked, turning her green orbs to glare at Ziradon.

"You were saved, and that is all that matters," he replied, lying upon the ground before her. "Will you be strong enough to hold as I fly?"

"Yes," she agreed. "Lamwen has carried me in such a manner, and I do not fear the fall."

Hoisting herself up, she settled into the grooves of his back, where the wings met his body and she could get her grip. The scales rough beneath her flesh, she smiled at the feel of him, alive and there with her. *"I have not spoken of my love for you,"* she plied as he took to the air.

"You need not speak of such things, Kaliwyn," he replied. *"Through the years and distance between us, I never doubted your devotion."*

Tears dripped onto her cheeks, adding a cold sting as the air rushed by. They flew north, tracing the path the group had taken on their quest to cross the sand. Arriving at the savannah that separated the mountain from the desert, the carpet of elves was gone.

"This holds my concern," Ziradon informed her.

"What does?" she asked, leaning forward and caressing him as his wings pumped beneath her.

"The elves had a garrison here, waiting at the edge of the sands. I noticed them when I searched for you, on my journey south."

"How long ago was this?" she asked, her fear heightening her need to breathe.

"Days, two at least. Maybe three."

"Dear God," she whispered.

Ahead, a dark shadow lay over the shifting dunes. Increasing his angle, Ziradon climbed as they approached, that they could inspect the troops without being observed themselves. From the greater height, he turned and made a circle, the girl leaning over the side and gaping at the ground below.

"There are thousands of them," she remarked airily.

"Yes. Enough to make the wizards beg for their lives, rest assured. They will reach the northern woods by way of the desert, I am assured."

"We must stop them," she panted. *"Take me now to the others, atop the dwarf cliffs. The battle there was all but won from what I saw before we left. We must rally our forces and make for Whitefair before it's too late."*

TWENTY-EIGHT

The Face of Danger

"WELL, it was close, but I believe we have won the day," Piers observed. "It was a miracle, to be certain, and one I hope we do not have to repeat." Yaodus stood with him, as did Baeweth, while Lamwen circled above. Looking up at the massive beast, he inhaled deeply, noting the smell of death and awaiting the captain's report.

Completing his assessment, the dragon landed nearby and picked his way towards them while taking care not to desecrate the corpses. "This is the bloodiest battlefield my eyes have ever seen," he growled. Turning with his wings spread wide, he observed the scene from their point of view. Walking on two legs during his days as a human had changed him and seeing the carnage through the lens of their eyes saddened him in a way he feared it would not have should he never have lived as one of them.

Across the field to the north, the dwarves worked their way through, killing any elves who had managed to survive and hide among the bodies. On the eastern edge, a triage had been assembled, and the injured dwarves and trolls were treated or transported to the Crimson Caves or Rhong if their wounds were severe.

Following his gaze, Baeweth agreed, "We have taken this battle, but the cost was great."

Each member of their group busy with the aftermath, Animir and Meena conducted the transports as Hayt and Zaendra nursed the fallen. Clomping across the bloody mud, the leaders joined them, as they each feared there would be little time to rest once Cilithrand learned of their victory.

No sooner had they gathered to converse about their intentions, when a dragon's shadow glided over the top of them. Looking up, they gasped to find Ziradon making a landing a few feet away.

"Oh my God, Ami!" Rey screamed, running up to the beast to help his wife to the ground.

"Rey," she replied, matching his enthusiasm as she collapsed against him.

The wound to her shoulder obvious through her torn and stained clothing, he ran his palm over it, seeing that it had been healed. "This is no ordinary wound," he observed, scooping her into his arms and carrying her to the others. Placing her feet upon the ground, she stood next to him as her father joined them.

"We must make haste," she announced. "The elves are on the move, and Whitefair will fall if we are not there to stand against them."

"Stand against them," Piers muttered. "Look around, princess. We have fought since yesterday noon without a break, and the battle here was scarcely won. We are exhausted and in need of food and rest before we even consider the next fight."

"The elves will be upon you whether you are rested or not," Ziradon informed him in his gravelly tone.

"You did not remain at the caves," Yaodus observed, glaring at the blonde in their midst. "It is good that you have found her, but we could have used your help in this battle if you were strong enough to fight."

"I'll make it up to you on the next one," the old dragon replied curtly. "For now, we must assemble at Whitefair if we are to have any hope of holding it."

"It is the oasis, the center of the desert," Amicia added. "If we allow the elves to take it, then the rest of the wizard communities will surely fall," she insisted.

Still tending to the wounded, her friends did not seem greatly moved by her words. Turning to the Mate, she urged, "Piers, please. This is vital, even more so than preserving the dwarf mountain. They will hold much of Eriden if they take the wizards, in population and land."

"We see the importance," he sneered. "We really do. But besides our exhaustion, we have no way to get there. It's over a week's march if we could find a way through this mountain range and then the desert besides."

"We must teleport," Ami agreed eagerly. "We can get there by magical means," she insisted, her eyes scanning the ruin for the ossci who could accomplish the task easily.

"I have ported people to the trolls and dwarves for hours," Meena complained. "My powers are spent."

"As are mine," Animir agreed.

"The gnomes can help," the girl pushed, unwilling to give up so easily. "But I don't see our small friends. Do they wait for us at the camp?"

"The gnomes are gone," the Mate informed her flatly. "Thirac has taken them back, as actually fighting goes against their principals."

Staring at him with large green eyes, Ami blinked a few times. "They have abandoned us," she breathed.

"Aye," he nodded, "before the battle even started. We tried to march to the dwarf mountain, but the wolves jumped us. We lost a few of the trolls then."

"Seventeen," Rey interjected.

"Yes, thank you," Piers spat sarcastically. "The point is, we were forced to spend hours and massive amounts of energy transpositioning everyone closer to get away from them. It cost us dearly in resources."

"How did you get up here?" Amicia demanded in a frustrated tone, his story falling short of explaining it all.

"Through Asomanee," Meena explained. "Baeweth agreed to join us in the fight, and we swept through the tunnels and reclaimed the halls. We spent the night at the camp in the valley and took on the elves here yesterday."

"I saw," the girl agreed. "I used my orb while the battle raged. I was not able to join you in my injured state."

"How were you healed so quickly?" Rey asked, his fingers tracing the remains of the bite.

"That I do not know," she sighed, cutting a cool stare at the old dragon. "Uscan and my father have declined to explain. I only know that I was mended during my delirium and made to rest until my thoughts had cleared. Ziradon has brought me here just now, and the discovery of the elves in the desert was made during our journey to this place."

"Then we are all understanding what has transpired, but that does not change the fact we have no way to get there, even if we were ready for the fight," Hayt observed.

"The gnomes can take us," Amicia declared. Her passion firm, she slapped her fist against an open palm to add strength to her claim.

"I just told you they have refused us further assistance," the Mate scowled at her obstinance, "and besides, the three of them would hardly be an improvement over what we have. It would still take us a full day to move our forces to the oasis."

"Three of them," she scoffed, her mind made up. "They are all capable of the task," she pointed out. "The ossci are their great and powerful ministers, but all of the gnomes have the ability as you may recall. I will go to Thirac and convince him they must do this."

"I doubt you would be able, my lady," Animir replied with a shake of his tired head.

"Doubt all you wish," she laughed. "I only require that you prepare. Assemble the men, any and all who can still hold a blade. I will go and convince the gnomes of their duty to our kingdom while you do," she informed them boldly before she disappeared.

Feeling stronger, Amicia transpositioned herself to the gnome village easily. Looking around at the empty trees and stones anxiously, her fingers moved to her mop of disheveled hair. *I guess I could have cleaned up a little.*

Adjusting her torn wizard's robe so it covered her new scar a little better, she slid a tentative foot forward to have a look around.

"Hello? Thirac?" she called loudly.

An odd silence met her, as if even the birds and bugs had forgotten to breathe. Her eyes roaming, she turned in a slow circle. The moisture dripped from the branches and leaves, the occasional plop of it hitting the dark damp earth the only noise she could decipher. Shuddering at the eerie reception, she refused to give up.

"Yimath? Ziyath? Mizath?"

She had gone through every gnome name she knew but one. *Sevoassi.* But the gnomes had denied knowledge of him.

"Sevoassi?" she dared, her voice quavering when she spoke it.

"I told you that name is not recognized here," Thirac scolded.

Spinning to face his warning, Amicia gasped down at the gnome before her. Reminding her of the day he had come out of the woods to more or less greet them, his hood covered his head and draped over him. His hands folded against his chest, the sleeves fell back just enough to give her a peek at his tiny hands.

"You said you didn't know him," she corrected.

"Same thing," he chirped, using the pudgy digits to remove his covering. His dark black hair and beady eyes exposed, he glared at her. "I told your friends our aid has ended. Perhaps they neglected to inform you."

"I wasn't here," she agreed. "I was detained," she added, her fingers brushing her hidden shoulder absently. "As far as your aid, I only require one more thing from you, and I will never ask for another."

"You require," he sniveled. "You may be heir to the throne of Eriden, but you are entitled to nothing in the marshlands."

Deciding to soften her approach, she knelt before him so that their height nearly matched. "Thirac, I do not know what has happened or why you have had this change of heart –"

"You took the ossci on a massacre," he shouted, cutting her off.

"I…" she stammered, recalling the attack on the wolves. "I asked them to go so we could test our new weapons and shields."

"You killed two magnificent creatures for a test?" he accused, his eyes narrowed into slits.

"No," she blinked, searching for the right words. "They had been after the trolls, and we feared they would move against us when we entered the forest." She justified their actions, her heart pounding with fear and regret.

"So, you plotted against them and set a trap."

Staring at him, she curled her tongue, losing patience quickly. "I really don't feel the need to defend our choices to you," she replied, her voice growing loudly vengeful.

"Obviously you do," he stated calmly, opening an empty palm to indicate her knees in the dirt.

Standing abruptly, she dusted at them angrily. "Listen, Thirac. The elves have been defeated on the dwarf mountain, and Rhong is safe, but another garrison marches on Whitefair. We must be moved to the oasis as quickly and as soon as possible to prepare for the attack."

"Then go," he mocked.

"We need you to move us. You said all of the gnomes have the capabilities of the ossci, and that means all of your people can transposition over the land of Eriden," she pushed.

His eyes narrowed, giving her pause.

When he said nothing, she added, "It would take a single trip in my estimation. Your people come and take a few and go. Drop us in Whitefair, and then they can get back to whatever it is they are doing."

"Most of the village is not here," he spat.

"Not here," she breathed, her eyes again roving over the emptiness around them. "Where have they gone? Why?"

"That is not your concern," he snapped.

"Look, Thirac," she almost shouted, "we do not have time to debate this issue. What is it that you want in return? You want me to beg?" she asked, her bottom lip trembling. She wasn't above groveling; she had done it before. "Just tell me what you want."

"All we have ever wanted was to be left alone," he sighed with a large nod.

"To be left alone," she mocked. "Thirac, you are part of Eriden, as much as any other creature who lives here. The elves –"

"Are not our concern," he silenced her words once more.

"Thirac," a small voice followed his interjection, freezing him in place if he had intended to say more. Pivoting slowly, he stopped to glare at Yimath, who stood almost hidden by the shadow of the trees. Coming in behind her, Happy and Grumpy also appeared.

A wave of joy flooding her senses, Amicia exhaled loudly but held her tongue.

Clasping her hands together, she wrapped her fingers and pressed the palms together, as if it would help her hold her excitement to silence. Pressing the sides against her lips to suppress her joy, she breathed against her chilled flesh and waited.

"We wish to return to the mortals," the tiny blonde said more loudly.

"It is forbidden," the older gnome gasped.

"Then we will accept our exile," Yimath agreed.

"Ossci in exile," their leader grunted. "Why would you choose this?"

"Our princess is correct," Mizath informed him, stepping forward and entering the light of the clearing. "Many days we have worked with them, side by side in their efforts. We do not feel compelled to abandon them in their hour of need."

"I knew I should never have allowed you to mingle with them," the king growled.

"What is done is done," Yimath soothed. "Allow us to help in the battle that comes. Surely you can agree that Cilithrand's hand across the land would be unfortunate."

Eyeing Ami with his dark orbs, Thirac considered the plea. "You have one day. When the sun sets tomorrow, if you are not back within the forest of Falconmarsh, you will be banished from it forever."

"Thank you, my lord," the gnome squealed, turning to clasp the hands of her two friends before they disappeared.

"Where did they go?" Ami whispered, surprised by her sudden turn of luck.

"To do as you requested," Thirac snapped. "We might as well mourn their removal now," he added, showing her his back and ambling between the trees.

TWENTY-NINE

Dragon's Flight

"OK, we have transportation, we should get moving," Amicia announced as soon as she materialized on the mountain, her hand flat to indicate the ossci.

"Three?" Piers asked doubtfully, pinching his lower lip as he studied them. They had gathered the troops, to an extent, preparing for her return, but at the moment, they were standing around waiting for help they apparently would not receive.

"We will be able to carry you," Yimath assured. "To where are we going?"

"Whitefair, of course," Ami stated firmly.

A stiff silence followed, and Meena pointed out, "The wizards probably are unaware of the pending attack. What is to say they will welcome our arrival or support?"

"Ok, then I'll go ahead of us and speak with the leader there," Amicia sighed.

"You look like a wild woman," Reynard laughed, indicating her current condition, then shook his head. "I doubt he will hear your words."

Her lip forming a pout, the girl crossed her arms over her chest and grunted, "Then what would you have me do?"

"Let's slow down and form a real plan," the Mate suggested, his stopping motion indicating the need for calm. Turning to the gnomes, he asked, "When you say you can carry us, how long will it take?"

His eyes scanning the men, Ziyath frowned in his grumpy way as he observed, "I dare say two trips, three at most. We can each transport fifty easily. Perhaps more if we pushed it."

"Fifty," Meena gasped. "I can hardly scrape a dozen if I dare."

"We've had a few more years of practice," Mizath grinned.

"Then the transport will not be the issue," Piers continued. "So, unless we want to move to the rocks outside of town and wait, which would be plain silly in my opinion, we should have a rest and a meal the best we can."

"We need to know the location of my kin," Animir added. "How long before they are in a position to strike."

"Agreed," the Mate nodded. "Perhaps the dragons can fly for us and keep watch. You are able to converse with each of them," he observed, raising his chin at Ami. "They can keep you apprised."

"Yes," she nodded, her head clearer as her adrenaline settled. "This is a good plan. I'll change into my second clothes and make myself presentable before I speak to…" She stopped short, perplexed. "I don't know who the leader of the wizards is. We never met him."

"Actually, Piers did," Meena informed him. "Gradien, or Gray as he is known. He organizes the market where we reclaimed the siren as he recieves a cut of all that passes through Whitefair."

"You mean that bald asshole who threatened to have us arrested?" Rey shouted.

"The same," the older woman sighed. "He is called the magistrate, and he takes care of the city ensuring what safety and security there is to be had."

"Plunders it, more like," the Mate scowled. "Must we save them?"

"Yes," Ami countered. "Their resources are too great to allow them to fall into the hands of the elves. We will go there and speak to him. We will convince him somehow that they must join our cause. Then, we will formulate our plans for defending the city and wiping out the elves."

Holding up the empty hamar gem, Animir shook his head. "We won't be able to repeat the battle plan from last night. The dark elf and her minions fought bravely, true to their word, but she chose to be destroyed by the light rather than return to her prison. We won't be able to use her again."

Taking the empty crystal from him, Ami studied it, a lump forming in her gut. "She gave up her life to help us."

"It wasn't much of a life," Piers sneered. "Trapped in that thing all the time."

"Still, it was a sacrifice," the girl insisted, turning it so it caught the light and shined brightly. Shoving it in her pocket, she mused, "We'll think of something. For now, we'll eat, rest and get a report on the elves. Lamwen, will you and my father see to what's going on in the desert?"

"Certainly, my lady," the dragon bowed.

"I am familiar to the wizards," Ziradon added. "I will make the flight to White-fair and prepare for your arrival to negotiate our cause."

"Very well then," the girl agreed, raising her chin with confidence. "We all have our chores, and we will meet back here in five hours to assess our progress."

"Here, love," Rey offered, her brush in hand, "let me tend your hair. We can wash it and the rest of you before you don your clean clothes."

"I'll warm a pot of water," Meena suggested, setting the fire.

"I can take care of our supper," Zae added. "The gnomes' fireplace and kettle are still inside their tree."

"Thank you," Ami agreed, casting a quick glance between them. "You are all very kind to care for me so." Noting their tense features, she pushed, "I'm curious as to the long faces, though."

"We were worried about you," Rey replied, pushing her to sit on the stone while he removed the clumps from her hair. Using the water, he cleansed it, the way he had the morning she awoke in the first mate's bed on the Sea Serpent.

"I was fine," she lied. Holding her slouched body stiffly, she allowed him to tend to her, but guilt ate at her gut.

Catching the quiver in her voice, he replied, "You don't look fine. You are covered in scrapes and bruises, and this scar speaks of a nasty wound. I've never seen anything like it."

"I have," Meena spoke up, cutting her eyes over at the girl as she busied herself preparing her clothes. "Piers has a similar scar upon his chest. A deep hole healed by magical means." She feared the girl had been close to death, pulled back from the brink of it by a powerful hand, and her unwillingness to share the details only added to her ominous absence.

Tracing the pink pucker with an extended digit, Rey asked, "Did you heal yourself? Who did this to you?"

"I did not, as I was unconscious," the girl whispered. "The wounds were inflicted by Uscan."

"Uscan," Rey grunted, clenching his teeth. "You went to the Shadowlands." He ceased his coddling and knelt beside her. Cutting his eyes up at her, he waited for to explain herself.

"Yes," she clipped. "I had to see if he had also aligned himself with the enemy." She kept her gaze on the fire, purposely avoiding his angry glare.

"And I suppose asking telepathically wasn't good enough," her husband growled.

"No. I needed to see face to face where he stood." Her features placid, she appeared tired. "I probably should have taken a few of you with me," she confessed.

"You don't say," Rey muttered, not taken to browbeating her with hindsight. "But that still doesn't tell us who healed the wound."

"Ziradon," Ami speculated flatly. "If it matches the one I healed on Piers, it stands to reason it was accomplished by a dragon. He was the only one there."

Nodding, Meena and Rey shared a glance, and he shrugged, "It sounds reasonable, don't you think?"

"Reasonable," the older woman also scrunched her shoulders. She had her doubts about the old sovereign's abilities reaching such a level but voicing those concerns would be unwise. Instead, she offered the warmed water. "We can strip these torn items off of you. I'll give them a wash while you help her to bathe."

"Aye," Rey agreed as he got to his feet. Helping Ami to stand and slip out of the garments, he let the interrogation end with the explanation she had given.

When her sticky flesh had all been cleansed, she slid her legs into the familiar pants; the ones that had belonged to Bally. Pulling the shirt on, the small gaps at the shoulders exposed only a peek at her new scar. Her fingers toying with the edge, she sighed loudly.

"Are you in pain?" Rey asked, his voice filled with concern.

"I'm fine," she countered, cutting her green orbs up at him. Taken with his tenderness, she added, "I should speak of my love for you while I can."

"Afraid you are going to die?" he teased, only half joking.

"I fear I won't get another chance," she moaned. "I do love you, Reynard Daye. I do not regret a single day of my life with you." Catching his hands, she stopped their motion and forced him to face her.

Staring into her emerald pools of light, he nodded, "And I you, Amicia. But you must forgive me if I am not ready to voice my goodbye."

"Then do not voice it," she agreed, her smile spreading over her lips. "Only know that my days as your bride have been happy. No matter what comes, I would not change the life we shared."

An uncomfortable silence followed, as Zaendra presented their meal. Placing the bowls on the table, she asked, "Will the others be joining us? I made enough for all."

"Pop up to the mountain and check on our progress," Amicia suggested, her gaze still locked with Rey's.

As soon as she disappeared, he dropped his mouth to hers, enjoying the taste of her and hoping it would not be his last.

THIRTY

Rain of Fire

"GOOD LUCK, MY KING," Lamwen called as he leapt into the air. Flying south, he would swoop across and trace the path of the elven forces to assess their progress.

Watching him go, Ziradon considered the other dragon and his loyalty to the crown. *You have been a faithful subject, Lamwen; captain of the king's guard.* He could not predict what would be the outcome of their struggle, even with the recovery of his daughter. The path before them dark and unsettled, he only knew they must make every effort to preserve the kingdom and hold it from the hands of the elves.

Satisfied with their plan, he also took to the air, headed west to Whitefair, where an audience with the magistrate awaited. He was familiar with the position, but since the wizards were a rough lot, he did not figure he had met the current one. *Not that I made any effort to know any of them well during my reign.* He had never cared for wizards any more than he held a deep regard for elves and would have considered the trolls more to his liking if he were to call any such creatures friends.

Staying low and following the rise and fall of the mountains, he searched the ground for any other nasty surprises the group would have to contend with. The terrain below almost exclusively wilderness, those who resided in the open mountains were mainly lesser beings; fairies, fauns and the like. A hearty bunch, as the winters there were long and harsh, they did not organize themselves into fixed communities, mostly keeping to mobile packs, herds, or family groups at best.

Spying a few such gatherings, his chest swelled with hope. His only child and heir to his throne understood the importance of even these, and she would protect them to the best of her ability. Thinking of her and the dragon that had flown to the south, he knew they would be the right pair to rule the Kingdom of Eriden, if Lamwen were to be her choice in the end. *I suspect that he will be, given what they shared when he walked beside her as a mortal.*

Realizing his thoughts had strayed, Ziradon quickly reined in his focus, as they had more pressing concerns. *Dreaming of the future will have to wait.* Returning to their battle plans, he recalled what he knew of the wizards, and hoped they would have a sufficient number within the walls of the oasis to augment their depleted numbers. Even if the ossci were to help bring their troops in full, there would likely not be enough to defeat the forces he had seen gathered on the edge of the sand and pouring across it as they moved towards the unsuspecting city.

Finding nothing out of the ordinary along the way, he soon arrived at the ancient walls. Floating in on a hot wind as the sun scorched the ground and sand-sculpted structures, he landed on the eastern barrier, not far from where the group had scaled it with the aid of Humphray and his associate. His view partially blocked by the dwellings below, those who could see him appeared unimpressed with his arrival.

Do they not know me? he pondered.

He had been held captive for two decades, and much had changed during that time. It felt odd not to cause a stir with his arrival, as there had been a time all in Eriden knew and respected their great king. He could not have gone anywhere that he was not recognized and revered before his fall.

Taking wing, he coasted over the streets as he had done when he searched for his daughter. The people below gave him hardly a second glance as his shadow passed. Reaching the market, he pulled up, landing on one of the adjacent structures and scouring the throng of people below.

On the far side of the auction house stood a stage, where a man offered goods for sale to the masses, which would go to the highest bidder. A long row of wooden planks, large boxes and crates lined the far end. A few casks of water also stood on the front side, and a trough provided water to animals as they were displayed for auction.

In the center, a small boy-sized body with cloven hooves for feet stood upon the wooden slats, his face long and narrow. "A woodland creature," Ziradon observed, as there were many types and forms on the inner mountain ranges. *He must have been hunted and trapped to be brought to market.* It saddened him that such dealings took place, especially in the bright light of day.

Recalling his reason for the visit, the great dragon decided this would make for a great opportunity to get the attention he deserved. Leaving his perch, he flapped his wings a few times to carry himself across the courtyard and landed upon the stage. "You there!" he shouted, sending the proprietor and his helpers scattering.

The faun in chains and bound by a rope tether, he did not try to bolt and instead stood petrified. Tilting his head back, long pointed ears protruded from beneath his shaggy hair. "A dragon," he whispered.

"Yes, a dragon," Ziradon bellowed. "Where is the magistrate?"

Excited chatter swept through the market as some dared to creep closer, while others hurried to get away, creating chaos in the shifting sea of bodies. When the auctioneer braved the platform to claim his unsold minion, the dragon blew smoke at him and growled, "You trap the creatures of my forest for gain?"

"I'm within my rights," the salesman countered shakily, pulling on the rope to lead the faun away.

"I'm the magistrate," a mid-sized man with no hair announced, approaching boldly. "What's the meaning of this, dragon? Why are you interrupting our sale? This lot must be moved, and quickly, as a new one will arrive tomorrow."

"I am Ziradon, the Supreme Dragon!" their large brown visitor announced loudly, but bouts of laughter and heckling prevented him from saying more. His large emerald-green orbs glaring at the crowd, he could feel their animosity radiating towards him.

"Excuse me," the bald spokesman joined in the laughter as he rubbed his barren scalp, "but if you want to impersonate a king, you shouldn't choose a dead one."

"Dead one?" Ziradon growled. "Who told you I was dead?"

"We heard he was killed a few weeks ago," the wizard elaborated, moving closer. Obviously unafraid of their giant patron, he divulged, "It would appear his prison fell down about his head, and none too soon I would imagine. Gwirwen has been fighting off a rebellion, and we can't wait to see if he holds on to the crown."

Staring at him through narrow slits, the rightful king seethed. "Interested in the politics of the council, are you?"

"Naw," the ring leader laughed. "We have wagered on the outcome. Care to place a bet?" he teased.

"I am not here to gamble," Ziradon thundered, spewing fire into the air and sending a few more locals scattering. "I have come to arrange a meeting with the magistrate," he insisted.

"Well, that would be me. Gradien Silversmith, at your service," the dignitary replied, his lips curled in an odd fashion. "Now, kindly get off the stage," he stated more pointedly.

Having heard all he cared to, the dragon smacked the wood beams with his tail, sweeping the appendage across the front. The motion caught some of the boxes piled on the end and smashed them, allowing a few dozen brightly colored forest fairies to escape, then spilled the kegs of water onto the thirsty sand.

"That's enough, dragon!" Gradien shouted, his face red as he poked a finger at him through the air. "We run a legitimate business here!"

"Not for long," Ziradon growled, his old body coiled for a fight.

"What, you made it a point to break out of prison just to shut us down?" the man jeered, keeping the dragon occupied.

Behind the old beast, a few of the vendors prepared to jump him, binding him before he could destroy anything else. Catching their scent as they worked their way around, Ziradon sneered, "My successor has allowed you too much freedom, I think. I will have to rectify that when I retake the throne."

Spinning, a stream of fire blew from his nostrils as he laid waste to their entire gallery. Taking to the air, he continued to burn the wood and bamboo, scorching any of the men who ventured too close.

The ground erupting into chaos, the people of Whitefair did not appear happy with their destructive visitor. Gathering arms and ropes, they prepared for another attempt to subdue him, cranking a large catapult out into the open and setting it up.

Seeing the device, the dragon scorned, "You insolent fools. I'm here to render aid, and this is the welcome I receive!"

"Render aid," Gradien mocked, shaking his fist at him and shouting. Smoke billowed around him and many of the townspeople worked to bring the firehose. Pumping precious water through it, the blaze had to be extinguished before it could spread.

Taking a higher circle, Ziradon watched them in disgust and was on his third slow loop when a dragon appeared in the distance. His green scales distinctive, Lamwen grew in size until he had closed the distance between them.

Daring to descend, they landed once again on the roofs around the blackened market, only this time Gradien appeared far more receptive.

"Lamwen," he gasped. "Two dead dragons in the same day!"

"I'm not dead," Lamwen growled, pivoting to take in the destruction.

"Yeah, that's what he said," the man chortled, indicating Ziradon with a shrug. "Why are you here, destroying our fine auction?"

"Your market is an abomination," Ziradon howled. "At least when I reigned, you kept such trade under cover. Gwirwen has allowed the open abuse of our creatures," he lamented, saddened at their suffering.

Glaring at the wizard, Lamwen confirmed, "This wretched place deserves to be destroyed. Perhaps we should let the elves have them," he called to his king.

"Elves? What elves?" the magistrate perked up, spreading his hands wide. "I don't see any elves here."

"The ones marching on your city, fool," Lamwen replied, adjusting his grip on the wall. "There is a garrison crossing from the south. They will be here in two days at most."

"A garrison," Gradien replied more quietly. Whitefair had a wall but had never needed it to fend off an attack. It was mostly used to ensure he got a share of anything that came in to or went out of the city.

"My daughter will be here in a few hours," Ziradon growled. "You will bargain with her for your surrender. Her army will provide you aid and protection."

"And if we refuse this… protection?"

"Then we will slaughter your people and take the city for ourselves," the old dragon challenged. "You deserve such judgement. However, we could be persuaded to bring you in with us if you were willing to accept unconditional terms."

"What matters to you is the city," Gradien said more calmly, the pieces fitting into place. "You worry for the oasis, not my inhabitants."

"As do you," Lamwen agreed tartly.

"Very well," the magistrate grinned, offering a half bow. "I will speak with the dragoness and come to an agreement we will both find satisfactory."

Turning to his crewmen, he shouted, "Get the fires put out and clean this mess up. Market's closed until further notice," he added over his shoulder as they left them to complete the task.

"Are we set?" Amicia called, standing on a rock so she could see across the heads of her troops.

"Aye, we are grouped and ready," the Mate agreed. "The gnomes will make two passes each to deposit our forces outside the city gates, with Meena and Animir bringing us and the captains to you."

They had eaten and rested, and the sun hung low in the sky as they prepared to transposition to Whitefair.

"My father says the magistrate will be agreeable to our terms, so I don't think it will take long to work out the details," she informed them. "Be ready to travel as soon as I call for you, and I will strike the bargain as quickly as I can."

Taking Rey's hand, she would transport him, Hayt, and Zae with her when she met with Gardien Silversmith, a man she despised on her husband's word alone. Shifting in an instant, they landed in a small square somewhere within the town, as Ziradon had directed.

Turning in a slow circle, Ami could see the taller, two-story buildings on all four sides had windows that opened to the ground on which they stood. *Nice place for an ambush,* she muttered to herself, wary of her soon-to-be ally. On one side, a long table with six chairs sat unoccupied at the moment. *Where's the council?* she mused.

"Welcome to the court of Whitefair," Gradien greeted, his bald head glistening in the waning light. Standing before them washed and wearing clean clothes, he made a handsome target, his smile too large to be genuine.

"Are you the magistrate?" Amicia demanded, taking charge. Her three friends forming a line behind her, each of them openly brandished a weapon and appeared unafraid to use them if need be.

Stiff, Rey recognized the man from the market the day he almost lost his small friend. "That's him," he whispered, clenching his fists around the handle of his sword but not moving to create a scene.

"I am, but I expected a dragoness, not a flimsy mortal girl," Gradien taunted. His eyes flicking between them, he considered these might be there to spring their trap before the real representative would appear.

Glaring at him, Amicia spat, "You are a wizard. You recognize the fire within me. And if you do not, then I am speaking to the wrong man."

Pursing his lips, he studied her bravado. "The dragoness Kaliwyn is legend, lost two decades ago when her father was deposed as king. You claim her rights as heir to the throne of Eriden?"

"I do, wizard," she sneered, lowering her chin as she glared at him. "I have an army ready to bring to the city. We must fortify the walls and seal the gates, as a battle will be upon us in less than a day… two if we are fortunate."

"And what are we offered in exchange for the use of our fortress?" he scowled. "Whitefair runs on coin, which I am sure you are aware."

"There is no profit in this for you," she coughed, her gaze fixed upon him as her companions watched for any sign of an ambush from above. "We will let you live," she continued, her voice low and even. "All those who survive the attack, at any rate. I cannot offer any more than that."

"You drive a hard bargain," he slurred while crossing his wide chest with his muscled arms. He realized they had little choice, but stalling their discussion was paramount. "How are you going to bring in your troops on such little notice? We are a bit out of the way," he chuckled, "and transposition has its limits."

"They will arrive outside the city in a few minutes. I have captains who will come here for the planning of the battle, and you will accommodate them as need be," she supplied coolly.

"Very well," he agreed, raising his hands in mock welcome, a signal to his men to hold their weapons for the moment.

"Piers, we are ready," she reached out, her eyes still fixed on the magistrate.

"Aye, we'll be right there," her old friend replied.

A few minutes later, Meena arrived with him, Yaodus, Baeweth, and a few of their captains. Only giving the magistrate a cursory nod, they took over the table and spread their maps and parchment to lay their plans.

"Well, this is an odd lot," Gradien observed, sidling up to the girl. "You were serious about getting right to work." He had intended to rain death upon them as soon as they arrived, but their number and mode of transportation had him intrigued, and the fact she did appear in charge even more so.

"We have less than a day to prepare, but we will work through the night to make it happen," she replied, her tone not so hostile. "Thank you for the use of your city. You have those who will join the fight?"

Studying her, his dark brown eyes softened. "I don't have an army if that's what you mean. Our guards are little more than mercenaries. Still, they have weapons and may be of some use to you."

"Then gather them," she agreed, offering her first real smile. "If the elf army is as massive as the one we defeated over the dwarf mountains, we are going to need every sword we can get."

THIRTY-ONE

In Our Defense

"SEND THE CRIERS," Gradien announced. Stomping through the entrance to an adjacent building where the court had really assembled, he met his head enforcer with a scowl. "We have a change in plans. We need to gather all of your men and have them bring their arms."

"You can't seriously be giving in to their demands," Corvack grunted, indicating the group within their trap. "We have them, Gray. Why not mow them down as planned and get on with our lives?"

"What, and hope the elves allow us to continue business as usual while the rest of Eriden burns?" the leader of their township growled. "We need every able-bodied man we can get to help with the defense," he continued giving orders.

"I won't allow it," one of the court members disagreed. "You've gone soft in the head, old man."

Turning, Gradien blasted him with a wave of power, knocking him flat against a wall and pinning him in place. "And you forget who you're talking to. I'm a wizard first and foremost, and I didn't get this post for my brains. I'm stronger than any of you lot, and I say when we stand and fight."

The wizard he held gasped for air, his feet not quite reaching the floor as he kicked them haphazardly. His tan skin taking on a bright red hue, the others backed away.

"I'll send the alarm," a third in their party agreed, turning to get out of there.

"Be sure that you do. Have them meet in the plaza," their magistrate decreed. "We will also need lamps for our guests, as we will work through the night to prepare," he addressed his aide.

"Right away, sir," a small servant agreed with a bow, scurrying away to secure them.

Dropping his rival, Gradien glared at the crumpled man who knelt on the ground and gulped for air. "You stand against me again and a pyre will burn in your honor," he warned.

"Yes, sir," he grunted, rubbing at his throat and chest. "I'll see that the blacksmith supplies all the weapons that he can."

"Good," the magistrate smiled. "I will rejoin the newcomers and help with the plans. I know this city like the back of my hand. If their numbers are great, we will be in for one hell of a fight, but we will give them a few surprises if we're able."

"How do you know they speak the truth?" Corvack pushed, blocking his exit. "She's just a girl."

"How many troops did they bring?" Gray asked calmly.

"Nearly a thousand from what I can tell," his scout spoke up. "They materialized outside the front gate in two waves. That's it – two."

Glaring at the court members to enlist their support, Gradien sneered, "So they are either all gifted with magical ability or someone can move a great deal over quite a large distance, a feat beyond any of us I am certain." Turning to his enforcer, he spat, "What other proof do you need?"

"They could be here to plunder the city," a hidden member offered, not caring to be recognized and punished.

"Pfft," Gradien spewed. "We are wasting time. They wouldn't go to all this trouble to steal from us. The city will fall if we don't help and still may even if we do. Follow my orders and prepare for our defense," he barked as he dodged the other man and continued on his way.

Stomping down the corridor, he rejoined the new arrivals, announcing in his robust voice, "We have unleashed the criers. They will sweep the streets in search of all who will join the fight. I have also arranged for lamps for you to work by, assuming this will be a sleepless night."

"As if any of us could," Amicia mumbled, earning a few chuckles from her friends.

Nodding, the town's leader noted their camaraderie, impressed with how easily they worked together. Going over their markings on the map, Gray continued, "Might I suggest we also barricade the gate. It would buy us at least a little time."

"Aye," the Mate agreed, tapping the crude drawing of the city. "We already have a group of dwarves working on the task. Hayt is a skilled engineer; he will know of its construction."

"Zaendra has transported him to Rhong, where they are gathering Firen's team, along with supplies to complete the task," Amicia commented. "Beginning construction with the rising sun, they hope it will be completed before the elves arrive."

"Then what else shall we need?" the magistrate asked, still studying their sketches and plans.

"Weapons," Animir interjected with a snap of his fingers. "Perhaps the armories have not been completely drained," he offered.

"Aren't you an elf?" Gradien observed in surprise. Noting him for the first time, he felt certain he had not come in with the others.

"Yes, but not loyal to Cilithrand," he countered with a shake of his head. Turning to Ami, Animir pushed, "I'll go and have a look. Whatever we find will be more than we have."

"That would be awfully risky," Amicia pointed out, "going back to Jerranyth."

"I won't be long," he assured, turning to Rey. "Come help with the supply?"

"No doubt," Rey chuckled, giving Ami a quick peck on the cheek before reaching for his arm. "We won't be long," he announced before they disappeared.

"My how talented you all are," the wizard breathed. "I've got my share of magic, but the great city of Jerranyth is far beyond my reach."

"The ossci gave us insight, to be sure," Meena informed him curtly, glaring at her adversary with thinly veiled hatred in her eyes.

"Wan," he growled in return. "Your blood should have been spilled long ago."

"Ah, but it wasn't. Justice served now that I should have a hand in the preservation of our people," she hissed, raising her chin.

Grinning at his wife's posturing, Piers felt confident she could take the man before him in a fair fight, and perhaps even a dirty one. "You should leave her be, Gradien. My bride is a skilled warrior, and we really don't have time at the moment to test your metal against hers."

"Agreed," Gray laughed, the rumble anything but amused. "But when there is time, I shall see her strength to be certain."

Rolling her eyes, Amicia pointed at the map and suggested, "We want to line the walls, and we have crews constructing scaffolding to support them, but I fear our men will be easy targets. If you can gather some stones, I will enchant as many as I am able."

"Enchant them," the magistrate grunted. "You people are full of surprises. What does an enchanted stone do?"

Unable to resist a demonstration, "Hit me," Piers offered, jutting out his chin.

Rolling a laugh, the other man wasn't born yesterday. Still, he took the baited offer and made the swing, the arch of blue light knocking him to the ground as his arm burned. "Holy Eriden, is that the charm? A shield of some kind," he groaned, flopping over and getting to his feet.

"Aye," the Mate grinned, showing him the small, smooth stone. "Amicia is quite talented with enchantments. Bring her stones that she may create as many as she can for our men who will defend the walls."

Sending a squire, the rocks were gathered in no time, and she began working on them in haste. She had only completed a few when Reynard and Animir returned from their quest to Lady Cilithrand's lockers.

Dropping a crate in their midst, Animir grinned, "They require assembly, but we have the means for many arrows."

"I'll get my people to work on them," Gradien informed him, opening and closing his hand with a scowl.

"What happened to you?" Rey wondered aloud.

"He tested the shield," Piers chuckled.

Laughing with him, Animir and Rey made a few more trips. Using a golden orb, they spent the rest of the night locating other armories in the elf mountains that had not been emptied completely and soon had a small cache of spears, bows, and more arrows to add to their stockpile.

Observing the natural light filtering in over head as they were given a meager breakfast, Amicia gasped, "The night is gone already."

"Aye," the Mate agreed, "but we accomplished much in the darkness," helping himself to one of the biscuits. "What else is on our list that hasn't been done or at least planned?"

"The weapons have been well stocked," Amicia observed between bites. "Excellent work on the part of Animir and Rey. They will need to be distributed, and I'd really like a count on our muscle."

"I'll see to the distribution and get a count on our numbers," Gradien volunteered. "You should get some rest. Everything we can do at this moment is under way, and you will need a clear head when the battle begins."

"I have to agree," Piers grunted, digging at his tired eyes. "We hardly napped yesterday when we finished on the mountain, and now we prepare to defend again."

Wafting to his aide, Gray directed, "See them to my lower suite. It will be cooler there so they can rest."

Following the smaller man, their entire party, less the dragons, made their way into a nearby building, but instead of climbing, the stairs descended into a cellar.

"Oh, this is nice," Amicia breathed, the difference in temperature quite noticeable. The sand walls held back by invisible restraints, the ceiling barely cleared Animir's head, as the tallest in their group. Around the walls, a selection of couches offered a comfortable place to sleep if they were able. Claiming one and a small square pillow, she waited until their escort had gone before she observed, "Do you think we are safe to slumber?"

"I'm sure if they intended to kill us, they would have already," Rey retorted, taking a blanket and the floor.

"You know, we could have gone back to camp for that matter," Zaendra observed, testing the cushions on one of the sofas.

"But then we would not be here if something happened and we were needed," her husband pointed out, also stretching out onto a section of the earth beneath them.

"We'll only get a few hours," Piers observed. "Let's get quiet."

Flat on the cushions, Ami stared at the ceiling above, her mind still listing things they needed to do and worrying if they would happen. When she awoke, she wasn't even sure she had been asleep. Lifting her head, she looked around at the others, their breaths and snores comforting her with their familiarity.

Rolling over to stand, she picked her way through to silently climb the stairs and return to their plotting. Finding her way on her own easier than she thought, she arrived at the courtyard formed by the four buildings and let herself in.

"Have I missed much?" she asked, looking up to see the sun almost directly overhead. "Oh, I have been below a while."

"Yes. I take it you slept," Gradien grinned. "A crier has reported we have just over a thousand gathered at the plaza," he informed her, rubbing at the sweat on his bald head with a swatch of cloth. "We near midday. How soon before our enemies arrive?"

Pouring herself a glass of water, she replied, "I can find out." Enjoying the drink, she called to the dragon. *"Lamwen."*

"Yes, my queen," he replied.

"How close are they now?"

"I hold my distance, but they are within view of the city walls, I am certain," he replied. At the height he circled, he believed the elves were unaware they were being monitored. *"Yes, the battle will come well before the sun sets if they continue this pace."*

"I fear the fight will arrive before dark," she said aloud. "Lamwen says they are within sight of the city. I will infuse more stones while we wait," she suggested, resuming her work.

"Do not spend long," Gray advised. "We will put everyone into their places soon enough."

Working until the others joined her, Amicia felt relieved at the freshness of their faces. "Well, at least you look somewhat rested," she observed with a smile.

"I noticed you were gone," Rey grumbled, suppressing a yawn.

"I've had more sleep than you the last few days. And besides, I still had work to do," she explained, indicating her collection of trinkets. "They are not enough for all, but some will have protection. Distribute the stones and instruct them how to use them," she commanded, pointing at the finished pile with an open palm.

"Yes, my lady," Animir agreed as he and Rey gathered the enchanted rocks.

"I guess we are as ready as we're going to be," Piers grumbled, noting their list had been completed while they slept. "I must say, I'm surprised our friend Gradien came through for us."

"I'm sure it was a matter of self-preservation," Meena pointed out.

"Whatever the motivation, I'll take it," Amicia countered. "But I believe we have done all we can to prepare."

"Not all," the wan disagreed. "Have you contacted the glen and informed them of our plight?"

"The glen," Ami breathed. "Of course. Perhaps a few more warriors can be gleaned."

Reaching into the abyss, she searched for her ally and friend. *"Uscan."*

"Princess," he replied in kind.

"How is the battle for Esterbrook?"

"We have pushed them back but have yet to eliminate them completely," he informed her evenly.

"Can you hold them without the aid of the dragons?"

"I believe we can at least do as much. Why?"

"We are gathered at Whitefair, and the elves march against us. If the dragons can mount an attack from the south..."

"Say no more. I will see they are dispatched at once."

"Thank you, Uscan."

"Certainly, my queen."

Blinking a few times, Amicia grinned, "The dragons will be here as soon as they can."

"And the glen?" Zaendra asked, having returned to provide her report on the progress of the dwarf engineers.

"Holding," Amicia assured with a nod. "How is the gate?"

"It will be finished," her smaller friend agreed. "As for the scaffolding, it will be in place as well."

"Then we line the walls and distribute the arms," Amicia stated with a firm jaw, "and then we wait."

THIRTY-TWO

Clash of Kings

"WILL THEY GET HERE IN TIME?" Rey asked gravely, standing with the others atop the tallest building in Whitefair. From their vantage point, they had watched the dark mass on the southern horizon growing as the sun hung in the western sky.

"I hope so," Ami whispered quietly.

The dragons had not arrived yet, but the elves were clear in their approach. When they reached the walls, the sea of soldiers broke upon them like waves crashing to the shore. Swarming around the installation, they dug in and hid between the rocks on the east side, picking off those who defended the walls when they could. Setting up larger weapons, their assault on the sandstone barriers would likely prevail.

From inside the city, the archers rained arrows down upon them to thin their numbers, but the difference would be of little consequence. Those who had shields were protected from the elf assault, but many did not, and they were killed or wounded by the flying arrows of the elves outside.

"It already isn't going well," Piers observed quietly, joining the couple as they observed the struggle.

"Dragon's fire!" Amicia screamed, pointing into the distance.

Flying in fast and low, six dragon forms blasted the backside of the elves with hot flame, Jarrowan in the lead. Turning on their massive catapults, the dragons would do their best to even the fight.

The sight of the reinforcements a jolt of hope, a cheer went up along the wall. Grinning up at the Mate, the girl cajoled, "We haven't lost yet. Continue the battle, and we will break them if we can."

"My lady," Yimath interrupted, she and the other two ossci appearing at her side.

"My friends," Amicia breathed, kneeling to speak with them. "I did not realize you were still here! You should be safe within the marshes before the sunset."

"We've been aiding in the transport of soldiers and supplies, but at last our time is spent," the small blonde replied, indicating the sinking sun with an open palm. "We were happy to help in all that we could."

"Yes, you must return to Falconmarsh before the day's end," Amicia agreed. "Thank you for all you have done in our honor."

"You are quite welcome, my queen," the gnome smiled, offering a small bow before the three ossci vanished.

Her mood quickly turned, Ami blinked back tears as she stood, her eyes sweeping the horizon as she fought the sorrow. The air felt cooler around her, but she surmised it was only an illusion created by the loss of her friends. "I wish I knew why they won't really help," she sighed.

"It's not in their nature to fight," Gradien observed, indicating a weak spot in the wall. "The elves are tearing us down, destroying our defenses. The dragon's fire doesn't seem to be damaging their cannons. They will be inside before the light is gone."

"Not damaging their cannons," Piers repeated, flicking his wrist to indicate them in the distance. Watching as a massive stone was cranked into place and hurled at the wall, he postulated, "Do you think they have discovered your anti-fire spell?"

"It's possible," Amicia shrugged. "Who knows, it could have originally belonged to them, and the ossci simply recorded it. Either way, we keep fighting until the last elf is dead, or we are," the girl countered, clenching her fists and willing them to victory.

Watching Ziradon and Lamwen join the other dragons in their runs at the enemy, she noted they were held at bay with powerful crossbows that flung massive arrows at them. "Do you suppose it was the elves who armed the satyrs?"

Shaking his head, the Mate sighed, "I don't know. Those weapons are similar, but if they did, why are they now fighting?"

"A double cross, maybe?" Rey joined in. "That would be pretty funny, actually. Cilithrand thought she was buying their loyalty by arming them, but in the end, they are using the weapons against them."

"Hey, guys," Gradien interrupted their discussion, "we are going to need a new plan, and we need it quick."

"What's going on?" Amicia asked. "So far our defenses are holding, despite our losses."

"Not anymore," he pointed. "They've breached the western wall. They'll be coming through that gap any time."

"Not if we push out through it first," the girl challenged.

"What, and fight them out on the sand?" Piers clipped. "There's daring and then there's crazy, love."

"If they get inside the city, can we pick them off as they enter?" Hayt suggested. "I mean, if they are ever going to take the city, eventually they have to come in."

Rubbing his hand roughly over his beard, Piers groaned, "We are heavily outnumbered. If we let them start pushing in, they will eventually overrun us."

"Then let's push out," Gray agreed. "Go down and lead the battle. Ami and I will stay up here and continue the watch on all sides, and she can reach out to you if we need to adjust."

"Yes, or I'll send Lamwen and Ziradon," she agreed. "I can reach them as well."

"All right," the Mate agreed reluctantly, glancing at his wife. "Who will join me?" he asked, as if he were headed to the pub for a pint.

"Aye," Rey and Animir agreed simultaneously, Hayt and Zaendra close behind.

"You know I'm no good hiding up here," Meena agreed. Holding out her arm, she waited for all their hands to join in the center before she transported them all to rally their forces.

"Wow," Gradien muttered. "Should I be glad we didn't have time to fight earlier?"

"I would be," Ami whispered, tears on her face. "I have this terrible fear they won't all be coming back."

"You can't think that way," he countered, dropping his hand on her shoulder and giving her a squeeze.

Wincing at the grip, she pulled herself free, reluctant to explain her recent injury. "Let's just keep a look out," she said instead, pulling away and pacing the edge of the walls.

Back on the east side, the dragons continued their heckling, but it was a battle of attrition. Just when they thought they had made some headway, one of them made a clean shot, taking one of the dragons down. Watching it fall to the ground, Amicia screamed, thinking of the night they had taken Lamwen in the same manner that night in the glen.

Tears in her eyes, she watched as the young beast was shown no mercy. Removing his head with a clean swing of a broad sword, his body fell limp, leaking his precious fluids upon the sand. "Oh God," she breathed, placing her hands over her face as her drops of sadness flowed, unable to pull herself away from the carnage. Her heart ached at the loss of her own kind, and she feared for them all, as none in the town of Whitefair would be safe from such an end.

Shifting her weight, her mother's dagger pressed against her leg. She had shoved it in her boot when she dressed after her bath the day before, thinking she might need it. Her mind drawn to it now, she clenched her teeth, wishing she could use it on the elf who had swung the blade. "They're monsters," she breathed. "Cold-hearted savages."

"They're elves," the wizard observed, as if that explanation should be clear. "They see all others as beneath them."

His words jolting her, Ami's mind slipped for a moment, and she thought of the oracle, the creator who had brought all of the inhabitants of Eriden to life. "Will it ever end?" she grieved, wishing with all her heart that their differences could be resolved. "None is greater than another, and all life is precious."

"Yeah," the magistrate coughed, as if he mocked her, "but damn few see it that way."

Turning her back as the fight continued, Amicia crept to the far side so she could watch their progress at the gap in the western wall. Animir had gathered their forces and would lead the charge through to the outside.

When they made the move, the elves fell back in surprise, not expecting to be assaulted from the front in such a manner. Reinforcements up on the walls rained down arrows, and she grinned to see those leading the charge carried her shields. "We're making headway."

"They will shift their troops soon enough," Gray countered, pointing at the southern side, close to the sealed gate. "They've already started to adapt."

"Jarrowan has them," she observed. "The dragons will curb their counter assault. The armaments may be enchanted, but their flesh still burns."

"Kaliwyn!" Ziradon's voice shattered her thoughts.

"Yes, father?"

"The dragons come, those who stand against us," he warned, beating his tired wings hard to meet Gwirwen over the open sand.

Her heart racing, Amicia leaned against the side of their rooftop, resting her hands on the raised edge as she searched. In the distance, Ziradon appeared hardly more than a speck when he collided with the other beast, rolling with him like a ball of hatred as they plummeted to the ground, landing on the fringe of the fresh battle.

Pointing them out to Gradien, she exclaimed, "More dragons come to reinforce the elves." Lightning catching her eye to the north, thick dark clouds formed on the horizon. "They bring the storm," she observed under her breath.

"They do not side with the elves," he denied. "They think we will have them beaten, but at great cost. They will swoop in and defeat our troops easily in our current state but not until we have removed the elves for them," he devised, indicating the new arrivals who circled above the city but did not engage. "A brilliant plan, actually. No matter which side prevails, they will easily come out on top."

Her eyes sweeping the sand, she shook her head in disgust. Picking out her friends among those on the ground, they each had their hands full with the fight swirling around them.

"We are so close to victory," she insisted.

"And yet we are so far," he growled.

"Father," she reached, unable to see him clearly at the distance where they had fallen.

The mass of bodies pushing out had reached them, engulfing the waring beasts with writhing arms, spears, and swords. Pacing side to side, Amicia watched the carnage all around them. To the north and south, the walls held, but those along the rim traded arrows with those upon the ground endlessly.

To the east, another of their dragons had been slaughtered. "Dear God," she wept, broken at the sight of the magnificent beast slain in such a fashion.

Pulling out her orb, she searched, locating Ziradon as he squared off with Gwirwen. Tears in her eyes, she sobbed, "They're out there. We have to help him." She couldn't contemplate seeing his blood staining the sand. "I must go to him. He cannot be lost!"

Pulling her arm so he could see, the magistrate growled, "You cannot help him, unless your wings are handy. Gwirwen would crush you in your current state."

"I have my shield," she postulated. "And we augmented the weapons to take on the dragon's scales."

"Save them," he warned. "Ziradon is a great warrior. Give him your faith, as we will need your trickery when the rest of Gwirwen's forces descend upon us," he added, indicating those who still circled above.

Gaping up at them, the wind caught her hair, whipping it around her face as she squinted against the glare. Feeling helpless, she watched as more of the elves pushed in at the gaping hole in their divider. *"Lamwen, they are breaching the western wall."*

Hearing her call, the dragon did not reply and instead made a pass over the section, dotting it with flame. Turning away, he did not repeat the pass, opting instead to follow the trail and setting fire to their reinforcements, further preventing them from crossing.

"Thank you, and well done," she praised, returning her attention to her orb and the fight across the sand.

The dragons tearing at each other, Ziradon howled, blasting fire at his enemy. Those who had fought near them fell away, their heat more than they could stand.

The earth around them emptied, they leapt and rolled, flying in short spirts to gain momentum before slamming into each other with their full force.

"You will not win this day," Ziradon challenged.

"I have already won," Gwirwen sneered. "The council is purged of those who opposed me. Once your forces have removed the elves, I will claim the cause as mine and restore order to the land."

"Kaliwyn will never allow it!"

"Kaliwyn will be dead," the beast threatened, leaping at the old dragon and clenching onto his throat with razor sharp fangs.

"Father," Amicia cried, still watching the battle from afar. In the distance, the horizon rolled as the dark clouds gathered, hiding the sun before it had completely set. If she were in her dragon form, she could join him, but time was against her, leaving her helpless. *"Fight, my lord,"* she urged.

Her words spoke to his heart, and Ziradon gained strength from their utterance. Thrashing, he wrenched himself free, the blood trickling down his chest as he slashed at his enemy with his talons.

Torn wings flapping in the growing wind, Gwirwen dove at his belly, searching for softer scales he could penetrate. Finding his mark, he scoured the flesh underneath as he ripped the protective layer away.

"I can't hold this much longer," Ziradon confessed, his eyes fixed on the dark layer of clouds that blackened the sky.

His words reaching her across the sands, Ami covered her mouth with a trembling palm. The orb displaying the carnage, she knew his end was near. *"Please don't leave me, father,"* she begged. Her face wet with tears picked up the splatter of rain, and she knew the storm had reached them.

"Kaliwyn," he called to her with his last breath, *"I am so proud of you."*

"No!" she screamed, transpositioning to his side, but it was too late. The massive dragon's eyes had closed forever. Spreading her arms, she pressed against him, lying against his still form. The roughness of his scales cutting at her flesh, the night she had been transformed into a mortal penetrated her thoughts as brief flashes of memory. *Father,* she sobbed as she wept loudly.

Her face pressed against his body, she seemed unaware as the other dragon hobbled around his prize. "Kaliwyn," Gwirwen sneered, wishing her to look at him when he scorched her.

Lifting her head to glare at him, she panted through clenched teeth. The wind rising, it swirled around them, hot and cold in turns as it drove the smattering of rain against them, it not yet falling in full force. Her hair blown back and forth, her face flushed with rage. "How dare you?" she snarled, unable to form a coherent insult.

Not waiting for her reprisal, the Supreme Dragon dropped his jaw and bathed her in flame. The hot blast pouring over her, Amicia leaned into the fire and held it off with her shield. Splashing against the protective force, the fire spilled to the sides and vaporized scattered drops of water with loud hisses.

Behind her, the thunderheads reached into the sky, blackening the sun completely as white streaks of death crashed to the ground. The deluge moving across the sand, it approached as the sound of horse hooves drumming against the earth.

Rage in her heart, Amicia lashed out, catching one of the bolts in her magical grasp and hurling it at her enemy. Stunned by the crack of thunder, Gwirwen ended his fiery assault, tumbling over the sand as he rolled away from her.

Ami's fingers crooked, she used them to call forth the power. Lamwen had told her once that the storm was their strength, and she turned it against Gwirwen with all that she had, her jaw clenched and eyes bulged with primal rage.

The flashes bright, the air crackled with the electric currents. Hitting him with bolt after bolt, the thunder rolled across the desert sands, shaking the earth with its fierce retribution as the heavens opened and the rain poured down upon them.

Snarling at her, the Supreme Dragon flung himself against the wind, blowing fire that would never reach her, carried away by the gusts. Snorting smoke, he pushed, knowing he could have her if only he could reach her small frail form. But her shield was strong, and he had little chance of getting past it.

Thunder crashed as the sparks flew. Almost to her, he swung his massive tail; victory was his. An instant later, it collided with a solid, immovable force as blue light flashed, hurling him across the sand once more.

Lying beneath the pouring rain, Gwirwen panted, huffing against the weight on his chest. On his side, he could see the small, brown boots as they walked straight up to him, no hesitation in their step. "You have not won," he growled. "I have destroyed your father, and you will never wear his crown."

"Be silent, traitor," she commanded. Kneeling beside him, she pulled Arely's dagger from her boot and plunged it into his neck, draining the last of his blood unto the cold, wet sand.

THIRTY-THREE

The Fallen

THE MORNING CAME with an eerie calm over the sands.

Bodies lay everywhere.

Kneeling beside that of her father, Amicia's loose hairs blew carelessly in the sporadic rogue gusts of wind. Her hand upon his massive head, she had cried until there were no more tears left within her eyes.

To the west, the ruins of Whitefair stood in the light of dawn. The great city had stood, but hardly so. Once Gwirwen had drawn his last breath, she had unleashed the storm upon them all.

Lightning had flashed, and thunder rolled as the power of her will streaked through the air. The elves had never stood a chance, but none were victors on that dark day.

The elf forces that remained gathered out away from the city to measure their strength. Cilithrand had demanded they push the fight, but it was hopeless to think they could push further; they were beaten, and they knew it.

Unwilling to let her slither back into her hiding place, Amicia had called to Animir, whispering to him what must be done. Staring at her with wide eyes, he had questioned the action, for once it had been carried out, it could not be undone.

"Yes," she had told him. "I respect all life, and because I do, hers must be forfeit. Be quick and return here to me when it is finished. We will present our prize for all to see, and the war will be ended upon my command."

Seeing the return of her faithful elf, servant and friend, Amicia left her father's body and marched slowly towards what remained of the town. Her arms hanging limply at her sides, her would-be mother's blade glistened in the light. Gripping the handle, as if it were her only grasp on the world, she squeezed it tightly, then lessened the hold to toy with the feel of the metal.

"No more killing," she announced loudly as she walked among the corpses. A few of the elves and dwarves were combing the battleground, searching for their fallen comrades. "It stops here," she added, her voice weak but her intent unshakable.

Coming to Yaodus, she paused, placing her hand on his shoulder. Kneeling over the body of his eldest, the great troll wept openly. "My son is no more."

"He will be remembered," Amicia replied with a squeeze of his pale blue flesh. "They all will be."

Running out to meet her, Rey's joy at her survival could not be contained. Falling against her, he hugged her tightly as he also wept. "I thought I had lost you," he whispered into her blond puffs of hair.

Her arms heavy, she forced them up to wrap him as well. "No, my love. I have been spared." Physically spared. But the pain and loss within her would take many years to heal, if those wounds ever did. Running her fingers over the scar on her shoulder, she thought again of how easily some injuries could be mended, while others would take a lifetime to accept.

Landing a few feet away, Lamwen announced, "The elves are gathered to the south, but scarcely a few hundred remain. I dare say the battle is won."

"The war is won," Amicia countered, extricating herself from her husband's grasp. "I must address all those that remain. Gather at the front, where the gate stood. Send for the elves and ask them to join us."

Doing as instructed, the call was made. Many who had lived in Whitefair remained, and they gathered on the inside of the demolished barrier. Those who had clashed in battle took to the opening and the sand beyond.

Standing on the tallest portion, a tower of rock that still stood, Amicia called in a shaky voice, "The war… is over. The dragons who rose against my father have been defeated, and the elf who used their plot for her own gain has also been brought down."

She raised her hand to indicate what remained of the elf troops. Before them, Animir appeared, having accomplished his final task in the darkness.

In his left hand, he held the head of Lady Cilithrand, and his bloodied sword remained clasped in the other. "Your wish is carried, my queen," he called to her loudly, offering her the severed member.

"Bury her head in the sand," Amicia commanded. "Claim her crown for your own. I discharge your banishment from Jerranyth and bid you lead the elves of Eriden in my name."

"I will accept the throne of my people as you command, my queen," Animir replied loudly, dropping Cilithrand's remains at his feet. It landed with a thud, her face up and glaring at the clear blue sky. Her eyes still open, as she had stared at him when he swung his blade and landed his final blow, tears touched his eyes. He had shared no love for their fallen leader, but he had respected her position within his people. Raising his sword straight into the air, he shouted, "All hail to the Dragoness! All hail to Kaliwyn!"

"All hail Kaliwyn!" his forces shouted back. If they were not eager to have him as their new king, they were at least willing to follow the command of their Supreme Dragoness.

Tears in Rey's eyes, he applauded, smacking his hands together loudly along with the others as they celebrated the announcement. "All hail the dragoness," he whispered, his heart torn with fear.

Amicia had said her goodbyes to him before the battle, when he cared for her at the camp. He wanted so desperately to hold her by his side, but with their victory, he had most assuredly lost the thing that mattered most in his eyes. Wiping at the drops of sadness, he observed the rest of the group that stood near, each of them dealing with their victory in his or her own way.

Standing next to his great nephew, Baeweth threw his arm across his shoulder and spoke loudly in his ear, "The elves have made amends. Return home with your bride to your place beneath the mountain."

Grinning, Hayt agreed, "On one condition, uncle. You will never ask me to wear your crown."

"I will find another heir," Baeweth agreed. "It will serve me well to simply have you within our halls."

Returning their attention to the new queen of Eriden, Hayt dabbed at the moisture in his eyes. "Hear, hear!" he shouted as the celebration over Animir's appointment finally died away.

"As for the sirens, they will be returned to their lagoon at Riran, and the glen shall be restored," Amicia continued. "The trolls will hold a place of honor, for their fallen were as dear as any other within our kingdom."

His heart heavy, Yaodus bowed his head towards her, placing his hand over his chest to swear his allegiance to her once more. Their losses had been heavy, but their people remained strong, and they would persevere in their home inside the Crimson Caves.

Pivoting, Ami's mind raced. She knew they wanted her to accept the crown and to proclaim her place as the Supreme Dragoness. The words tight in her throat, she swallowed, pushing at the lump that refused to go down. "Lamwen," she croaked, calling him to her side.

Walking over the rubble, he worked his way towards her, sitting back on his haunches so that his head sat within her reach. Her hand trembling, she rested her palm against his snout, as she had done the first time she touched him. "You are a beautiful creature and the truest of friends," she whispered.

"Yes, my queen," he agreed, his dragon tears large drops as they dripped upon the broken stones.

"Lamwen, I here by proclaim you the King of Adiarwen and the Supreme Dragon of Eriden," she announced loudly.

A rolling gasp echoed across the masses, as the weight of her words pressed upon them.

"My lady," Animir huffed, taking a single step towards her. The lump where he had placed Cilithrand's remains covered behind him, he had not expected this turn of events any more than his friends had.

His hand in Meena's, she held him in place when the Mate almost moved towards her. "Be still," she hissed, knowing he should not interfere.

"Hear me," Amicia called more loudly. "I have chosen this dragon with no shortness of consideration. He is a good and faithful servant. He has, dedicated his life to the cause and the kingdom. He will wear the crown with pride, his heart understanding the role he must play. He will act in my stead and lead us, as it should be."

The applause slow, it started as a few random claps but built into a crescendo of approval as all who were gathered eventually gave in to the sanctity of her bequest. Smiling into her dearest friend's features, she spread her arms and hugged his neck, inhaling his scent as he pushed against her.

"I will always love you, Lamwen. Lead our people as you know is right and have faith in the future that lies before us," she instructed him as the applause sounded around them.

Hearing her words, the dragon growled his agreement. Her speech ended, the search for survivors resumed, and those who had fallen would be gathered for their funeral pyres. The day had been hard fought and the victory bittersweet. In his heart, Lamwen knew he would endeavor to carry out her wishes, his heart filled with joy at the conviction her promise meant their separation would only be for a while, and one day she would return to the rocks of Adiarwen to be his mate.

THIRTY-FOUR

Tears for Tomorrow

LEAVING HER PODIUM, Amicia walked towards Reynard, holding a smile she did not feel. When he stood before her, she offered him her hand. "Walk with me?"

Taking the appendage, he studied it for a moment, the stiffness of her frame causing the hairs on the back of his neck to prickle. "Of course, my lady," he teased, his mirth not reaching his eyes. Opening his free hand in the direction of her fallen kin, they ambled towards the pyre that the wizards had been constructing.

When they arrived at the massive structure, the old brown dragon lay upon it, his body cleansed by the rain his daughter had poured over him in her rage. The slats set, Gradien offered her the torch, that she might light the fire.

"I did not know your father long," the magistrate offered, "but if his daughter is any indication, he was a fine king."

"Indeed, he was," she agreed, accepting the flame. Inhaling deeply, she paused, not ready to set the blaze.

"We'll allow you to say goodbye in private," the wizard informed her, calling to his men to move on to the next.

"You will provide a proper burial for all of them?" the girl asked, turning to stare at his feet as he moved away from her.

"Only if it pleases you," he called back.

"It pleases me," she agreed with a small smile. "Gwirwen was my father's friend before he betrayed him. I hope they have found their peace in their passing."

Nodding, Gradien twirled his hand in the air above his head, calling the others to follow and complete the task.

"It is very gracious of you to be so kind with the dragon who overthrew your kin," Rey observed. "His actions have cost us dearly."

"I have chosen to forgive him. Holding my rage would only add to my suffering," she replied. Squeezing his hand, she released him, stepping forward to place the torch against the lumber.

Catching fire, the flames spread quickly, and Ziradon's body became engulfed in the conflagration. Watching the dancing light, Amicia sighed. "Where will you go?" she asked quietly.

Caught off guard, Rey gasped, "I thought we would finally find that place where we belonged and settle down."

"Oh, Rey," she whispered. "I have much left to do." Cutting her eyes over at him, she smiled enticingly. "Remember when we made a plan and I would wait for you to come to me?"

"Aye," he replied warily, "so long ago."

"Yes, many moons have passed. You spoke once of returning to your parents' farm. I think that you should," she offered.

"Domania?" he gasped. "Firstly, it's part of the rim, so you know –"

"I know it is part of the rim of mortals," she laughed, catching her hair and pulling it out of her face. "I will see that you are transpositioned there. And I will further promise no more dragons will burn your crops and scorch your cattle."

Studying her in the warmth of her father's pyre, sadness filled his eyes. "Will I wait for you to join me?"

Swallowing, she held the grin. "My dearest Rey, I cannot promise we have any days left between us." Turning to face him squarely, she added, "But in my heart, I wish that it were so."

"Then I will return to the farm of my youth, making milk and cheese and awaiting your arrival," he agreed, sweeping her into his arms for a final hug.

Unable to hold back the tears, he cried against her. "I wish you could promise my wait would not be long."

"I will be there with you, always, so long as you carry me in your heart," she replied.

Sighing, he could only agree, as he had always agreed with the wishes of Amicia Spicer. But deep in his heart, there was room for little more than the girl in his arms, and that tiniest of things was fear – fear she would return to her dragon form and spend her days with Lamwen, instead.

THIRTY-FIVE

Dragon's Heart

SAUNTERING up to Lamwen's massive form, Amicia grinned as he barked orders. They would have the walls of the city cleared and construction under way in no time.

"You will change the heart of these people, my love," she cooed.

"It is you who have changed their hearts, my queen," he teased, sitting back, then lying on the sand beside her. "Shall I gather the others that we may finally call forth your dragon form?"

"Not yet," she replied, shaking her head as her hand traced the scars on his jaw. "My bravest admirer," she sighed.

"I am more than that," he growled playfully. "A dragon's heart beats within your chest. My only desire is to see her freed."

"In time," Amicia agreed, dropping the touch and turning to amble out away from the others.

Rising, the new king followed, not dissuaded by her refusal. "There will be plenty of time," he agreed. "Will Rey be returning to the beach at New Abolia with Meena and the Mate?" he asked, changing the subject. "The trolls have offered to help them rebuild the cabin, and they are going to place Baldwin's remains there in the forest, erecting his stone above them."

"It will be good to have them back where they belong," she agreed, speaking of the older couple. "Rey will be returning to his people and his family across the sea."

"My queen," Lamwen gasped, "you wish to return him to the rim?"

"Yes," she agreed, stealing a glance at him after his shocked reply. "I am removing the barrier between Eriden and the rest of our world. It is time that the humans were returned to the magic of our kingdom."

"You are the destroyer," he whispered, swallowing and pausing his step to glare at her.

Her gaze narrowed, she agreed, "As it should be. None in our world hold a position one above another. It will take time for us to adjust, but we will manage. An ancient wrong will be set right beneath your reign."

Catching her words, he blinked rapidly. "But I reign in your stead. You will join me and take your place at my side."

"Oh, Lamwen," she sighed, reaching for the rough feel of him once more. "You have my undying love and deepest devotion. I promise I will come to you when I am able."

Turning, she walked a few steps before she disappeared, leaving him with the belief she had chosen the mortal over him in the end.

THIRTY-SIX

Sevoassi's Secret

MATERIALIZING next to their camp in the marsh, Amicia looked around anxiously. She knew the gnomes were there, watching from the shadows. They were always there, always watching, even if she had not seen.

Sinking to her knees, she crawled inside the leaning shelter, her hands roving over the blanket. Locating a strap, she pulled it, freeing her bag from beneath the jumble of their meager belongings. Studying the worn material, her mind drifted, and she recalled the afternoon of Arely's funeral. *The day I packed this with all that I owned and set out on the grandest of adventures.*

The journey had been long, and seldom easy. Her discoveries had been immense, and yet new ones still lay before her; she felt certain of it. Working the pack open, she shoved her hand in, her fingers wriggling as she searched the contents. Pulling out her brush and mirror, a brief smile crossed her lips at all they had meant to her.

Dropping them on the blanket, she resumed her fondling, until they brushed against a smooth round surface. Clasping it gently, as if it were easily cracked beneath her hold, she withdrew her arm from the pouch.

Opening her hand, the red orb fell against her flesh. Shimmering in the bright light, it awaited her command to open and reveal its secrets to her. Closing the digits around it, she pulled the globe to her chest, wrapping it with her other hand as well. "I'm ready," she panted, closing her eyes and enjoying the feel of the magic that enveloped her.

Getting to her feet, she left the rest of her belongings, taking only the orb and nothing more. Moving away from the structures, she closed her eyes and instantly transported to a small cottage beneath a tree in the northern woods.

Her smile broad, she rested her hand against the rough bark. "Sevoassi?" she called loudly, turning her gaze into the leaves above her as she awaited his reply.

Hearing nothing, the grin faded, and she turned her back on the tree. Kneeling, she shoved her feet into the opening and climbed down into the darker room below. The air cooler, she shoved the orb in her pocket and rubbed her hands together briskly.

"Winter is coming to the north," she giggled, surprised at how quickly the summer had been and gone. "With all the running and fighting, we hardly noticed," she sighed to herself.

Tossing a few logs into the hearth, she located the flint and set the blaze. Smiling at the flames as they licked at her, she breathed deeply, exhaling the breaths to calm her.

"Sevoassi!" she tried again, standing to have a look around the home that had been his. "I know you're here," she added. "You might as well come out. I'm going to look inside the orb."

Silence the only reply, she stamped her foot in mild disgust. Her eyes roving again, she pondered, "Maybe he wants to wait and come after I have seen."

Sitting on one of the new stools before the fire, she thought of the small siren that had once held the chair. Pulling the red orb from her pocket, she turned it gently, slowly observing the beauty of it once more. *It's ok,* she soothed. *You can look.*

"I don't have to look," she countered, sparring with herself. "I know what's in it." *The truth.*

Cilithrand had claimed as much the first time Amicia had been shown such a trinket, but this one was real. *The only one.* That's what Sevoassi had told her.

All the others could be used by any who had the gift to wield magic, but not this one. *This one requires a special magic,* she assumed. *It shows the things the other orbs cannot reach.* This was the orb of the oracle.

Taking another deep breath, she willed the orb to reveal its secrets; *Sevoassi's secrets.*

The mist swirling within it, the view cleared, exposing a group of wolves. Standing in a ring, they glared down at a creature in their midst. "Oh, no. It's me," she whispered, falling into the images as if she were there.

THIRTY-SEVEN

Lost Time

THE AIR COOL AROUND HER, Amicia lay against the hard earth. Above her, Uscan's large head occupied most of her view. "I'm so cold," she whispered.

"Rest, princess," the alpha replied, his eyes focused on the darkness of the woods.

Above, the air swished a moment before a large dark shape blocked the stars, then landed a few feet away.

"Dragon," Uscan growled.

"Tis I," Ziradon spat, catching the scent of the girl. "You do have her. Why have you prevented her return to the others?" he growled.

Not backing away, the rest of the pack held their ground, baring their teeth and their intentions.

"Leave him," Uscan commanded. "We have had enough unfortunate turns of events as of late." Shifting to reveal the girl he cradled, he added, "I'm afraid I do not have the strength to heal her. I have called for the nymphs, but I fear they will not arrive in time."

"Kaliwyn," Ziradon breathed, able to make out her injured form in the dim light. "What have you done, wolf?" he growled, the fire hot within his chest. It would only take a single blast to rectify the transgression.

"My deepest regrets, old friend," Uscan sighed. "I was moved by the lies of my kin and struck her down before the truth had been revealed."

"Oh, my sweet dragoness," the old dragon breathed, lying across the dirt and stones to rest his head beside her.

"Father?" Amicia breathed. Her eyes fluttering, the gravelly tones of his voice soothed her. "I'm hurt," she coughed.

"Bitten," he growled. "You must be strong, my love. Help is on the way."

Her shoulder ached as she lifted her hand, it falling short of her target before it dropped back against her side. Pushing his nose down, he nuzzled her flesh and inhaled the smell of her and he recalled the night she had been given the flimsy form. "It will be a shame that she should die this way," he observed, his words heavy with regret.

The pack had relaxed around them, but a stir beyond the edge of the ring roused them to their feet. Forming a line between the trio and the intruder, they growled, ready to defend their dying queen.

"Stand way," a voice called from the darkness. Taking a few paces, a massive red wolf appeared. "There is no harm," the powerful jaws bade.

Rolling over, the dragon sat up, glaring at the intruder. "You may not take her," he snarled.

"I have not come to remove her," the wolf replied.

"Will you preserve her?" Uscan asked of his relative. Not part of the pack, a wolf nonetheless, he considered the newcomer a friend.

Trotting a few steps closer, the auburn-colored beast placed his nose against her cheek. "Her end is near," he announced.

"This we know," Ziradon sighed. Using his talons, he scraped a few pieces of the dead wood around them into a pile and blasted them with a short burst of flame. Glowing, they warmed the air. "A few more hours we can buy her if we keep her warm."

"Would you wish her saved if you knew her destiny?" the new wolf whispered.

Studying each other in the dancing light, Uscan growled, "If it is our place to keep her on her path, then so be it."

Sitting, the red wolf produced a brilliant flash of light. In an instant, the shape of a man sat in his place, his bright red hair shining in the light of the fire. Raising his hands, he warmed them. "Your daughter is very brave, dragon," he offered.

"As is fitting," Ziradon replied. "She knows her place among our kind."

"Among all of Eriden," Uscan countered. "She holds no creature above another. I have seen it within her many times."

"And yet you doubted, spilling her blood in your weakness," the man pointed out, indicating her wound with an open palm.

"Do not punish her for my transgression," Uscan urged. "Please, restore what I have taken."

Leaning towards her, the stranger laid his hand across her wound. Closing his eyes, he called to her, "Amicia, mortal of the rim!"

"Yes," she breathed, fighting to open her eyes against the weight of the lids; for thin slivers of flesh, they had never been so heavy.

The stranger smiled at her efforts. More quietly, he offered her comfort, "Do not struggle. You are safe within the power of your kind. Rest, and on the morrow, you shall be healed." Giving her a squeeze, she shrieked in agony an instant before she fell silent, the darkness overtaking her.

THIRTY-EIGHT

From the Ashes

SITTING in the safety of the gnome's cottage, Ami blinked at the orb. Tears wet her cheeks, the feel of her father's love in the vision so real. Sitting up straight, she wiped at her eyes and stretched.

"Was it what you expected?" a male voice startled her, causing her to jump.

Swinging her head around the small space, she located him as he stood next to the exit. His hand resting on one of the small steps, he held it fondly.

"You remembered every detail," he grinned, his free hand wafting to indicate his previous home.

"Meena and the ossci completed the restoration," she replied gently, still drying her face. "They sheltered me here after the transformation stole my strength." Glaring up at him, the light of the fire played tricks with his features. "I know you, but you are not who I expected," she confessed. Shaking the orb, she added, "You healed me and left the food and water for me to regain my strength, but why are you here?"

Ambling forward, his movements unrushed, he stopped next the second stool. His clear green eyes sweeping over her, they met her gaze. "You are looking for the gnome," he agreed, finally taking a seat next to her.

"Yes," she breathed. "Sevoassi."

"I am Sevoassi," he replied. "I have spoken to you many times, Amicia Spicer. Brief visits as I have watched and waited for you to reach this place."

"Then you are a gnome," she agreed. "Thirac gave you away, claiming they had never heard of you."

"How did that give me away?" he replied, his features scrunched with doubt.

"Later, when I asked, he said your name was not recognized there in the marsh," she informed him, her conviction growing strength. "You were banished from them, and that is why they do not know you. They choose not to see you, or the part you play in the world."

Nodding gently, he shrugged, "I have been alone for many centuries, but once they were my people, before I grew beyond them. Some think the dragons are the most powerful of Eriden, but they are mistaken. The greatest of all our inhabitants are the gnomes. So strong are they that they have sworn never to interfere in the affairs of others in our great kingdom."

"You are the oracle," she said quietly. "The creator."

"Oh, that's a stretch," he laughed. "Surely you have seen past such fairy tales."

Her brow furrowed, she disagreed, "Many of the creatures of Eriden shared this story with me, and I hardly wish to disparage it."

"The number who believe in a lie does not increase its measure of truth. They believe because they seek to understand something that is beyond them," he explained, holding out his empty hand.

Looking down at the orb, she gathered his intent. Placing the sphere in his grasp, she grinned, "You were the boy at Arely's funeral. You gave me a rose and suggested I should travel."

"Yes," he nodded, turning the globe as it glowed, showing her the scene just as she recalled it.

"You were here again, in Heewan. As you are now, the weaver." Staring at the orb, the scene shifted, and she watched as she and Meena discussed her love for Piers in his shop. Spilling a tear, she swiped it once more. "I'm so glad he was not taken from her."

"You prevented it," Sevoassi clipped. "I thought then you would recognize your inner self, but you failed to make the connection."

"No. I wasn't ready," she swallowed. "It took me months and a trip across the continent to open my eyes. Even after I was told of Ziradon and had spread my wings as a dragon, I did not understand."

Swiping the orb, the image changed, and Kaliwyn flew across the surface. "You have not taken her form again," her companion observed.

"No," she agreed, shaking her blond locks. Turning to the fire, she held up her fingers to warm them. "I don't know that I ever will return to it."

"You are afraid you will be trapped to her forever," he surmised, his voice tender as he addressed her concerns.

"Yes. I'm not certain I wish to spend all my days as a dragon," she coughed in a half laugh. "Besides, would I not need the help and power of my friends to make the transformation?"

"You wouldn't have to use their power. You could simply use your own." His lips hinted at a smile as he leaned towards her. "You have the magic within you. You always have."

Staring at him with clear green orbs, her lips parted in awe. "That's why I'm different, isn't it? I'm not really a dragon, any more than I'm a mortal of the rim."

"You are whatever you choose to be," he whispered. "You may take any form you wish, as easily as I do."

"And how do I choose?" she sighed, more tears trailing her cheeks. "With the world laid before me..." she sobbed. "How can one life I would live be greater than another?"

"Think of the happiest you, the one that you always want to be. That is the life that is yours."

Pursing her lips, she stared at her hands, occasionally flicking the gaze to see that he studied her intently. "I have sent Rey to his home. I could join him there."

"Yes."

"And I have given Lamwen cause to rule the land and lead Eriden in new hope," she gushed between breaths.

"Yes," he agreed again with a firm nod.

"But I'm not ready to settle with either of them," she confessed. "There is so much more to see and do now that I know of my kind." Hesitating, she cut her eyes up at him and dared, "Our kind."

Opening her palm, she offered him her hand, her lip trembling as she waited. His digits warm when they touched her, he curled his fingers with hers. "Neither of us will be alone on this journey," he agreed, leaning patiently closer to her.

Licking her lips, she recalled the kisses she had shared with Lamwen and all the many more that had belonged to Rey. "I'm the destroyer," she confessed. "I am a lover of dragons and men."

"My silly girl," he replied, still waiting for her to choose. "You have ended the separation between Eriden and the Rim. The world has been made whole once again. If you insist upon the fairy tale, then the creator and the destroyer are one."

"I am happy for this, Sevoassi," she breathed. "But I am curious. Which name will you now call me?"

"The name you were born to carry. One that truly suits you, I should think. For a dragon's heart beats within your chest, Kaliwyn, my dragon of Eriden."

Her lungs tight, adrenaline coursed through her veins. "Will we be watchers, like the gnomes?"

"I doubt it would be so," he sighed. "I refused to stand on the side. It was how I earned my exile, as you have earned yours."

"Why didn't they destroy me?" she whispered curiously. "They are such powerful creatures, I'm sure that they could have."

"Yes, but it is not in their nature to interfere, my sweet dragoness," he explained. "Banishing you was sentence enough to rid you from their concern. Imagine their surprise to learn the path you chose in becoming a hatchling and living as Ziradon's heir."

"But you weren't surprised. You knew I would find my way home," she concluded. "Even hundreds of years ago, you knew."

"Oh," he gasped, as if a distant thought had suddenly been thrust into the light. "I made my prophecy at the time you were banished. Do you not remember your crime?"

"I honestly don't remember anything except small bits of my time as Kaliwyn and the life I have lived as Amicia. Any such past as you speak of is forgotten, and the rest I have had to work out from the facts as they have unfolded. But your final prophecy as the oracle was said to be from the great war and at least two hundred years old," she accused with a small pout forming on her lips. "How could it have been so long ago and yet it come true?"

"It wasn't long, not in the life of a gnome. Kaliwyn, we are the ossci."

His words fell flat across the room, the pop and hiss of the fire the only sound to follow for several minutes. Her thoughts churning, Ami searched through her memories, every instance that she had seen in the marsh and in the presence of the gnomes. The three she had met and held so dear were born after her exile, but little else could be ascertained.

"Why did they punish me?" she asked at last, unable to discern the reason for herself.

"You destroyed Galiodien. He instigated the great war and took the lives of Ziradon's mate and sons. When you discovered his treachery, you could no longer resign yourself to simply hide and watch, recording the events as they unfolded. Did you not recognize your own hand?"

"My own hand," she whispered. "You are talking about the tomes in the libraries."

"Yes, my love," he replied gently. "You loved Ziradon so much you recorded every detail of his life, right up to the point they banished you. Someone else took over his story and left it there for you to discover as of late. You bore your exile until you could stand it no more, and then you chose to be reincarnated as his final offspring."

Swallowing, his lips grew thin in a forced smile before he continued.

"But obviously, choosing such a path cost you all that you knew of your previous existence. The prophecy wasn't a prophecy at all. I simply stated what I saw to be true. Your pure heart, a lover of dragon and man, the highest and lowest among us. It never sat well with you that they had banished the mortals to the rim, even if you failed at the time to act. You abhorred the deeds that had been done. The wrongs that were inflicted. I knew when they decided not to destroy you that it was only a matter of time before you would bring the separation of our worlds to its rightful end."

A flicker of recognition in her green eyes, she gasped, "You prevented the mortals from being destroyed. It was through your influence that they were spared and moved to the rim to begin with. That's when you were banished from the marsh."

"Yes."

"But I wasn't strong enough then," she croaked, tears welling in her eyes.

Swallowing, he nodded.

"And you have waited for me all this time."

"And now you know the truth," he managed in a less than masculine voice. "You have at last returned to me," he grinned, "and you have chosen me."

Smiling, she leaned towards him, her supple lips finding his. Searching, yearning, her hand resting against his cheek, she enjoyed the taste of him. Breaking the connection, she placed her forehead against his. "I understand."

Raising his arm, he pressed his fleshy palm against the back of hers, enjoying the warmth of her touch. "Then you know we have centuries ahead of us," he whispered. "And we have each other's company in which to spend them."

"Aye," she giggled, "in the form of any creature we want to be." The thought drew her mind to the dragon skeleton she had spied in Meena's golden orb while they hid in the Crimson Caves. She had thought they were a trick, when she had doubted the intentions of Yaodus. Her thoughtful mood returning, she shrugged. "I saw your bones, or at least I believed that they were. Why did you pretend to be dead?"

"I never pretended to be dead," he chuckled. "I took my leave of world, secluding myself more fully and they assumed my absence heralded my passing. I'm afraid the body you found was yours, left behind when you fused yourself with egg of a dragon. I have visited the cave and stood by them often in my grief," he confessed."

"Mine," she gasped, the thought of such a thing giving her a shudder. "Then how do I still breathe? I doubt stealing a dragon's life could bring about such a thing."

"Of that, I have no firm explanation. I only know that some truths cannot be denied, and all have been shocked to find that you were able to take on a new life. You left your bones behind and were born of the flesh to walk the earth in a second life. You were reincarnated as Kaliwyn, almost as if you had planned it all along."

"Rubbish," Ami giggled, her eyes bright. "No one could have planned such a twisted tale as this."

Epilogue

IN HER ORDINARY MORTAL FORM, Kaliwyn arrived home to their tree-cottage in the northern woods, where she lit the fire and placed a kettle over the flames. Taking a seat at the table, she opened her single tome to a new blank page and began to write. After a few minutes of dipping and scrawling, she laid her pen aside and stood to pace the small space.

Sevoassi would not return for hours, and normally she would enjoy her quiet evening, but tonight her heart felt heavy. Much had weighed on her mind as of late, and although her life was more than she ever could have dreamed, she felt as if she had left business unfinished that she needed to attend to, and soon. Hearing her water hiss inside her pot, she added the leaves to the vessel and set it aside to steep. When it was ready, she poured her cup and reclaimed her seat at the table. Flipping her memoir to the beginning, she began to read...

If you have discovered my tome, then allow me a short preface to the contents. Herein lies the eventual ends of our journey as we have been scattered across the globe to while our days on separate paths. However, we once walked as a group and lived as a family. We were a collection of souls with a single purpose: to save ourselves and our beloved mother earth from the squabbling of her children in the two realms... the Kingdom of Eriden and those called the Mortals of the Rim.

. . .

Her fingers skimming over the words and chapters that followed, she picked out brief passages to relive parts of their adventure, turning the pages that recorded all the events she had recalled and documented within the binding. They were the details of her life from the moment of Arely's revelation to the night she sat in that very room with Sevoassi and learned the final piece of her truth.

But that was only the beginning, she contemplated with a crooked grin. She and the one they called oracle were destined to become lovers, sharing beliefs and abilities few if any could understand. Their lives together had unfolded slowly as the years passed, and she loved him deeply. Her memories of her previous self had never returned; an unfortunate consequence of her choice to don Kaliwyn's wings and live the life of a true dragon. Staring at the words of her diary, it was all that she had, but it was enough.

Her eyes flicking around at the flame-kissed walls, she closed the tome and sighed. In the back, she had been adding updates to their adventures, as she visited many of her friends often. *Or at least those who have remained in Eriden.* Tonight, her thoughts were of Reynard Daye, and she could feel the ache in her chest. The longing to know of the man she had once wed.

Rey had remained with Oldrilin and the Sirens for some months after the battle at Whitefair, but eventually Meena had delivered him to the Rim and he had returned to his childhood home of Domania, or so it had been decided. Kaliwyn had no real knowledge of what had become of him, as she had feared what she would find. She wanted so much for him, but she could not be a part of his future, and that had kept her away.

Leaning back in her chair, she rested her hand on her belly and the movement of the growing form within pressed against her fingers. It had surprised her and Sevoassi both that she had conceived, but they had grown accustomed to the idea of raising their young and future ossci. It would arrive in a few months, and her life would again undergo a drastic change, only this one felt more right than any other she had experienced so far.

A tender smile painting her lips, she could not shake the curiosity that had twisted her gut, the pending arrival perhaps feeding her desire to know. Biting her lip, she flicked her eyes around the room once more, then cut them up at the tree above her as she considered the trip she had previously not dared to take. *The orb won't do. I have to see for myself.*

Pushing the chair back, she left all as it was and made the distance in a single leap. She was an old hand at transpositioning these days and could visit anywhere on the earth in the blink of an eye.

Arriving in a sun-drenched village on the isle of Domania, she hid her features and her condition with a clever disguise; one of long dark locks that hung straight to her waist and clear blue eyes that took in the world with a gleam. With her deeply tanned flesh, she wished to spy upon her old friend with no intention of alerting him to her presence. She had visited with the others of their group often, openly sharing when she chose to call, but this was different. Her being recognized would be a disruption for him, or so she firmly believed.

Stepping out from her hidden location, she breathed deeply. Some commotion was currently under way there in his peaceful village, and she was met with a throng of happy islanders swarming around her. Making her way forward, she relaxed into the crowd, confident she would reach her target among them.

"Amicia?" A male voice came from over her shoulder.

Frozen in place, the girl did not turn. Her eyes adjusted to the bright light, she skimmed over people coming and going in the town square. *A festival.* Brightly colored dresses and decorations adorned the area, and music floated on the air.

"Ami, is that you?" Rey persisted, seizing her arm and forcing her to face him.

Gazing in awe at his full beard and unkempt hair, Ami managed a small grin. "I didn't think you would know me."

"How could I not, with a fire as bright as yours?" he teased. Turning as he released her, he welcomed a second woman into their conversation. "Ami, this is my wife, Felice."

At her introduction, the young woman stared at the girl. Her obvious condition formed a large bump beneath her gown, and her hands traced the mound affectionately as she breathed, "Amicia Spicer. I've heard so much about you."

Glancing at her old friend, Ami could see the flush staining his cheeks and the tips of his ears that peeked out from his long ringlets. "Have you, now?" She grinned knowingly, glad her disguise was complete, and he would not be aware of her own pending arrival.

"Papa! Papa!" A young boy broke between them, calling to his father. "May we have six pence for the show?"

"Stand," Rey ordered gruffly, using their shoulders to turn his sons as he presented them. "Amicia, these are our boys... Piers and Baldwin."

Smiling down at the two young men, Ami grinned at their likeness to their father. "Hello," she stated matter-of-factly as she knelt before them. "And how old are you?"

"I'm seven," little Piers informed her confidently, then indicated his younger brother. "Bally's five." Unimpressed with the strange woman, he returned to his begging, "Please, father? A few coins for the afternoon."

Retrieving the sum from his pocket, Rey grinned broadly as he offered them to his progeny. "Do not leave the village," he called as the pair scampered away.

Standing slowly, Ami's gaze met the dark brown orbs of Rey's bride. Seeing the smile on Felice's lips, a twist in her gut unleashed a flood of emotions, ones she hoped remained hidden behind her disguise.

"I'm going for a visit at the parish," the other woman announced, giving Rey a firm pat on his broad chest. "Invite your friend to supper, like a good host," she reminded before she turned and floated away, leaving the pair to talk in private.

After she had gone, a strained silence settled over them, and Ami looked around her anxiously. The town square filled with people, happy sounds of celebration rose and fell like a tide. "What's the occasion?" Amicia finally asked, grateful for the safe subject with which to begin.

"It's the dragon festival," Rey informed her. Taking her arm, he led her at a slow pace, guiding her through the crowded space to the edge of the noise and down a quiet path that would take them out of the village. When they were away from the rest, he said more quietly, "They don't really know why the dragons no longer come. They only know that they do not, and each year we hold a celebration. This is the tenth."

"Ten years," Ami quietly echoed, the idea of it stealing her breath. Looking up at him, she stared into his hazel orbs with regret. "I'm sorry it has taken this long for me to come to you."

"Rubbish." He laughed, coming to a full stop. He released her arm and shoved his hands in his pockets. "I doubt you are here to rekindle our flame." His eyes roaming up and down her slender frame, she had taken great care to hide her identity, and he wondered briefly how many times she had made the trip before he had noticed her. "Do you watch me often?" he asked pointedly.

"Never. Not so much as a peek with my orb," she confessed, a tear spilling over and streaking her cheek. Wiping it away quickly, her chest felt tight. "I've been so afraid to see you. I feared what I would find... to discover how you had faired."

"I have faired well," he whispered, his hand brushing her shoulder to comfort her. "I'm a happy man, Ami."

"Tell me about her then," she replied, meeting his gaze and forcing a smile. "Your wife. Leave nothing out."

"Well, I stayed at Riran until it had been rebuilt. Leaving Lin was difficult, but in the end, we both knew it was for the best," he began. Using the hand that rested on her shoulder, he gave her a nudge to follow as he ambled along, putting more distance between them and the others.

Understanding his silent desire to keep their words private, Amicia followed, her grin shifting to genuine. "Yes, I was aware of your aid in their reconstruction. And when Meena delivered you back to the Rim."

"Yes, at my request she placed me at Myrth and I caught a ship to here. I arrived at Domania under the firm conviction that I would never see you again and would spend the remainder of my days pining for you while I worked for my brothers on our family farm," he said with a chuckle.

"But that's not how it turned out."

"Oh no. When I arrived, I had only been here a week before I discovered my real reason for coming home. For the first Sunday service, I sat in the church feeling sorry for myself and happened to be two pews back from Felice. During the sermon, she glanced at me over her shoulder, and in an instant, I knew. We grew up together, here in this village, and I had known her my entire life, but it was as if I had seen her for the first time." His words gentle, he hoped he would not upset his first wife with his confession.

"Oh, Rey," she reassured, stopping to face him squarely. "You have found love again. I'm so happy for you!" Throwing her arms around him, she pulled him into a firm hug. "I was so scared."

"My beloved Ami," he whispered against her ear, a little sad that she no longer donned her unruly golden locks. "I will never forget you. I promise. But my life has continued and I..." His voice trailed away.

"I'm not here to steal you from it," she assured, still holding him. "I only wanted to see. It pleases me greatly you have done so well. But what of your brothers and your family's farm?"

"They still run it. Felice had suffered her own tragedies in my absence. That day in the church, she felt the connection as strongly as I did. We left there together, and I dined at their house that very eve. Her parents had passed, leaving their lands to her and her brother. He had taken a wife, but it was a great deal of work for them. It still is, but we share the land, and our families are as one."

"Oh, Rey," Ami giggled, "and I'm sure your cheeses are the best in the land."

"Of course they are!" He laughed as well. Walking for a few minutes in silence, he inhaled deeply and breathed out in a long, relaxed breath. "Our third child will be here soon."

"I noticed," she agreed, clasping his hand and folding their digits like old times, as if the merdoe rested between them.

"How are the others? Have they faired as well in the land of Eriden?" he prodded.

Nodding slowly, Amicia glanced around them. They had left the village behind and were currently walking down a dirt path with open fields of green on either side. Not a soul in sight, they would be free to speak of the place they had shared and the people they had grown to love.

"Meena and the Mate have rebuilt at New Abolia," she began. "The cabin is very similar to the one we held there, but of course, the vessel was not reconstructed," she informed him.

"I shouldn't think that he would need it," Rey agreed.

"No, he is vastly content to share his days with her. He has a small dingy that he uses to putter around their bay. He fishes and wanders, and the like, but always returns to her. They are loved by the trolls as well, and Yaodus has decreed that there will be a mortal village built for the time the two lands again become blended."

"But that hasn't happened yet. I'm sorry, Ami. I thought surely what you did would have brought about such change."

"In time. The barriers have been broken, but it will take the passing of people between them to spread the word and create the bonds necessary to heal the rift between."

"And you do not think it will harm those of the rim to learn of Eriden?" he asked doubtfully. He had kept his stories to a select few for fear of being thought mad and doubted many would be brave enough to break the silence on the subject.

"No. I think it will be a blessing for mortals to see their place in the grand scheme of things," she stated firmly. "You hide what you know of Eriden, but others will return and bring the tales of a foreign magical land. Their knowledge will grow, and all will be as it should be."

"Yes, I hide it well." He laughed loudly, thinking of the few people he had shared his adventures with. "Most would be unreceptive of such revelations, but Felice believes me."

"As she should," Ami confirmed. "Anyway, as to the others, the rest of Eriden has been rebuilding, but it is a slow and painful process. Animir has worked to bring the elves down from their lofty ideals, if you will. It was quite a shock to them, learning that they are not really better than everyone else. The elf kingdom will be many years in the making, to be certain, but they are adjusting."

"I'm glad his place among his kind has been returned. It wasn't right that he was stripped of his rank on his father's deeds."

"Yes, but it will be many moons before his heart is fully healed. His time apart changed him, but it has given him perspective that is invaluable now as their leader. He is a young elf and will have many centuries to guide his people and experience his own healing."

"How are our dwarf and nymph doing?" he asked, swinging her hand playfully as he thought of their ebony-skinned friend and her diminutive husband.

"Oh, if you can believe it, Hayt and Zae have a daughter who is five. They split their time between Rhong and the glen so that she can learn and experience both worlds of her heritage."

"Esterbrook has been restored?"

"Yes, greatly, but there are still burned out places where the trees are barren, and the creatures have not returned," Amicia informed him with a shake of her head. "I still hope they will come back, and it will not become another cursed forest and blot upon the land."

"And Adiarwen?"

"Lamwen is well. He rules over all with an iron claw and a loving heart," she informed him with a large grin. Suspecting he believed the dragon to be her mate, she allowed him to think so.

"I'm glad you put him in charge. We may have had our disagreements, but he has a head for what's right," Rey stated agreeably.

"Yes, and he has no fear of doing what is necessary. Whitefair has been put into shape, with the market permanently closed. The city thrives, and the traffic between the east and west flourishes, with the north to south growing as well."

"Gradien was such an ass."

"Yes, but he is a smart man. He knew right away if he did not affect the changes our new king desired he would be replaced. He has become a great leader in the end."

"I once feared you would become Lamwen's mate," Rey dared, cutting his eyes over at her. "He has not claimed another?"

His words stung her, and she struggled to breathe. Glancing up at his brooding hazel orbs, she stopped abruptly and gasped, "You knew I would not return to my dragon form."

"I believe you have kept some truths for yourself," he confessed with a shrug. "Even now, you are careful not to speak of them."

"Oh, Rey," she sighed. "No, that was not my place," she informed him, shaking her head. "In twenty or thirty years, when he has settled into his position more firmly, perhaps he will claim one of the new females and begin to build his line. But you are correct, I will never be his dragoness. Have you known of this for long?" She wondered if her visit had given away as much, as she had always been careful to keep her truth hidden, as he had pointed out.

"Aye," he breathed. "It took me many months of pondering, but I finally realized what made you so special. And why you stand before me as a stranger."

Swallowing, Ami dropped his fingers as she studied him. "Go on." She curled her hands together, her palms damp with uncertainty.

Pursing his lips, Rey's face flushed with self-doubt. "Well, I should expect you would simply tell me and not cause me to guess."

"I have told no one," she whispered. "Even as I visit the others, I hide all that I can."

"You hide little, I assure you," he chuckled, lumbering on and forcing her to catch up. When she strolled beside him once more, he stated confidently. "Sevoassi. He was the piece that never quite fit, with his magical red orb. A gnome that wasn't a gnome, I am certain. And you with all your surprising powers and attributes. Almost dragon, but always something more. You had abilities that scared the hell out of Meena. She never spoke of them, but I'm certain she knows as well."

"Perhaps she does," Ami quietly agreed, glancing at the sun that had traveled a fair distance while they ambled along. "Will your wife be looking for you?"

"Aye. We should turn back," he agreed, pivoting and offering his left arm for her to take. With the glare at their backs, he kept their pace slow, the fingers of his free right hand lying over hers as she gripped his left elbow. He toyed with the soft flesh of her digits, as he wanted to enjoy every moment they could share. He felt certain she would not come to him again. Not now that he had revealed he knew her secret. "It's ok that you are with him, and I promise I will never reveal what I have surmised. Not to anyone. I'm glad you have found the one who is your equal."

"Yes," she said in a meek and hushed tone, nodding her agreement. "Sevoassi and I will enjoy many years together." *Or centuries,* she silently mused. "It surprises me though that you have guessed what it took me years to figure out."

"Because I'm a mortal?"

"Well, that's part of it. But our magic is different. It is extraordinary that you could see me through my disguise, much less understand the depth of my being."

"I see because I loved you, Amicia Spicer."

His gravelly tone dug at her heart, and his words gave her a chill, the past tense bringing a frown to her features. Leaving it, she sighed. "I loved you as well, Reynard Daye. I loved all who shared my journey. And I am glad that so many of us have survived to help rebuild our great and wonderful lands."

Arriving at the edge of their village, a dull ache had settled into Amicia's gut, and she felt the strong desire to flee. "I need to go, love," she announced when the sounds of the celebration grew sufficiently loud. "Please, give your wife my regrets."

"As you wish," he replied, unwilling to add guilt to her drawn features. Bending, he placed a gentle kiss upon her cheek, again certain he would never see her again but comforted that she had made the journey and peace would stand between them.

In an instant she was gone and stood once more in the small cottage in the northern woods. Her fire had been stoked, and her mate sat at her table looking over her tome.

"I was beginning to wonder," Sevoassi informed her with a wink when their gaze met.

Her heart fluttering, Kaliwyn had returned to her ordinary self, and her golden waves shimmered as she caught the curve of her round belly and sat in the second seat. "I had a visit to pay among the rim."

"At last. I wondered how much longer you could stand it."

"But you have been watching," she accused. "You knew what had become of my Rey."

"I knew. And you would know when you were ready." Reaching for her hand that lay on the table between them, he caressed her fingers, sensing that the man in question had done the same only a short time ago. Their love did not bother him, as he understood far more than he could put into words. Instead, he changed the subject, allowing her some privacy of their visit. "I believe I have found a more suitable location for us, now that we will be three," he informed her quietly.

"Is that what kept you out so late? Searching for a place to raise our pending arrival?" She enjoyed the way that he fawned over her. The entire world was his for the taking, but she was all that he needed and had been for near an eon.

He laughed at her choice of words. "How deeply I love you, Kaliwyn," he confessed. The red of his hair catching the light, his smile covered his face and gleamed in the blue of his eyes. He had waited for her so long, nothing could spoil the moments that they shared.

Standing in unison, she wrapped him in her arms, her lump sandwiched between them as they embraced. "My life is so full, and I am so happy with our days," she breathed against his neck. "We will go there tomorrow, and I will make our new home to prepare."

Squeezing her as firmly as he dared, Sevoassi's heart raced. During her walk as a mortal, he had almost always felt certain they would one day stand together in such a way. Almost always. But there had been times he had feared what would become of her and her rag-tag group of friends. That night, he was very grateful things had worked out the way they had, and she would be his to hold and to love for eternity. His Dragon of Eriden.

Books in the Dragon of Eriden Series
Whisper of Suffering
Journey of Darkness
Betrayal of Honor
Kingdom of Ruin
The Complete Set (All 4 Books in 1)

Maps of Eriden & The Rim of Mortals

Characters by Race

Humans

Amicia Spicer is a young woman from Nalen discovering her true identity as the story unfolds. Her mother has revealed a secret about her origins upon her deathbed, and Ami is looking for the place she belongs in the world.

Reynard Daye is a young crewman aboard the Sea Serpent. He survives the destruction of the ship and joins the unlucky group of mortals as they crash upon the shores of Eriden.

Piers Massheby is the first mate aboard the Sea Serpent. He is a strong leader and guides the group through their perilous journey in search of a way home.

Baldwin Carter is the cabin boy on board the ship. He is mostly along for the ride, being young and inexperienced at handling the hardships that the group faces along the way.

Minor Human Characters:
    Rupert Miller – Amicia Spicer's friend from Nalen, he expects that she will become his betrothed when her parents no longer need her.
    Gus Spicer – Amicia's father.
    Arely Spicer – Amicia's mother.
    Shamus Smith – blacksmith in the desert city of Whitefair.

Geoffrey Tabard – trader from Whitefair.
Humphray Heron – trader from Whitefair.

Sirens

Olirassa is queen of the mermaids. She is the sovereign and protector of the city of Riran.

Oldrilin is Reynard Daye's caretaker in Riran. She becomes caught up in their escape and is swept away onto their adventure through Eriden. Her devotion to Rey is sincere, and she proves to be a valuable member of their group. She seems to have little magical ability but is able to transform into a large black fish.

Elves

Cilithrand is the queen of the elves. She resides in a magnificent palace in Jerranyth, located on the southern end of the elf lands, which consists of the lower end of the central mountains of Eriden.

Animir is an elf of higher class that has been outcast from his station. He no longer feels a part of his elf kin, and helps the group to escape Jerranyth, thereby joining them on their quest to find a way home. He had been banned from using his innate magical abilities, but with the freedom of the group, he explores his talents and regains his ability as a strong wielder of magic. A resourceful member of the group, they value his friendship and utility.

Minor Elf Characters:
Sadrir – serves the group while they are in Jerranyth.
Anerion – lead huntsman to Lady Cilithrand.
Galiodien – Cilithrand's father and former king of the elves.
Cothiel – female companion to Piers in Jerranyth.

Nymphs

Preivia is queen of the nymphs. She is the sovereign and protector of the city of Esterbrook and the surrounding areas known as the glen and the meadows.

Zaendra is an earth nymph. She is pleased to meet the group when they come into the glen and attaches herself to their company. Spending time with them while they reside in their cabin, she packs her things to leave with them at their departure, as she has always wanted to explore more of Eriden and sees this as her chance. She has some magical abilities and proves to be a valuable member of the group.

Wolves

Uscan is the alpha of the southern pack of grey wolves. His loyalties are often murky, but he holds an affinity for Amicia Spicer. He acts in her best interest both as a friend and advisor. As for the southern pack, they protect the Shadowlands, a cursed area of woods that acts as a natural barrier between the glen and the mountains of the elf lands.

Edeill is the alpha of the northern pack. His loyalties are also in question. His pack of great white wolves are the protectors of the northern woods, and they patrol a much larger area than their southern kin.

Minor Wolf Characters:
Mirean – scout sent to Esterbrook for the southern pack.
Aelalle – beta of the northern pack.

Wizards

Meena Gavaan is a wan, a female wizard, but unlike most, she was born with the ability to use magic, which is forbidden within their people. She has led a difficult life and faces tough choices throughout the story. She meets the group upon their arrival in the desert community of Whitefair and agrees to help them for a price. She leaves with them when they flee the oasis and travels with them on their journey, earning her place within the group with her special magical skill set and talent for using her powers in practical ways.

Minor Wizard Characters:
Jaco Gavaan – Meena's deceased husband.
Gradien Silversmith – magistrate of the wizard city of Whitefair, he is a powerful wizard, but also a bit of a scoundrel.
Corvack – head of the security force in Whitefair.

Trolls

Yaodus is the king of the trolls. He is a powerful wielder of magic, which is rare but not unheard of among the trolls. He is distrustful of everyone outside of their community and takes his role of protector of his kind with the utmost of dedication. He is an unlikely ally of the group after Amicia convinces him of her worth, and his help is often the difference between life and death for the mortals and their friends.

Traok is Yaodus's eldest son. He is met several times, as he acts as the liaison between the group and the troll community on several occasions.

Dwarves

Baeweth is the king of the city of Rhong. As their sovereign, he is the protector of the growing city beneath the mountain. However, his family and people have endured a great deal in the last few hundred years. They have denounced the use of magic and are rebuilding after a daemon drove them from their previous home of Asomanee.

Hayt is the king's great nephew and heir to the throne. He holds no desire to ever be king and devises a way to win the trust of the group, then helps them escape rather than see them handed over to the dragons. He is a skilled engineer, and his abilities and knowledge prove useful to the group on their quest.

Minor Dwarf Characters:
Asyng – the king's sister and Hayt's grandmother, she is Baeweth's advisor.
Firen – Hayt's good friend and fellow engineer.
Vael – Another acquaintance of Hayt's, he is the guard on duty when the group prepares to escape.

Daemons

Kedoria is the queen of the daemons. Her loyalties to the elves are shaken when she is captured by Animir and recruited by Amicia. She commands the daemon forces, but they are only able to live in total darkness, which severely limits her utility within the group. She has a few named minions, but they are only briefly mentioned in the events of the story.

Gnomes

Thirac is the sovereign or king of the gnomes, also called the head of the elders. He is untrustworthy and holds little concern for the Kingdom of Eriden. Their people watch events unfold and record them in their tomes, which are stored in their great libraries hidden inside of the old trees of the marsh lands.

Sevoassi is the gnome the group encounters in the northern woods. He is a trickster who helps them escape the northern pack and gives Amicia a special red orb of unknown origin or purpose.

Minor Gnome Characters:

Ziyath (grumpy) – member of the order of the ossci, the highest and most powerful of the gnomes.

Mizath (happy) – member of the order of the ossci, the highest and most powerful of the gnomes.

Yimath – member of the order of the ossci, the highest and most powerful of the gnomes.

Dragons

Ziradon is Kaliwyn's father and rightful Supreme Dragon of Eriden. He is overthrown at the beginning of the story by Gwirwen, who imprisons him that he may suffer for the rest of his days. A powerful wielder of magic, he is seven hundred years of age. During his life, he has lost two wives and all of his sons. Princess Kaliwyn, his dragoness and heir to the throne, is all he has in the world.

Gwirwen is the current King of Eriden, but only because he was successful in taking over the throne. He is not as strong as Ziradon, and certainly not as wise. His poor choices lead to certain destruction, as the prophecy of the destroyer appears to be fulfilled by his doing.

Kaliwyn is the daughter of Ziradon and rightful heir to the throne of the Supreme Dragon of Eriden. Forced into the form of a mortal as a young dragoness, she is taken away to Nalen, where she is found and raised by human parents. She is not aware of her true self and must discover her dragon heart before it's too late.

Lamwen is the captain of the king's guard. He is assigned to protect the coast of the continent and leads the guard in that role. When the group makes it ashore, it is the guard's job to eliminate them. When their attempts prove unsuccessful, he is reassigned to spy on the group, where he learns of Amicia's identity. Becoming her friend and guardian, he is eventually welcomed by the travelers and becomes vital in their success.

Minor Dragon Characters:

Ziewen – female dragon, loyal to and eventually mated with Gwirwen.

Pardodan – loyal to Gwirwen, he longs to improve his rank in the king's guard.

Vaudien – loyal to Gwirwen, he takes Lamwen's place as captain of the king's guard when he is removed.

Kilawon – Kaliwyn's mother and Ziradon's late mate, who was murdered by Gwirwen.

Jarrowan – Lamwen's friend and supporter, he spends time with the group and even experiences human form for a few days.

Putwyn – a less than decisive member of Lamwen's followers who betrays him, then wishes to rejoin them. Most noted for helping the group escape the dragons by arranging for Baeweth to help them.

Onothwyn – a lesser member of the king's guard who helps to hunt the group.

About the Author

Anyone who knows me could tell you, I am a friendly kind of person, never met a stranger and take up conversations anywhere at any time. I work hard, and my mind never seems to shut down, as I wake up often in the middle of the night with ideas pouring out and demanding to be dealt with. Of course that means much of my books were written in the middle of the night.

I grew up and still live in the great state of Texas where everything is bigger, where we have warm weather and a central location. I love my state, my town, and my family, which includes my four sons, my significant other, and many friends as well.

I have thoroughly enjoyed writing this story and hope that you will love reading it just as much. And of course, there will be many more adventures to come.

You can follow Samantha Jacobey at:
Website: www.SamJacobey.com
Facebook: https://www.facebook.com/SamJacobey
Twitter: https://twitter.com/SamJacobey

Also by SAMANTHA JACOBEY

A New Life Series

http://myBook.to/ANewLifeSeries

An epic adventure, TORI FARRELL's life IS one wild story... escaped from a biker gang and running from drug lords... used by the FBI and hoping to protect her present from her past... IT'S DARK - IT'S BRUTAL, and it's WORTH EVERY MINUTE OF IT!! (Mature Adult, 18+)

Summer Spirit Novella Series

http://myBook.to/SummerSpiritSeries

No one EVER had a summer romance like this... Charlie visits another plane, parallel to our own, where Summer Angels and Dark Angels battle over the fate of man. A unique twist on an old idea that will keep you guessing; will Charlie and Clarisse ever find their HEA? (New adult)

Irrevocable Series

http://mybook.to/IrrevocableBoxedSet

From affluent beginnings, BAILEY DEWITT's life has become a broken mess... after her parents died unexpectedly, she didn't think it could get any worse. But when the arrogance of man catches up and puts the entire world into a dooms-day spiral, there will be only ONE PLACE she can run to - the ONE PLACE she wanted desperately to escape. (New Adult)

Teach Me to Prey

http://hyperurl.co/e9qs9f

In this standalone thriller, JASON TRUITT and his friends have gotten their way for years. Deceit, sex, and foul play aren't normally covered in the curriculum, but they're doing whatever it takes to get under BECKY STEWART's skin. When one of the boys turns up dead, it's a race against time to save the others; a STUNNING STORY that will get your heart racing and leave you breathless by the end... (New Adult)

The Wicked Awakened

http://hyperurl.co/2qsgl6

A Halloween novel; a five-hundred-year-old witch wants to turn SARAH MATTHEWS' body into her new home… A twisted tale involving a coven hell bent on seeing that she succeeds. Who will come out on top in this epic battle of wills? (Mature Adult, 18+)

The Binding

http://myBook.to/TheBinding

One cursed diary will change two strangers forever...Can Meri and Rider use her mother's old book to figure out why someone is after them? Or will the guilty party succeed, ripping the tome away before killing them and then slithering back into the darkness…

Also From Our Lavish Family

The Norn Novellas

A. Nicky Hjort

https://www.lavishpublishing.com/authors/nicky-hjort-1/

The Norn Novellas are all chapters in the epic saga of the youngest and most fickle of the four Norn Sisters. The same feisty immortal creature who must escape her inherent inner darkness to learn the meaning of life.

Each story takes a classic fairytale and spins it on its head, as we learn that maybe Norse Mythology was so much more than legend. And to think, you thought you knew those old tales so well.

Meet Za and find out what really happened...

When Tundra Turns to Ardnyt - Book 1: In the center of a magical world there grows a beautiful and terrible chasm of climbing plants. On one side of the Ivy Wall we find the hell-of-Tyndra, on the other, the heaven-of-Ardnyt. But legend has it that in the middle...lives a preternatural beast that imprisons and tortures the children from both sides.

When the war against time begins, Azza will have to cross over the Ivy Wall, something that has never been done before by a living being. But if she does make it through, she just might discover who she really is and how she became trapped in this alternate reality.

A fairytale at heart, this is the first chapter in the epic saga of the youngest and most fickle of the four Norn Sisters. The same feisty immortal creature who must escape her inherent inner darkness to learn the meaning of love.

A veritable palindrome from start to finish, the narrative of Where Tyndra Turns to Ardnyt journeys through duality to discover what shocking truths emerge when up becomes down, life becomes death, suffering becomes release, and the most unexpected endings become the most surprising beginnings.

Welcome to a place where forwards and backwards are exactly the same direction. Here Where Tyndra Turns to Ardnyt.

Where Ebon Sounds Like Ivory – book 2: Norse legend has it that the arms of the Yggdrasil tree—a sacred instrument of Odin—are ever-reaching, and its survival is necessary for life itself to continue.

During Winter's Solstice, when the search for her mortal mother begins, Za will have to cross over the Ebon Branch of the Dead—a feat that has supposedly never been survived intact. But if she does make it across and back home, she just might discover why she and the other three Norn Sisters of Fate came to be.

A fairytale at heart, this is the second chapter in the epic saga of the youngest and most fickle of the four Norn Sisters. The same feisty immortal creature who must discover her true origins to understand her inherent inner darkness. Only this way can she learn the meaning of unconditional sacrifice in the name of impenetrable love...when, as her destiny would have it, all the branches of such a powerful tree tremble treacherously in her tiny little hands.

A veritable unraveling of Snow White, the narrative of Where Ebon Sounds Like Ivory journeys through the most horrible of realms where shocking truths emerge. Here where death mimics life, obsession masquerades as devotion, and the most unexpected endings become the most surprising beginnings of a classic tale. One...you thought you knew so well.

Welcome to a place where the darkest of melodies births a miraculous tune of surrenderance. Here Where Ebon Sounds Like Ivory and Christmas, as we know it, begins.

Behind Blue Eyes Series

Sara J. Bernhardt

https://books2read.com/BlueEyesBeginner

A father's desire to save his child presents him with an unthinkable choice that leaves him darker than human, forced to roam through time alone as he searches for the place he belongs.

Adam Gold – Book 1: Fleeing the French invasion of Geneva Switzerland in the 1700s, Adam Gold books passage to America with his family. On the ship, Adam's daughter falls fatally ill. A mysterious man comes to Adam with a way to save his child by turning Adam into something darker than human.

The Medallion – Book 2: Adam Gold, an immortal with sweet eyes of blue, rushes through the centuries on a quest for reason and a thirst for revenge. To cope with his pain and regret, he sleeps away the years and awakes in a new era with a powerful, ancient vampire who sets her sights on him.

Golden Shackles – Book 3: When the ancient queen, Sekhmet snatches up Adam, he is faced with a terrifying decision. To help aid her in her vile plans or dare to stand against her.

Plus 3 more segments!